THE DUKE'S BRIDE

FENELLA J MILLER

Boldwood

First published in 2018. This edition published in Great Britain in 2025 by Boldwood Books Ltd.

Copyright © Fenella J. Miller, 2018

Cover Design by Colin Thomas

Cover Images: Colin Thomas and iStock

The moral right of Fenella J. Miller to be identified as the author of this work has been asserted in accordance with the Copyright, Designs and Patents Act 1988.

All rights reserved. No part of this book may be reproduced in any form or by any electronic or mechanical means, including information storage and retrieval systems, without written permission from the author, except for the use of brief quotations in a book review. This book is a work of fiction and, except in the case of historical fact, any resemblance to actual persons, living or dead, is purely coincidental.

Every effort has been made to obtain the necessary permissions with reference to copyright material, both illustrative and quoted. We apologise for any omissions in this respect and will be pleased to make the appropriate acknowledgements in any future edition.

A CIP catalogue record for this book is available from the British Library.

Paperback ISBN 978-1-83678-344-2

Large Print ISBN 978-1-83678-345-9

Hardback ISBN 978-1-83678-343-5

Ebook ISBN 978-1-83678-346-6

Kindle ISBN 978-1-83678-347-3

Audio CD ISBN 978-1-83678-338-1

MP3 CD ISBN 978-1-83678-339-8

Digital audio download ISBN 978-1-83678-341-1

This book is printed on certified sustainable paper. Boldwood Books is dedicated to putting sustainability at the heart of our business. For more information please visit https://www.boldwoodbooks.com/about-us/sustainability/

Boldwood Books Ltd, 23 Bowerdean Street, London, SW6 3TN

www.boldwoodbooks.com

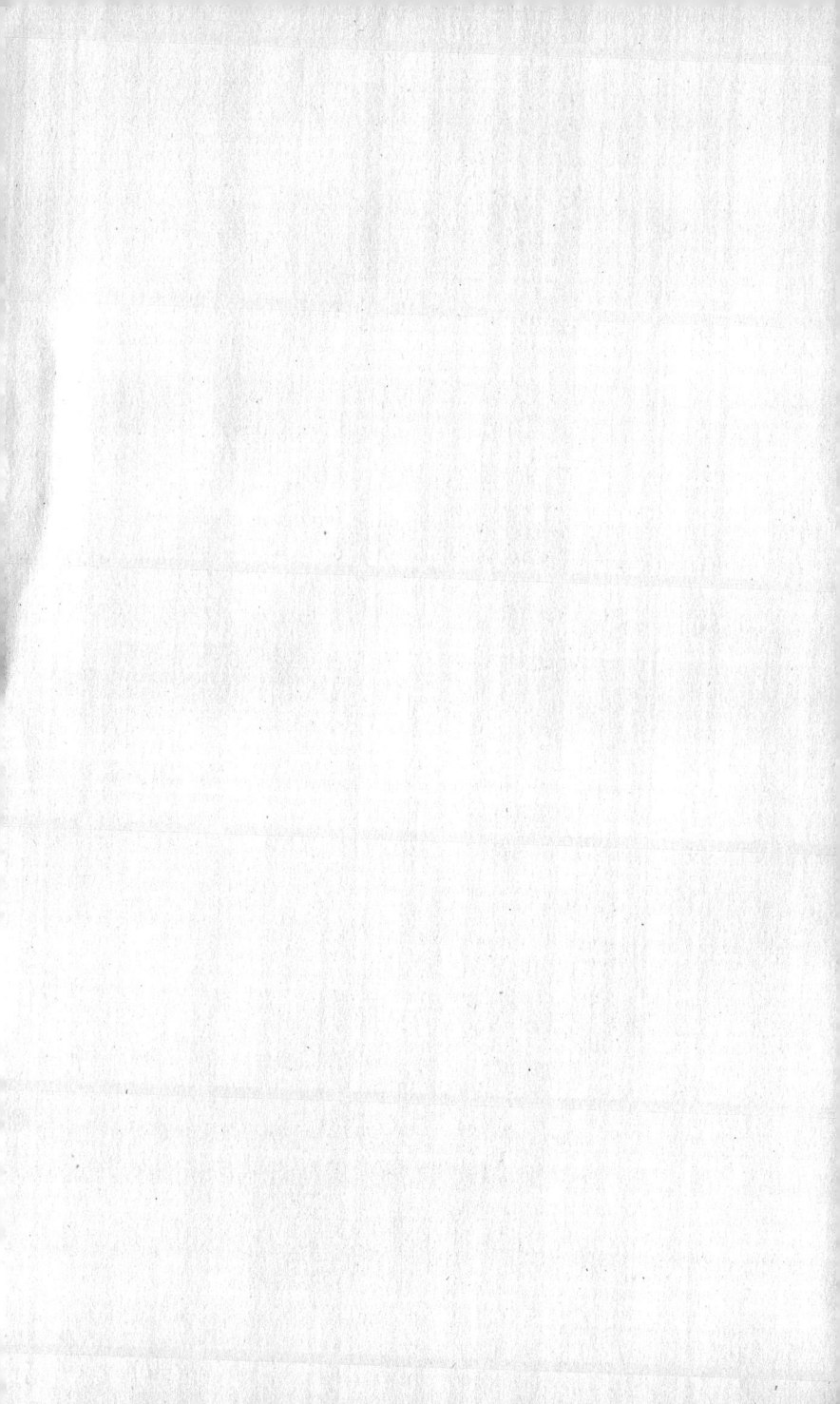

1

SILCHESTER COURT, FEBRUARY 1814

Beau would have preferred to be able to depart without a fuss, but his siblings had decided there must be a family party to send him on his way. For the next six months at least, he would not be known as the Duke of Silchester, but as plain Mr Sheldon.

'Your grace,' Peebles the butler said. 'The carriage with Lady Giselle and Lord Rushton has just arrived.'

He nodded. 'Do not look so dismayed; my brothers Lord Peregrine and Lord Aubrey can take care of things as well as I in my absence.'

The old man looked unconvinced. 'Forgive me for saying so, your grace, but there has always been a duke in residence here. Silchester Court will not be the same without you.'

'Good God, man, I was away for four months last year and the estates did not suffer then.'

His butler sniffed but made no response. No one on the staff knew where he was going or that he was intending to live as a commoner and spend time pursuing his interest in music. When a small boy, his father had told him in no uncertain terms that composing and playing could not feature in the future life of the

Duke of Silchester. Therefore, Beau had had to play and compose in secret and not until recently had any of his family realised how talented he was.

Bennett, the brother closest to him in age and his heir, met him in the passageway outside the study. 'Are you having second thoughts? No one will think the worse of you if you do decide to stay.'

'I cannot wait to leave. The thought of having until the summer without the responsibilities of this title, to be able to pursue my music, is something I never thought to experience. I have Sofia to thank for this life-changing occurrence. I thank God every day that Perry married her.'

'So, you will ride away from here without a second thought? To be honest, I do not blame you one jot. Others envy us our status, titles and wealth, but with these things come burdens and responsibilities that a commoner does not have.'

Beau slapped him on the back. 'Enough sermonising, brother, we are a close-knit and happy family and I think that it is what other people must envy.'

As they reached the vast entrance hall his younger sister, Giselle, stepped in through the front door. She was so muffled against the elements that she was scarcely recognisable. His closest friend, her husband, strode across and shook his hand vigorously.

'It seems only a short while since we were here for Christmas...'

His sister laughed. 'That is because it is only a short while, my love.' She threw herself into his arms and he hugged her.

'You have left the children behind this time?'

'The baby is too small to travel so far and the girls were quite happy to remain and keep him company.'

'If I tell you I am relieved that children are not included in this farewell party, I hope you will not be offended. I much prefer the company of adults, which is one reason I have never made a real effort to find myself a wife.'

'You're becoming a curmudgeon, Beau, and you are not yet five and thirty. We are all hoping being away from us, being able to spend time doing something that has been denied you all your life, will restore your *joie de vivre*.'

The drawing room was overflowing with those he loved most in this world: Madeline with her husband Grey, the twins Aubrey and Perry with their wives, Giselle and Rushton, and Bennett with his wife Grace. He would miss them all but not enough to prevent him from departing tomorrow morning.

The remainder of the day was spent in convivial conversation, lively debate and ended with him giving them a recital of his latest composition. When he played the piano he became someone else entirely, not a man who was known by his title nor his abilities.

He embraced them all and retreated to the privacy of his study for the last time. He would be travelling to a small estate, which only his man of affairs, Carstairs, knew the name and whereabouts of. This was a small but prosperous estate in Suffolk called Elveden Hall. The previous tenant had died suddenly, leaving it unoccupied but fully staffed. He had purchased a modest travelling carriage and a pair of nondescript bay geldings to pull it. He was travelling to London by the common stage, which would be an experience in itself, and would rendezvous with his vehicle and two newly appointed coachmen on his arrival in the metropolis.

His trunk had been conveyed there in advance. He was leaving his valet behind and would have to appoint someone new to fulfil that role when he was settled. It was imperative that no one accompanied him who knew his real identity and the only way to ensure this was by starting afresh with his servants.

One of his coachmen drove him in a gig to a coaching inn in a town where he was not well known, and he took his place inside the waiting vehicle with some trepidation. The interior was malodorous, the occupants little better, and for a moment he regretted his decision to travel this way.

All his life he had been fêted and lauded, and for the first time he would be treated like everyone else. If he was liked it would be for himself, not for the fact that he was a duke.

The journey to London was mercifully short and he disembarked with alacrity. He discovered his own vehicle on the far side of the large, cobbled yard and introduced himself. He was surprised both coachmen behaved exactly the same way to him as if he had been a duke.

His trunk was tied securely at the back of the carriage and they were ready to depart immediately. The distance to his new abode from Town necessitated stopping to allow the horses to rest and for himself to get refreshment, as well as an overnight stop in Colchester. The Red Lion in the High Street was perfectly satisfactory and after having spent four months living rough in Spain whilst he was searching for his brother, Perry, he found he was less fussy than he had used to be.

Elveden Hall was but a few miles from the market town of Ipswich and it was here that he must go if he wished to attend an assembly – not that he thought this was something he would do. The carriage turned into a well-weeded drive that stretched arrow-straight to an ancient but substantial building. The surrounding parkland was kept trim by a herd of deer.

The windows on either side of the front door were sparkling in the winter sunlight. The turning circle had recently been raked, no doubt in advance of his arrival. As far as the indoor staff and outside men were concerned, he had purchased the property and was not a tenant as the previous occupant had been.

The front door opened as the carriage turned. A surprisingly young man dressed in black appeared on the doorstep. Presumably he was the butler and the older woman in brown bombazine was the housekeeper. A footman in smart bottle-green livery hurried over to let down the steps and open the door for him to descend.

He was bowed in with as much ceremony as when he arrived at Silchester and he began to suspect that somehow the servants were aware of his true identity.

'I am Foster, butler here, sir, and this is Reynolds, housekeeper at your service.'

'I have no valet. I recently returned from abroad and have not yet had time to find someone who will suit. Is there a footman who can serve me for the moment?'

'Bishop has served in this position occasionally for visiting gentlemen. I shall have him attend you at once, sir.'

Beau paused to speak to the housekeeper. 'I prefer plain food served hot. Apart from that I have no need to be apprised of the menus unless I am entertaining.'

The woman curtsied and seemed satisfied with his request. 'Would you like me to show you around, sir, or would you prefer to do this alone?'

'It is a small house. I doubt that I shall get lost.'

He handed the butler his caped coat, gloves and beaver and then began his exploration. The moderately sized entrance hall had two sets of double doors, one on either side, as well as the passageway that led from the rear. He assumed that was to the servants' quarters.

On the right was a small but beautifully proportioned

drawing room and a single door at the far end led into a dining room that would seat at the most twenty people. This chamber had two doors, one of which led to a small, more feminine sitting room and the other to the breakfast parlour. He retraced his steps and crossed the hall.

His breath caught in his throat when he saw the magnificent piano standing at the far end of this second large reception room. There was also a harp and a harpsichord – neither of which interested him. He strode the length of the room, revealed the keys and ran his hands along them. The instrument was perfectly tuned. He pulled out the piano stool and sat down. Within minutes he was lost in his music and knew that he had made the right decision to abandon his responsibilities and spend time on his passion.

* * *

'My dear Viola, I have so much to tell you. Will you not sit down for a moment and listen to your mama?'

'I cannot do so until I have located the twins. Thomas and Elizabeth have been absent from the schoolroom without permission for over an hour and, despite sending out every available servant to look for them, they have not yet been located.'

'They are missing their papa, my love. If you were to allow them a little less freedom and take a tighter grip on the reins then you will find things easier.'

Viola bit back a sharp retort. 'Rupert died three years ago. I doubt that they can even remember him as they were only five years old at the time. Thomas has inherited the earldom and will be in charge of vast estates when he reaches his majority and must learn to take responsibility for his actions even though he is still a child.'

'I did not mean they were missing your husband any more than you do yourself; what they are missing is the firm hand of a gentleman. You spoil them both and it is doing them no favours.'

'I worry about my son, Mama. He has his head in the clouds and no aptitude for figures at all. He would spend all day sitting at the piano if I would allow him to. Whereas Elizabeth is normally studious and well behaved. Indeed, she would make a better Earl of Fenchurch. I fear the good Lord made my daughter best suited to the duties of a title and my son to live a life of idleness.'

'From the way you are gazing across the park you must think they have gone outside despite the inclement weather?'

'I am certain of it. They were determined to take Brutus for a long walk but I said it was too cold.'

Her mother laughed. 'As usual they have ignored your orders. Did you know that a single gentleman called Edward Sheldon has taken residence at Elveden Hall? He has recently returned from travelling overseas and arrived yesterday.'

'How in the world do you know this?'

'Do not forget that I was visiting my dearest friend at the vicarage yesterday. News travels there first and is then spread widely around the neighbourhood by dear Sarah. Being the wife of the vicar is the perfect position for someone who is an inveterate gossip.'

'I am intrigued to know more about this new arrival. Is he a handsome man? Is he old – young? Tell me more.'

'I would if I had anything else to tell you. I do know that he arrived yesterday but that is all. I assume you will send your card in the next day or two?'

'I shall certainly do no such thing. If he sends his then I will receive him, but I have no intention of initiating our acquaintance.' She shuddered. 'The only good thing to come from my marriage to Rupert was my children. I did as you and Papa wished, but if he had not broken his neck riding to hounds I would have disgraced the family by running away from him. He was a brute, a drunk and a bad landlord.'

'That's as may be, my love, but you are now a wealthy widow, the Countess of Fenchurch, and have complete control of your life and that of your children. It is fortunate indeed that your dear papa insisted that your brother would be guardian if you were widowed.'

Viola blinked back tears. 'I miss Papa every day. It must be so much worse for you.'

'The good Lord saw fit to take him back too soon, but we had thirty wonderful years together. The only regret I have is that he did not live long enough to see you free of that monster.'

'Richard is doing a splendid job of running the businesses. Papa would be proud of him. Our fleet has grown in size and his investments have paid dividends. I suppose I should be grateful that my obnoxious husband was not a gambler or no doubt he would have run through the fortune Papa gave him upon my marriage.'

'It was always his dearest wish for the family to be part of the aristocracy. Now his daughter is a countess, his grandson is an earl and his granddaughter Lady Elizabeth. Although if we had known that man's true character we would never have accepted his offer for you.'

'He was a handsome man, charming and witty, everything a young lady could wish for in a husband before we were wed. I thought of myself as a fairy-tale princess and was happy to marry him. I never loved him, but I thought those feelings would come with time. In fact, what came was the opposite.'

'Your brother would have torn him apart with his bare hands if he had known that man was beating you.'

'Then it is fortunate I kept it to myself until after I was widowed. I believe that is why my brother is leaving me to run the estates and bring up my children without his interference.'

'Did I tell you he is about to make an offer himself? Not for the daughter of an aristocrat, but for Amy Frobisher, his childhood sweetheart.'

'They are perfectly suited and have been in love with each other for years. I cannot think why he has taken so long to propose.'

'Silas Frobisher had the same ambitions for his daughter as we had for you. He was hanging out for an earl, for someone higher up the ladder than your brother. However, even he has been forced to admit that it would be better to have his daughter married to Richard than remain a spinster.'

Viola had been staring across at the woodland that edged the park. 'Look, Mama, I have just seen Brutus emerge from the undergrowth so the children cannot be far behind. I thank God every day that Richard gave them that dog, as at least I can be sure they will remain unharmed with him at their side.'

Her mother came to join her at the long window. 'Yes, I can see the children. That dog is even bigger than his sire. I swear they could ride on him if they so wished.'

'Rupert would never have allowed them a puppy and certainly not one that size. Neither would he have countenanced such a huge animal living in the house with us.'

She continued to watch until the twins were close enough to see her and their grandmother standing in the window. The children waved frantically and then broke into a run. They were both such delightful offspring that she found it impossible to discipline them with any enthusiasm. However, as she had absolutely no intention of ever being married again she would just have to hope that her lax approach to their upbringing would not ruin them entirely.

2

Beau rather liked the compact nature of his new accommodation. Despite the temperature the house was warm; even the passageways were bearable. His new staff were well trained and efficient – what more could he ask? Bishop, the young man appointed to be his temporary valet, had proved himself adequate to the task and so would remain in that position.

The estate was efficiently managed by the factor and he had no intention of interfering in that department. His intention was to spend the entire six months composing, playing and being free of his lifelong responsibilities.

The day after his arrival he was comfortably settled at the piano playing something that had come to him in the night before he committed it to paper. He paused and glanced up whilst he thought. His eyes widened. Peering back at him were three heads – two children and a dog that reminded him of Zorro, the enormous hound Sofia and Perry had brought back with them from Spain.

He stood up, expecting them to run away, but they waited as if expecting him to open the window and allow them into the music room. They were not afraid, which surprised him as he was more than two yards high in his stockinged feet.

He smiled at them and gestured that they came around to the front door. He was damned if he was going to shout through the glass. They understood immediately and vanished from sight. They must have been clinging on like limpets to have been able to see above the windowsill.

There was a footman standing to attention in the entrance hall, waiting to run errands. 'Two children are about to knock on the front door. You will let them in but on no account allow their dog inside. Then have refreshments sent to the music room – something suitable for children as well as myself.'

To give him his due the young man moved swiftly to the door as if it was the most normal thing in the world to be letting in two unknown little ones. He waited by the music room and was amused to see them stand to have their coats removed by the footman before they walked towards him. These were no village children – that much was obvious from their appearance and behaviour.

The girl curtsied and the boy bowed. 'Thank you for inviting us in, Mr Sheldon. We could hear you playing from across the park and just had to come and listen. I am Lady Elizabeth Fenchurch and this is my twin brother, Lord Thomas, the Earl of Fenchurch.'

Beau bowed. 'I am Edward Sheldon and delighted to make your acquaintance. However, might I enquire if your parents are aware that you are wandering about my property uninvited and unsupervised?'

Again, it was the girl who spoke. The boy was staring at him with something that could be interpreted as awe. 'I would have thought, sir, that someone who could play as sublimely as you would have realised we have no papa. If we had, my brother would not hold the title.'

'Of course, a commoner like myself could not be expected to understand these things. Then I shall rephrase my question, young lady: is the Countess of Fenchurch aware that you are here?'

'I expect she will have guessed as we have not returned for luncheon. My brother does not often take the lead, but today he was insistent that we come and listen to you play. He is a talented pianist but sadly lacking in technique.'

Beau was finding this entire conversation quite extraordinary. The child, and she could be little more than eight or nine years of age, addressed him like an adult. He was unused to being put in his place by anyone and certainly not by a little girl who thought she was his equal.

Finally, the diminutive earl found his voice. 'I do beg your pardon, Mr Sheldon, for intruding on you in this manner. Before we are sent packing could I beg you to play for me again? I did not recognise the tune – is it something new?'

'I have no intention of sending you away until I have fed you and then I shall take you myself in the carriage. I shall have a note delivered to your mama explaining where you are and that I will bring you back safely before it gets dark.'

The rattle of crockery on a tray heralded the arrival of the refreshments. 'Come into my music room and warm yourselves in front of the fire. You should not have been wandering about outside when the temperature is below freezing.'

'We did not intend to come this far, sir; we were just exercising our dog, Brutus. As no doubt you observed, he is a very large animal and requires a deal of exercise.'

Beau hid his smile. The child was quite delightful and unlike any he had met before. He knew the daughters of his best friend,

Rushton; they were about the same age but neither of them were as poised and grown-up as this girl. The boy was eyeing the piano longingly and taking no notice whatsoever of the delicious treats that had been placed on a table near the fire.

Should he address the child by his title or by his given name? He had never been in this position before as being a duke meant he was always the most important person in the room – unless a member of the royal family happened to be present. He was not sure of the correct etiquette for a commoner to address an earl.

He erred on the side of caution. 'My lord, would you care to try my instrument?'

The boy was on the stool before he had finished speaking. Then he began to play the recently composed sonata that Beau had been playing moments before.

He made several mistakes but he had the melodies exact. How was this possible when he had only listened to the music once and that through the window? The boy was a musical genius. Beau turned and saw the girl was listening as intently as himself.

Hearing his own composition played with such talent, such enthusiasm, made him decide to change his plans for the next few months. His mission now was to teach this child prodigy the technique he lacked and help him to develop his undeniable genius. He had been denied a music teacher in his formative years because of his position in life; he could not let that happen to another who had even more ability than he did. Like this boy, he had been self-taught and was then obliged to unlearn his bad habits when as an adult, and able to organise his own life without interference, he employed a teacher.

Whilst up at Oxford he had indulged his passion knowing that when he returned music would have to be a secret part of his life – at least whilst his austere father still lived. He had inherited the title three months after reaching his majority and had then assumed responsibility for his five younger siblings and had no time for himself. Their mama had died when Giselle was still in the schoolroom and he had devoted himself to making his brothers and sisters happy as well as keeping the estates functioning efficiently.

He walked across to the piano and gently removed the child's hands. 'The refreshments have arrived. We shall talk whilst we eat.'

With some reluctance he guided the boy to the fire. Soon they were all munching happily on the delicious pastries. 'What would you like to drink? There is buttermilk, chocolate or coffee.' He was unsurprised when they both chose the dark, aromatic brew he preferred himself.

Once they were replete he indicated they should put their used utensils on the tray. They seemed surprised to be asked to do so but did not cavil. He doubted they ever did anything for themselves at home.

'I should like to give you lessons, my lord. Do you think that is something your mother would agree to?'

His smile and the way the boy nodded his head so vigorously answered his question. 'I am Thomas, if you please, sir. I do not care to be addressed so formally.'

'Then, Thomas, shall we begin?' He turned to the girl. 'Are you content to listen or would you like to be shown to the library to find yourself something to read?'

'The library, if you please, Mr Sheldon. Shall I ask for the tray to be removed?'

He nodded. 'Do that. There is a footman outside the door who will take you. The house is small enough for you to be able to find your way back without any difficulty.'

Thomas was already back at the piano, his eyes alight with

excitement, his fingers poised above the keys. Beau thought an hour sufficient for a first lesson but they both would have been happy to carry on for the remainder of the afternoon.

'Practise what I have shown you. I take it you have an instrument?'

'It is not as good as this but serves the purpose. At what time shall I present myself for my next lesson, sir?'

'I must speak to your mama before we make any firm arrangements, young man. If she does not want me to teach you then that is the end of the matter. You will not sneak off to visit me in the hope that I will ignore her wishes. Do I make myself clear?'

The child grinned. 'Mama will agree; she wishes us both to be happy.'

'If that is the case then no doubt she will arrange for you to be brought here by carriage. Presumably you are in the schoolroom with your tutor in the mornings, so it will have to be the afternoon.'

Elizabeth joined in the conversation from her position by the fire where she was busily reading a book of sermons. 'We are in between governesses, Mr Sheldon. Miss Brown left somewhat hurriedly just before Christmas and our mama has yet to find a replacement.' She looked hard at him. 'A tutor would be just as good as a governess.'

Beau laughed. 'If you are trying to suggest that I apply for that position, Elizabeth, then you are in for a disappointment. I am happy to help develop your brother's talents on the piano, but I draw the line at anything else.'

There was a polite tap on the door and the footman came in to announce that the carriage was waiting to convey them back to Fenchurch Manor. He had quite forgotten about the massive dog, which had been waiting patiently outside the front door for his young owners to emerge.

'That animal is not coming inside my carriage. He can run behind.'

The children exchanged glances and sighed in unison. 'That is what Mama always says and it is a great disappointment to all three of us,' Elizabeth said sadly.

* * *

When Viola had received the note from Mr Sheldon her first thought had been to order her carriage and drive over there immediately and retrieve her errant children. Then she reconsidered. The children were rarely wrong in their assessment of a person's character and if they wished to stay she trusted their judgement. After all, had they not been correct to distrust the previous governess? The wretched woman had falsified her testimonials and she never would have discovered this if the twins had not insisted she wrote to the three people concerned. Miss Brown had been dismissed without references and she had allowed the children to run wild for a few weeks.

There were half a dozen new candidates coming for interviews. This time the women would spend a day with her children so they could be involved in the choice. Every reference had been checked before inviting the governesses to come. This meant that whoever the children preferred could be appointed without fear of disappointment.

Allowing the two of them to roam free for so long was perhaps not the wisest move, but she had felt guilty that they had been obliged to endure inferior teaching for several months before she had believed their complaints.

At three o'clock she saw a carriage turn into the drive and

hastily moved away from the window in case she could be seen. She took her place on a comfortable chair in front of the fire and her mother bustled in from wherever she had been to join her.

'I wish to meet the gentleman who has been able to entertain my grandchildren for several hours. I wonder what it was about him that persuaded them to call there?'

'I am surprised Brutus did not return hours ago. One can be very certain that he was not allowed inside the house so, unless he found refuge in the stables, he will have been outside in the elements.'

'He has a thick coat; he will come to no harm. Did you honestly think he would leave the children?'

'I suppose not. No doubt Mr Sheldon will be shocked to find he is allowed inside this house as if he were a lapdog.'

'What you do and do not do, my love, is no concern of anyone but yourself.'

'I shall order tea and almond biscuits to be served. It has been so long since I had a morning caller I have quite forgotten the procedure.'

'As all our neighbours were close friends of your obnoxious husband they can hardly be surprised that you did not wish to see them once he was dead. I do wish that you had someone of your own age with whom to converse, my dear. You spend all your time with children and old people.'

She smiled. 'Old person, Mama, as there is only one of you.'

A further twenty minutes passed before the carriage pulled up outside. The tea urn was already in place, but she had dismissed the maid and decided to serve this insipid beverage herself if it was needed. Nursery tea would be waiting for the twins so they would be sent straight upstairs. It was Mr Sheldon she wished to converse with.

A footman stood in the doorway. 'A Mr Sheldon to see you, my lady.'

There was no obligation on her part to stand but her innate good manners made her do so. She was glad she was on her feet as the gentleman who strode in was enormous. He must be a foot taller than herself. He was also a prodigiously handsome man and that would not go unnoticed by her mother, who had remained seated.

'My lady, I must apologise for keeping your children with me for so long. I do hope you were not worried by their absence.'

'I was not, sir, as you had sent me a note to that effect. Would you care to be seated and take tea?'

'No tea – I thank you for the offer. I am not fond of it. I prefer coffee.'

She caught the eye of the footman and he vanished and would return with a jug of freshly brewed coffee in no time at all.

'Allow me to introduce you to my mother, Mrs Alston. I shall pour tea for her as she is very fond of it.'

He bowed to her mama. 'I am delighted to make your acquaintance, ma'am.' Then he flicked aside his coat-tails and took a chair opposite the one she had been sitting in. He was assured, obviously well used to moving in the best circles, which was more than could be said for herself.

'Lord Thomas is a musical genius, my lady, and it was his talent that kept us busy these past hours. I am a musician and composer myself and would like the privilege of teaching your son. He is eager to have lessons with me if you agree.'

She didn't hesitate. She trusted this man on sight. 'They are without a governess at present so he can come at whatever time suits you best. However, I am in the process of appointing another and, once she is in place, he must have his piano lessons with you when his schoolwork is done.'

'Then I shall expect him at ten o'clock tomorrow morning.'

The footman placed the silver coffee pot on the table next to the tea urn. Whilst she busied herself pouring tea he was conversing politely with her mother.

'As you see, Mr Sheldon, we now have coffee. Can I tempt you to some of these freshly baked biscuits?'

'No, coffee is all I require, thank you.'

She was in the process of pouring him a cup when disaster struck. Brutus, on seeing Mr Sheldon, bounded forward and nudged him firmly in the back. His hand flew up knocking the coffee jug from her hand and sending a scalding arc of liquid into the air closely followed by the priceless cup and saucer.

The hot liquid landed on the dog who yelped and continued to whine and frantically attempt to bite his back. One might have expected her visitor to have been appalled but instead he snatched up a vase containing hothouse blooms, tipped them onto the floor, and then emptied the water over the dog.

He dropped to his knees and, regardless of the immediate ruination to his smart jacket, rubbed the dog dry with the tails of his coat. The whining ceased and Viola joined him on the floor in order to examine any damage that might have been done.

'Is he badly burnt?'

'No, the cold water prevented that.' He rose smoothly to his feet and offered his hand.

Without hesitation she took it and he pulled her to her feet. He was so substantial that she felt like a child beside him. She had never before regretted the fact that the good Lord had made her a little over five feet tall, but now she wished she was not so petite.

She was about to apologise for the dog when he snapped his fingers and pointed to the door. To her astonishment the dog trotted out and she heard the ever vigilant footman opening the front door to let him into the garden.

'Good gracious! I never thought to see the day that that animal would heed anyone but the children.'

'He will do better in the cold.'

'Of course he will. I must thank you for your prompt action. You saved my dog but have ruined your jacket.'

He smiled and it quite took her breath away. 'I have other topcoats, my lady; do not concern yourself. However, if you will excuse me, I shall depart. I am not comfortable in your drawing room as I am.'

He bowed to both her and her mama and then took his leave. The room seemed strangely empty after his abrupt departure.

3

Beau travelled back to Elveden Hall with his thoughts in as much disarray as his appearance. First two delightful children had insinuated themselves into his life and now their mama was having the same effect on him. He closed his eyes and immediately her face was clear to him. She had glorious golden hair the colour of ripe corn, periwinkle blue eyes and a perfect feminine figure. She laughed readily, was without doubt intelligent, and obviously a devoted mother to her children.

What had Sofia said to him before he left? 'Beau, there is a woman out there somewhere for you to fall in love with. One day you will meet her and you will know at once she is the one you will marry.'

He was the only one of his siblings unmarried and his brothers and sisters had all made a love match. They were blissfully happy and he certainly envied them that. He sat straighter on the squabs. He was almost five and thirty, a confirmed bachelor, had no wish to disrupt his well-ordered life with a wife and possibly a nursery full of squalling babies.

Would he ever be prepared to sacrifice all this for a woman

he had just met? He smiled wryly. He almost thought he would, but that would be the height of folly. Romantic love was not, despite his siblings' experience, the basis for a lifelong partnership. He would need to know a lot more about Lady Fenchurch before he made a commitment.

He was chuckling at his foolishness when he strolled inside his own domain. He had spent barely a quarter of an hour in her company and most of that had been spent dealing with her scalded dog. Thinking about such an animal being allowed into the drawing room against all common sense and decency made him push away the romantic nonsense.

Teaching Thomas was another thing altogether. It would enhance his own determination to improve his composition and ability on the piano. He would ask Bishop for information about the family, for they must be the most prestigious in the neighbourhood.

He had informed Foster that he would not dress for dinner, did not wish a formal meal to be served in the dining room, but instead would eat simply in the breakfast parlour. He had also insisted that he would eat no earlier than five o'clock, which gave him ample time to change out of his ruined jacket and into something dry. Then he would spend the remaining time preparing tomorrow's lesson for the boy.

The child was adept at his scales but his fingering was incorrect, which meant he would not be able to play some of the more complex chords as he progressed. This was what he would begin with. He became so immersed in his music that a servant was obliged to bang a gong loudly in the doorway to attract his attention.

He was sharp-set, had eaten nothing since he broke his fast at seven o'clock that morning. The children had fallen on the pastries with such enthusiasm he had not had the heart to take any for himself. He drank two glasses of excellent claret with his dinner and then returned to the music room for a further few hours.

* * *

He was waiting in the entrance hall when the carriage from Fenchurch Manor rolled to a standstill. The massive dog had trotted alongside as it had the previous evening. He had already instructed a groom to find the animal somewhere warm to wait.

The coachman would remain here with his team until the lesson was finished. It made no sense to tire the horses unnecessarily by making them do four journeys instead of two. The horses would be unharnessed and put in the stables until word was sent for them to be got ready for the return.

The footman opened the door and Beau was surprised, and a little annoyed, to find the girl had accompanied her brother. They seemed oblivious to his disapproval.

'Good morning, Mr Sheldon, my brother and I are grateful to be...'

'Lady Elizabeth, have you come for a piano lesson?'

She looked at him as if he was speaking in tongues. 'I have not. It is my brother who is musical, not I.'

'In which case you will not come again uninvited. I am not your nursemaid. I am surprised that the countess has allowed you to accompany him.'

For the first time in their brief acquaintance she looked uncomfortable. Her cheeks coloured and she would not meet his eye. 'Mama is not aware that I have come too, sir. She believes me to be in the schoolroom attending to my embroidery.'

The two of them were still waiting to have their outdoor

garments removed by the footman. 'Escort Lady Elizabeth back to her carriage. She is to return home.'

The child's demeanour changed from embarrassed to furious in a second. She stamped her foot and pointed to him as if he were her servant. 'I do not take orders from you, sir. I shall stay here with my brother and that is the end of the matter.'

He stepped forward, picked her up and tossed her over his shoulder like a sack of corn. When she kicked him, he laughed and she remained still from that moment onwards. The footman had had the sense to stop the carriage disappearing to the coach house.

Beau opened the door with one hand and tossed the snivelling child inside. He slammed it shut and waved to the coachman who made no effort to hide his inappropriate smile of approval. The carriage moved forward and he could hear the yells of rage coming from inside as it disappeared down the drive.

It only then occurred to him that Thomas might react with equal violence after seeing his sister being treated so cavalierly. The reverse was true.

'I say, sir, that was capital. I love my sister but she believes she can do as she wishes and Mama finds it easier to let her get her own way than suffer from her tantrums.'

'She is a spirited and intelligent young lady, but my interest is in you and your amazing talent. I see you have divested yourself of your outdoor garments, so shall we begin our lesson?'

* * *

Viola had almost accompanied Thomas to his music lesson. Mr Sheldon would be spending a considerable amount of time with her beloved son and it behoved her to know as much as possible about him. She wished now that the carriage would be returning rather than remaining at Elveden. The weather was far too cold for her to use the gig.

She had no pressing engagements as she had seen her estate manager already this week, had spoken to the housekeeper about menus, and did not receive invitations, or any sort of correspondence that required her attention. Her mother had taken on the role of charitable giving on the estate and was out delivering comfort parcels to various deserving tenants and villagers, so there was no point in searching her out for company.

Elizabeth must be lonely on her own in the schoolroom. She and her brother were inseparable and this would be the first time Thomas had gone anywhere without his sibling for support. Viola wondered whether Brutus had decided to remain here or go with her son. She frowned. She had not seen the dog since the carriage had departed half an hour ago.

The schoolroom was empty – as far as she could see her daughter had not even been up here today. This could mean only one thing: the naughty girl had gone with her brother despite being told she must not do so. Mr Sheldon would not be pleased. This explained why the dog was also absent.

As she arrived in the hall her carriage arrived at the front door. The footman, an intelligent young man, was on his way to let down the steps and open the door for her daughter to descend. Mr Sheldon had done exactly the right thing, but she was certain her daughter would not see it this way and no doubt would treat the household to one of her infamous tantrums.

This time she would not give in to her daughter's rage. She would stand firm and send Elizabeth to her room in disgrace. She braced herself as a red-faced, furious little girl erupted into the hall.

'Mama, he threw me into the carriage. You must go at once and fetch Thomas back from that monster.'

The Duke's Bride

For a second Viola almost responded to this outrageous statement by dropping to her knees and offering her sobbing child a shoulder to cry on. However, she restrained the impulse. 'Elizabeth, whatever happened to you was entirely your own fault. You were expressly forbidden to accompany your brother. You will go to your room and remain there until I give you permission to come down.'

If she had tipped a bucket of icy water over the child's head it could not have had a more dramatic result. The crying ceased. Her daughter stared at her open-mouthed. Then without a word she fled upstairs. The force with which she slammed her bedchamber door echoed throughout the house.

The children had moved down from the nursery floor when Nanny had departed after Rupert had died. The only good thing about her marriage had been that once he had his heir he'd had no interest in producing another and therefore had mercifully left her unmolested in her own apartment.

This had not prevented him from beating her when the mood took him. She had endured his punishments silently, not giving him the satisfaction of hearing her cry or beg for mercy. The scars on her back from the whip he had used would remain a permanent reminder of the miserable years she had spent married to him. If she had not allowed him to take out his rage on her, he would have vented it on the children. She would never remarry and thus repeat her first mistake.

The carriage was still outside. 'Tell the coachman to wait, I wish to go to Elveden Hall.' The footman nodded and went out to deliver her message. She must not keep the horses standing in this weather. She flew up to her rooms and with the help of her dresser put on her outdoor half-kid boots, her winter cloak and matching bonnet. She was downstairs and on her way in minutes.

'Coachman, I shall not remain at Elveden for long, so you will have to walk the horses. There will be little point in unharnessing them.'

He touched his hat with his whip and nodded. He was a taciturn old man, someone who had worked for the family his entire life and his loyalties still lay with her deceased husband. She really should dismiss him but hadn't the heart. Unless she was prepared to give him a cottage on the estate and a pension he would starve. No one else would employ such a man.

The journey was short but it gave her sufficient time to organise her thoughts. Why was she going? Did she believe her daughter had been mistreated? Surely the gentleman she had met yesterday could not do such a thing to a child? Mr Sheldon had appeared to be an honest, trustworthy sort of person, not one who would mistreat a little one.

Elizabeth was a demanding, autocratic child but she was not a liar. Thomas must return with her immediately and there would be no further association with this man.

The air was crisp, the sky blue, and the sun bathed the frost-covered trees with golden light. Everywhere looked quite enchanting but she knew this to be a deception. It might look lovely, but if one remained out here for long one would perish. One could not trust one's eyes. What might appear perfect, inviting, would prove to be the reverse. This might seem a pessimistic outlook but her own experience had shown her view to be correct. Appearances were usually deceptive.

She sailed into the house and expected to be greeted by Mr Sheldon looking suitably apologetic. What met her was the beautiful sound of the piano. For a moment she was mesmerised by the liquid notes as they drifted from behind the closed doors of the music room and quite forgot why she was there. Then she recalled her sobbing daughter and her resolve hardened.

She was not going to be sent into the drawing room to wait on him. She would speak to him immediately. Ignoring the butler, who was attempting to speak to her, she pushed open the doors and stepped inside. He was the one playing, her son sitting beside him on the piano stool. They ignored her even though she was certain Mr Sheldon was aware she was there.

Viola stood, tapping her foot, becoming more incensed as the minutes passed and he continued to play. The notes died away and he rose smoothly from the stool and turned to face her. His expression was bland, his eyes watchful, but he did not look at all surprised to find her there.

The silence stretched between them. Thomas wriggled from his seat and ran to her. 'I do not know what my sister told you, but it will be a tale to her advantage. She refused to leave and so Mr Sheldon picked her up. He was savagely kicked and he laughed at her. That was all that happened. I should never have allowed her to come.'

The weight that had been pressing on her chest immediately lifted. 'Indeed, you should not have, my dear, but we both know that when your sister decides to do something it is almost impossible to dissuade her.'

Mr Sheldon nodded politely. 'Welcome to my house, my lady. I wish it were in more convivial circumstances.'

She waited for him to apologise for mistreating her beloved daughter but instead he said something else entirely.

'Lady Elizabeth is sadly spoiled. The child mostly behaves like an adult and expects to be treated like one. I think it might be wise if you found something to occupy her fierce intelligence before she is quite ruined by your overindulgence.'

How dare he speak to her like that? He scarcely knew Elizabeth; he could not possibly be in a position to pass judgement in this way. 'Come, Thomas, you will return home with me this instant. You will not be having music lessons in future with Mr Sheldon.'

Her son nodded, did not argue, but his slumped shoulders and tear-filled eyes told her more than his protests ever could. She raked the offending gentleman from head to foot with a steely stare, expecting him to look uncomfortable. He merely raised an eyebrow, which only enraged her more.

If she said anything further it would be so impolite she would regret it later. Therefore, she took her son's hand and led him away, knowing even as she did so that she was being unfair to both Mr Sheldon and her son. Too late for regrets. The matter was settled.

Thomas said nothing on the return journey. If he had cried, begged her to reconsider, she might have done so immediately. His stoic silence, his sitting as far away from her as he could in the carriage, his refusal to meet her eye, pierced her heart. She prayed she had not irretrievably damaged her relationship with both him and her daughter. She would have a deal of fence-mending to do before this matter was settled between them.

4

Beau saw the butler holding Thomas's coat and muffler and swore under his breath. He had been behaving as if he was the Duke of Silchester and not a humble commoner. Small wonder Lady Fenchurch had been so angry that her precious daughter had been manhandled by himself.

'Have a horse saddled and waiting for me out front. I shall be there in ten minutes.' He gave this command without any servant being visible but was confident someone would have heard him and followed his orders.

Upstairs Bishop tossed him his greatcoat and the other necessary items and he was still fastening buttons as he bounded down the outside steps that led to the turning circle. There was no mount waiting for him. He had not thought to enquire when he had arrived yesterday if there was something up to his weight in the stables.

The sound of hooves on cobbles heralded the arrival of an animal equal to anything he had in his own stables at Silchester. The black stallion was magnificent and seemed an unlikely horse for an elderly man to have kept. No time to investigate this oddity; he would do so on his return.

He swung into the saddle, rammed his boots into the irons, and was away across the fields. He took the direct route and thought he should arrive ahead of the carriage despite the fact they had left before him. During the wild gallop he realised two things. One, he intended to take this horse back with him when he returned to his own home and two, he was behaving like a lunatic. The boy would have several outer garments and would come to no real harm during the short journey from being only in his indoor clothes.

A huge hedge loomed in front of him. He pushed his concerns aside and concentrated on remaining in the saddle and not breaking his neck. The stallion soared into the air and cleared the obstacle with a foot at least to spare.

He was committed to travelling as if his breeches were on fire so did not check his horse until he arrived. Lady Fenchurch was standing in front of the house as if expecting him to come. He dismounted with more speed than dignity. Thomas was hiding in the stable somewhere and he ran through the arch, determined to find the child and take him in before he suffered any ill effects from the elements.

* * *

Viola's son was out of the carriage ahead of her, not waiting for the steps to be let down, and vanished with his dog in the direction of the stables. Good grief! In her hurry to leave she had neglected to collect her son's outdoor garments and now he was unprotected in the treacherous February weather.

The carriage vanished to the coach house whilst she stood undecided in the turning circle. Would it be best to go after

Thomas immediately and persuade him to come in and put on something warmer, or should she send Elizabeth with the necessary items?

As she dithered the sound of a horse galloping across the park made her turn so suddenly she almost lost her footing. Thundering towards her was Mr Sheldon. He pulled his stallion to a rearing halt and tumbled from the saddle.

'Is Thomas inside?' She shook her head but was unable to speak a word. 'Where will he hide? I have his outdoor garments here. He cannot remain outside without them.'

Too shocked by his inexplicable and sudden appearance to do more than point in the direction of the stables, she watched him race away, unsure what to think. How could he have arrived simultaneously? When she had left him, he had been in the music room and yet here he was in his greatcoat. Her thoughts were rudely interrupted by something heavy shoving her in the small of the back.

Then an enormous equine head rested on her shoulder and instinctively she raised a hand to stoke the nose of the magnificent horse. Sheldon appeared to have forgotten his mount in his hurry to find her son.

'Well then, sir, it is I who must take you to a warm stable. Does your master often abandon you in this way?'

She reached up and took the reins and the animal did not object to her leading him. For such an enormous horse he was remarkably docile. She continued to talk nonsense to him as she led him through the archway to the stable yard. Belatedly it occurred to her that one of her own grooms should have realised they were needed at the front of the house; Mr Sheldon could hardly have arrived so quickly on his own two feet.

* * *

Unfortunately, as the lesson had only lasted an hour, he had had little time to talk to the boy so had no idea whether he would be inclined to hide with the horses or find somewhere away from the stables. Brutus appeared at his side and nipped him sharply on the thigh and then dashed off towards the barn in which the fowl were kept.

He followed the dog into the building, gagging at the smell. Why would anyone wish to hide somewhere so pungent? The dog had stopped at the rear of the barn beside a huddled shape in the far corner. This was not the time for sympathy, but for firm action.

'Thomas, you will put on your coat and scarf.' He handed them to the child who scrambled into them without complaint. 'Good, now we shall return to the house. Do not look so despondent. I give you my word your lessons will resume. Maybe not tomorrow, but within a day or two at the most.'

'When Mama makes up her mind she is like my sister – she will not back down. I have never known her to alter her opinion on a subject once she has stated it so positively as she did about the lessons.'

'I am a very persuasive gentleman when I set my mind to it. Never in my life have I been gainsaid and I shall not allow that to happen this time. It stinks in here, my boy. Why on earth did you not take refuge with the horses?'

'I do not like them. No one in the family has ridden since my father broke his neck when out hunting.'

'God's teeth! I abandoned my horse. I hope someone has gone to fetch him from the turning circle.'

'Mama does not approve of such language, sir. That is because my father used a lot of bad words.'

The more he heard about this dead earl the less he liked him.

'That's as may be, lad, but as she is not present I cannot see she can object. Now, you must go inside and I must find my stallion.'

The boy obediently trotted away with his massive pet beside him, leaving him to go in search of the horse he had ridden across country, at breakneck speed, without even knowing the animal's name, or how he came to be in his stables.

A groom greeted him cheerfully. 'Her ladyship fetched your horse, sir. The beast's warm and snug in a stall for the moment. He were too hot to water but will be taken care of when he's cool.'

'Excellent. I doubt I shall be long, but I will send word when I require him to be saddled.' He looked around to see if there was a path that led directly to the house and saw it immediately. It ran between two immaculately clipped privet hedges.

He wondered who was now running the estate and was guardian to the children; whoever they were, they were doing an excellent job – at least with the estate. As far as he was concerned the children were in need of more discipline, and less spoiling from their mother. This might be true, but it was none of his business and he had no intention of interfering further.

As soon as he had persuaded the countess to allow him to continue to teach her son he would be on his way home. He was forced to admit it wasn't just for the child's sake but also for his own. He would gain as much from their interaction as the boy.

The side door was unlocked and he stepped through without announcing himself. He marched to the entrance hall and tossed his coat and other items to a somewhat startled footman. 'Where shall I find the countess?'

'Her ladyship is upstairs with Lord Thomas and Lady Elizabeth. I do not believe she is receiving at present, Mr Sheldon.'

Beau ignored the remark. 'Inform her ladyship that I shall be waiting for her in the drawing room. First, I need somewhere to remove the mud from my person. I shall require coffee but nothing to eat.'

'If you would care to come with me, sir, there is an anteroom where I can attend to you.'

Less than five minutes later Beau's boots were restored to their previous shine and the worst of the mud brushed from his breeches. He returned to the main part of the house, leaving his caped riding coat in the capable hands of the footman.

Again, he did not knock but walked into the drawing room as if he had every right to be there. The coffee was ahead of him. He poured himself a cup, drained it in one swallow and then refilled it. The vista from the long windows at the far end of the room was impressive but did not compare with Silchester. His coffee slopped on his fingers.

What the hell was he doing? The person he was supposed to be would not have had the effrontery to take possession of this drawing room, make demands of the servants and insist that Lady Fenchurch come down to see him. He should have accepted the footman's comment, left a message, and departed, yet here he was strolling around her house as if he were a member of the family.

* * *

Viola was just stepping into a fresh gown when word came up that Sheldon had taken occupancy of her drawing room and was calmly drinking coffee and wandering about the place like a welcome guest.

'Hurry up, Hughes. I have to be downstairs immediately.'

One of the two nursemaids who attended to her children had sent word that Thomas was safely indoors and reconciled with his sister; they were both happily engrossed in a game of soldiers

The Duke's Bride

in the nursery. Elizabeth, who had been instructed to remain in her own bedchamber, had obviously ignored this order. She would deal with her daughter's disobedience when she had dispatched the unwanted visitor.

She rarely noticed what she was wearing; she left her choice of garments entirely in the hands of her very efficient abigail as she had absolutely no interest in her appearance. Hughes had been appointed by her husband and was not someone she particularly liked. However, the woman was efficient, did not bother her with idle chatter and knew her place.

She ran lightly down the staircase, but instead of dashing in to confront the gentleman who had invaded her house she paused in the shadows to study him more closely. He was sitting, relaxed, his long, booted legs stretched out towards the fire, drinking coffee. She would have expected him to be pacing anxiously, not lounging about as he was.

He wore his dark hair fashionably short; his eyes were some shade between blue and green; his features were regular, aristocratic even; and as he swallowed the strong column of his neck drew her attention. She was sure that his topcoat was from Weston's, his boots from Hobbs – but then why should they not be as he was a wealthy man?

Then to her horror he looked directly at her. 'My lady, do you intend to lurk out there indefinitely or are you going to join me in a cup of your excellent coffee?'

One would have thought she would be embarrassed at being caught staring like an urchin, but for some reason she laughed. 'I beg your pardon, sir, I was lost in admiration at your ability to behave as if you had every right to be here and were not an uninvited guest.'

He rose smoothly to his feet and bowed. His eyes were

glinting with amusement. 'I apologise for my intrusion, my lady. Can I pour you a cup?'

'That would be splendid, thank you. Do sit down; you are looming over me. Being so small myself I find overlarge people quite intimidating.'

He folded his considerable length elegantly back onto the chair before speaking. 'Then I apologise a second time for being too tall. I shall do my best not to loom in future.'

His hands were strong, lean and sun-browned as if he had spent some time in a hot country lately. 'Are you recently returned from India?'

His smile was warm and she responded to his charm despite her reservations.

'No, I am not a nabob if that is what you were thinking. I was travelling for some months in Spain last year.'

'I see. It is none of my business and I apologise for...'

'Enough, we have both apologised sufficiently for one visit. I would like to explain what happened.'

'There is no need, sir, my son told me what transpired. I do not agree with any form of physical punishment, which is why I was so angry when I came to collect my son.'

'In that case if you ensure that Lady Elizabeth does not accompany Lord Thomas then can I expect him to come tomorrow morning? Although we only spent a short time together today it has served to reinforce my opinion that he is a very special boy. I believe that I have a modest talent for both playing and composing, but your son is quite extraordinary. He can hear a piece of music once and then replicate it note for note.'

'I had no idea he was that good. Yes, of course he must continue to come to you. My daughter will not be best pleased but it is time she learned she cannot always have her own way.'

The Duke's Bride

'Perhaps there is something that she shines at? She is a most intelligent child. There must be an interest she has that you could encourage her to pursue?'

'She loves to read the driest things. Books of boring sermons seem to be her particular favourite at the moment.'

He smiled. 'That is exactly what she selected from my library when she was there yesterday. Does she write a journal? If you provided her with a suitably important-looking ledger she could record her thoughts in that every day.'

'I think that an excellent notion. Your mention of a ledger has given me an idea. She is also better at computation than I am myself. I shall give her the household accounts to oversee – that should keep her busy.'

He looked at her as if she was an escapee from Bedlam. What could she possibly have said to cause him to look at her like that? Surely, he had not taken her suggestion seriously?

'Are you honestly intending to allow your eight-year-old daughter to see how much is paid to each number of your staff, or how much you donate to charity, and then be able to compare it with the amount you spend on yourselves?'

He sounded so outraged she could not hold back her laughter. 'I think it will be an excellent lesson for her. With any luck she will become a radical and give her inheritance away.'

'I beg your pardon, I honestly thought you were making a genuine proposal...'

'I thought we had abandoned further apologies, Mr Sheldon. You do not know me well enough to realise whether I am being sincere or not.'

'That is something I hope I can remedy over the coming weeks. I am, as you know, recently arrived in the neighbourhood and having no wife to make morning calls and leave cards for me I have no notion to whom I should extend an invitation to dine.'

'I would suggest that you make no push to become acquainted with anyone locally.' She hesitated, not sure if it was right that she told him about her husband. 'No doubt you will hear all this from your staff so I might as well tell you myself.'

When she had finished explaining the true state of her marriage, the character of her husband and the fact that all the families locally were supporters of his, he looked appalled. For a second she thought it was because she had been so indiscreet.

'If I had known the true facts, my lady, I would have treated your daughter differently, however hard she had kicked me. You are well rid of him. If you have an adult brother, why did he not step in and deal with the matter?'

'I told no one until after the earl was dead. Do you think I wished my brother to dangle at the end of a rope on my account?'

He ran his hand through his hair, making it stand on end. He now looked less formidable, more approachable somehow. 'You are the most courageous woman I have ever met. I suppose you were taken in by his appearance, wealth and charm and did not realise what you were stepping into until it was too late.'

'That is exactly how it happened. My papa, who died four years ago, had always dreamed of bringing his family up in the world. He was a very wealthy man but his money came from trade. This estate is only in such good heart because of my inheritance. When I arrived, matters had been sadly neglected.'

He leaned forward, his eyes intent. 'How on earth did you persuade the earl to use the money in this way?'

'Papa had it written into the agreement. Half the amount was to be used at my discretion; the other half he was free to do as he wished with.'

His brow creased as he digested this extraordinary statement. 'All I can say, my lady, is that your father was a wise man. Forgive me for being impertinent, but might I enquire if your brother is now in charge of the family and estates?'

'Legally he is, but he is far too busy managing the family businesses to bother himself with us. He is a loving brother, a good uncle and son, but we see too little of him. I am sure that if I requested his assistance he would make time for me.'

He nodded. 'I have outstayed my welcome by a considerable amount. Thank you for being so open about your situation.'

He was on his feet now and a smile played around his lips. She could not take her eyes from it. 'You do understand how this changes our circumstances, my lady? If I am not to make the acquaintance of anyone else in the vicinity, then there is only yourself and your family I can entertain at my home.'

She too rose and as before she found his size rather intimidating. He sensed her unease and increased the distance between them. 'Is that a roundabout way of asking me to invite you to dine here?'

'I should be delighted. When am I to come and at what time?'

'Would tomorrow be convenient, Mr Sheldon?'

He half-bowed. 'Time?'

'We keep country hours here, so four o'clock.'

'I prefer to eat later so when I return the invitation, you will be dining at six o'clock. Would that be a problem?'

'I cannot see why not. It will mean travelling in the dark, but it is no distance to Elveden Hall so I doubt I shall come to any harm.'

'Then I shall see you here tomorrow at four, my lady.' He turned and strode out. He had a military bearing – she wondered if this travelling overseas that he had mentioned could have been with the army on the Peninsula.

5

Beau had neglected to send word to the stables so his nameless stallion remained unsaddled. His tack was neatly arranged on the peg outside his stall so he took care of the matter himself.

'Well, old fellow, I wonder how you came to be at Elveden and what name you go by.' He pulled the massive animal's ears affectionately and the horse responded by slobbering down his greatcoat.

He was just tightening the girth when a flustered groom skidded to a halt beside them. 'I beg your pardon, sir, I didn't know you wished to leave.'

'My fault – I forgot to send notice of my departure.' With the reins hooked over his arm he led his mount out of the stable block and into the yard. Despite the fact that the horse was well over sixteen hands he swung into the saddle without recourse to the mounting block.

This time he would return at a sensible pace and use the lanes rather than the fields. He leaned forward and patted the gleaming black neck of his horse. 'See there, old fellow, those

The Duke's Bride

three men are replacing the divots you kicked up when we arrived half an hour ago.'

Beau squeezed gently and the stallion moved smoothly into a collected canter. They passed nobody on the journey so he was not obliged to slow his pace until half a mile away, when he instructed the horse to walk. This would ensure the animal would be cool when he arrived. He dismounted outside the stables so he could talk to the head groom who had come out to take the reins.

'As you can see he is not hot so can be fed and watered immediately. Tell me, how does this animal come to be in my stables? When I purchased this estate all I knew was that there were two teams of farm horses, two hunters and a second team to pull a carriage.'

'The master saw Titus as a colt at a gypsy fair and could not resist him. I broke him in myself and he was never gelded because he is so sweet-natured. I reckon his sire was a thoroughbred for him to be so fine.'

'He is a splendid animal and I have no need to purchase anything else as he is exactly what I need.'

The remainder of the day was spent preparing both lessons and passages that Thomas could practise for the next day. He dined as before in the breakfast parlour and retired early. He did not miss the responsibilities that came with his heritage but he did miss his siblings and their families.

Silchester Court was a massive barracks of a building with more rooms than he had ever cared to count. At least when he did return in a few months he would still have Aubrey and Mary living in the wing he had converted for them. Perry and Sofia would be departing for their new house in Derbyshire as soon as he got back.

He did not consider himself a sociable sort of fellow, but he had not realised how much time he spent in conversation with his brother Bennett and his brother-in-law Grey, who both lived nearby. Also, he was finding it uncomfortable having to tell Banbury tales in order to maintain the pretence that he was plain Mr Sheldon.

For all the disadvantages he did not regret for one moment having come. Now he was able to spend as much time as he wished on his passion without feeling one iota of guilt that important matters were being neglected. The fact that he would become better acquainted with Lady Fenchurch and her children was not something he'd anticipated, but he was looking forward to some lively conversations with all three of them.

The following morning he got up to an eerie whiteness. There had been heavy snowfall overnight, which would mean the lanes would be impassable – even the high hedges would not prevent them becoming blocked. He was disappointed that his pupil would not be able to come for his lesson but more for the fact that he would not be able to go to dinner as planned at Fenchurch Manor.

'Bishop, how long are we likely to be cut off here?'

His valet poked his head into the bedchamber from where he had been busy laying out Beau's clothes in the dressing room. 'We've not had much snow so far this winter, sir, so I think it might well be here for a week or two, possibly more.'

'Then the horses will get no exercise and neither shall I. From the look of the sky we are in for more snow later today.'

And so it was – that afternoon he watched morosely as the flakes drifted to the ground, adding to the six inches that were already obliterating the landscape.

* * *

The thaw arrived as suddenly as the snow. Beau got up two weeks later to find he was no longer cut off. However, the deluge that had fallen would make the lanes fetlock-deep in mud so he doubted Thomas would be able to come to him, as a carriage would get stuck. Instead, he would ride across the fields and give him his lesson on the inferior instrument that he owned.

He was well aware his real motive for going was not to teach, but to speak to Viola – she was no longer Lady Fenchurch to him in the intimacy of his head. Over the past few days he had had ample opportunity to think about this delightful young widow and the more he did so the more he came to believe that perhaps he had at last met the person he was to fall in love with.

* * *

Viola was overjoyed to see the snow had melted at last. Even the children were no longer interested in making snowmen or having snowball fights. The first candidate that was supposed to arrive for interview had, not surprisingly, failed to come. The second and third were due this week so no doubt she would find herself involved with three young ladies, who all wanted the position as governess, at the same time.

Thomas, who should know better, burst into her bedchamber in his nightshirt. 'Mama, the snow has gone so I can start my lessons again.'

'Unfortunately, the lanes will still be closed. We must wait for it to dry out or the carriage will come to grief.'

'How long will that be?'

'I have no idea, darling. You would do better to ask one of the outside men as they seem to be knowledgeable about the weather.'

He was about to ask another question but she stopped him.

'Go back to your bedchamber and allow me to get dressed in peace. We shall continue the conversation over breakfast.'

One would have thought that after only spending an hour in Mr Sheldon's company she would have forgotten the details of his appearance, the timbre of his voice, but this was not the case. His image invaded her every waking moment as well as her dreams. This was not something she wanted and it made her feel vulnerable. She had never been attracted to a gentleman before. It was most unsettling, almost unpleasant.

Despite her good intentions to discipline her children – well, to be honest it was only her daughter who needed a firmer hand – she had abandoned her attempts to check Elizabeth's strong will after a second tantrum that lasted an entire morning.

Her mother was already in the breakfast parlour helping herself from a tasty array of items. 'Good morning, Viola, I'm sure you are as relieved as I am to see the back of that nasty white stuff. Do you intend to reissue your dinner invitation to Mr Sheldon?'

'I can hardly do otherwise, Mama. At least I do not have to worry about it until the lanes are safe for a carriage to pass through. I am more concerned about the three would-be governesses who are likely to arrive together. I am not sure how to organise interviews if they are all under my roof at the same time.'

'If you intend for them to spend a morning with the children before you make a decision then they will be here for three days. I suppose it will not hurt to see how they interact together; a little healthy rivalry never did anyone any harm in my opinion.'

'I dread to think how Elizabeth will behave by the third day. She does not like to be constrained, and to ask her to be on her best behaviour for so long will be doomed to failure.'

Her mother chuckled. 'Then so much the better, my dear –

whoever you appoint must be able to manage that girl's tantrums.'

'I think it more likely they will all turn tail and run away. I would much prefer them to see her when she is being cooperative.'

'By the by, did you know that Mr Sheldon bought the estate unseen? I have never heard the like. To spend so much money without even a single visit beggars belief.'

'I am sure he had someone make thorough investigations. He does not seem like a gentleman to do anything without serious consideration beforehand. Anyway, Mama, it is none of our business.'

Her mother looked at her through narrowed eyes. 'He is not the gentleman for you, daughter, so if you are thinking of him as a possible husband...'

Viola dropped her plate and the ham, coddled eggs and toast landed on the carpet. 'How can you say such a thing? You know I shall never marry again.' Her heart was pounding, her hands clammy at the thought. 'Please, do not say you think he is interested in me in that way.'

'Good heavens, I am certain he is not. However, you are halfway to falling in love with him yourself even if you are denying it. If you would like my advice, I should find some excuse to cancel the dinner invitation. The less you see of him the better. I can only see it ending in heartbreak.'

The footman who was in attendance had already cleared away the mess but her appetite had deserted her. She would just have coffee this morning. Now her panic had subsided she was curious to know why her mother thought Mr Sheldon would not consider her to be a suitable wife for him. She was shocked to the core by the answer she got to this question.

'Think about it, Viola. There can be only one reason why a

wealthy gentleman of almost five and thirty, who is a fine figure of a man, is not married and that is because he has chosen to remain single. Therefore, he is unlikely to change his mind so late in the day, even for you.'

'I can assure you, Mama, I have no more interest in marriage than he has, so I can see no obstacle to us continuing our acquaintance.'

'It has occurred to me, my love, that he could be a widower himself or...'

'I have no wish to discuss this subject a moment longer. I wish to enjoy my breakfast without interruption.'

At ten o'clock the twins burst into the drawing room. 'He is coming; we saw him cantering down the drive. Mr Sheldon will be here at any moment. I am to have my piano lesson today after all,' Thomas said as he danced from one foot to the other.

'I do not like Mr Sheldon, Mama. I insist that you send him away.'

Viola put down her book and stood up. 'You will not speak to me like that, young lady. Go to your bedchamber at once and remain there until I give you leave to come out. Your behaviour is unacceptable and inappropriate for a young lady of your station.'

Her daughter hesitated. Then her cheeks flushed. With a sinking heart Viola knew Mr Sheldon was going to witness the most appalling tantrum. She would not blame him one jot if he refused to stay and teach Thomas.

The fact that this gentleman had ridden to Fenchurch Manor today rather than wait until it was suitable for a carriage meant he was as eager to resume the lessons as her son was to participate.

Thomas grabbed his sister's hand. 'Don't do it, Beth, please don't, not when Mr Sheldon is coming. He will be horrified. You

The Duke's Bride

must go upstairs and behave yourself and allow me to have my music lesson.'

Elizabeth snatched her arm away, clenched her fist and punched her brother in the face. He reeled backwards and fell heavily to the floor. Viola dropped to her knees to attend to him but was hindered by Elizabeth's flying fists and feet. The child had lost control of her senses and seemed determined to injure her brother.

Then Mr Sheldon was there. He picked up her screaming daughter and vanished up the stairs, ignoring the blows and kicks he was receiving. If ever a little girl deserved a spanking it was Elizabeth, but she knew he would not go back on his word.

* * *

Beau walked into the first room he came to. It was not a child's bedchamber but it would serve the purpose. The fact that there was no fire lit and it was decidedly chilly was all the better. Elizabeth was still screaming as if she were being murdered but she was no longer kicking or punching him. He dropped her to the floor so suddenly the racket stopped and her legs folded beneath her so she was sitting at his feet.

There was a bentwood chair close by, which he picked up, turned and straddled, then folded his arms across and rested his chin on them. Her cheeks were scarlet and tear-stained but she looked anything but unrepentant for her misbehaviour.

He stared down at her but said nothing. She was obviously expecting a bear-garden jaw and in the growing silence she began to fidget. Then she attempted to get up and he reached down and gently pushed her back to the floor. This was repeated several times over the next twenty minutes. He was waiting for her to calm down, for her face to resume its normal colour, before he attempted to talk to her.

After the sixth time she pulled her feet under her and folded her arms across her chest. 'Why don't you smack me?'

'I do not believe in physical punishment if it can be avoided.'

She almost smiled.

'You certainly deserve a sound spanking, young lady, but I would not have given you one even with your mother's consent. I am no relation to you therefore it is not my place to discipline you or your brother.'

Her interest was piqued as he had hoped. 'Might I be permitted to get up please, Mr Sheldon?'

'You may, but you will sit on that chair opposite me and remain there until I give you permission to get down.'

She nodded and was soon curled up looking at him thoughtfully. She really was a most remarkable girl. 'Are we to freeze together in here?'

'I shall not do so as I am warmly dressed. It is unfortunate that you only have on your gown and pinafore. So, for your sake I hope this conversation can be completed speedily.'

'You could always light the fire then we can converse in comfort.'

'We shall proceed as things are, my girl. It was the most unedifying spectacle I walked into. Are you in the habit of kicking and punching your brother whilst screaming like a banshee?'

She had the grace to look away. When she looked up again there were tears trickling down her cheeks. 'I have never done that before. I love Thomas more than anything in the world. He is my twin – my other half. Please, please, will you let me go and apologise to him and my mother for my dreadful behaviour?'

In one smooth movement he was crouching next to her and

offered her his handkerchief. 'There, that was not so difficult was it?'

She sniffed loudly and blew her nose. 'I do not mean to be horrible – something comes over me and I cannot control it.'

'Then, little one, I suggest that when you know your anger is about to overwhelm you that you absent yourself from the situation. Then return when you are calmer, apologise and talk things through as we are doing.'

'You are a kind man and I thank you for your understanding. I do not deserve it as I have shown you disrespect and have both punched and kicked you.'

'And you, Elizabeth, are wise beyond your years. Have you started to write your journal?'

'I found that tedious, sir, so have decided to write a book instead.'

He could not prevent his look of horror and she giggled. 'I am not going to write sermons; they are even more tedious than writing a journal. I only read them to appear interesting.'

He joined in her laughter. 'You have certainly succeeded in that, as it has been a topic of conversation between myself and your mama. Come, I am sure you wish to find your family and make your apologies.'

She jumped off the chair and held out her hand for him to take. It wasn't an imperious gesture but one of friendship. 'Will you come with me please? I believe that if they see that you have forgiven me and we are now the best of friends they will be more ready to accept my regrets.'

Hand in hand they made their way to the drawing room. Thomas was sitting with his mother and, apart from a bruise on his cheek, appeared undamaged from his encounter with the little termagant he was leading in. Strangely she kept hold of his hand and didn't run to her mother or brother as he had expected.

6

Viola was moved by the sight of her turbulent daughter walking peaceably beside Mr Sheldon. It was quite obvious that there was absolute trust between them – they had come to an understanding. Thomas was about to get up but she touched his arm and shook her head. He nodded and sat back once more.

'Elizabeth, Mr Sheldon, I am delighted to see you in accord.'

Her daughter glanced up at him for reassurance and then seeing approval on his face finally released his hand and stepped forward to stand in front of her.

'Mama, Thomas, I most humbly beg your pardon for my atrocious behaviour. I cannot promise I shall never behave so again, but what I can promise is that I shall do my very best not to. Mr Sheldon has given me some good advice and I intend to follow it.' Elizabeth then curtsied first to her and then to her son.

'Thank you for apologising so sincerely. You were forgiven before you had left the room by both of us.'

Her son jumped up and flung his arms around his sister. 'You're my favourite person in the whole world and there's nothing you can do that would make me change my mind.' He released her and grinned up at Mr Sheldon. 'Can we have a lesson now, please, sir? I have practised and practised and believe I have mastered the new fingering.'

'If your mother is agreeable, then I am happy to oblige.'

'Yes, go at once to the music room. Thank you for making the effort to ride over. It is much appreciated by all of us.'

He followed Thomas from the room and she could hear the boy chattering and laughing in a way that he had never done before. Whilst his father had been alive the twins had been kept away from him, remained on the nursery floor as much as possible. Only when Rupert was away from home did they venture down – if she wished to spend time with them she had to do so without letting that monster know. He did not want her any more himself but was not prepared to share her attention even with his own children.

She held out her arms and Elizabeth fell into them. 'Mama, why am I so horrible? Is it because I take after our papa? He was a horrible man too. Thomas and I were glad when he died.'

For a child of her age to say such a thing was deeply shocking. She hugged her close and tried to reassure her.

'Neither of you look the slightest bit like him. You both have my colouring, so I think it highly unlikely you have inherited any of his less pleasant traits. Remember, my love, you are in control of yourself regardless of who your parents are. If you behave badly then it is up to you to curb this.'

'Grandmama told the vicar's wife that I am horribly spoilt. Is that why I get in such a rage and cannot bear to be thwarted?'

'Eavesdropping, Elizabeth, is not acceptable. One will always hear things one does not want to. I do indulge you both – that is my prerogative – but from this moment on we shall work together to help you and your brother learn to behave as you should.'

Her daughter wriggled onto her lap, not something she had done since she was in leading strings. 'I love you, Mama, almost as much as I do Thomas. I also love my grandmama but not as much.'

'And I love you, my darling girl – nothing will change that.' She stroked Elizabeth's soft, golden hair and tightened her hold. With a sigh of contentment, the child fell asleep. They remained in this way for an hour and then her daughter began to stir.

'Shall we go and listen to your brother playing? But first can I ask you to pull the bell strap and order coffee and pastries to be served in here in half an hour?'

'I think Mr Sheldon was shocked that Thomas and I prefer coffee to anything else. Is it bad for children? Was that why he was concerned?'

'I think he was more surprised than concerned. It is certainly unusual for children to like coffee.'

When she offered her hand, her daughter took it – this too was a rare occurrence. Surely it could not be the influence of a music teacher that had changed her daughter so radically?

She had expected to hear the wonderful sound of the piano as they approached the room but this was not the case. She increased her pace. Elizabeth let go of her hold and ran ahead, as eager to discover the reason for the silence as she was.

The door was open and the room was empty. Why had the lesson been cut short? She sincerely hoped nothing had gone awry between Mr Sheldon and her son. She would be disappointed if there was no reason for there to be any interaction between them in future.

'Look, Mama, Thomas has left us a note.' This was waved triumphantly above her daughter's head.

'Read it to me then. I wish to know where they both are.'

'If you are looking for us, you will find us on the nursery floor. I

have taken Mr Sheldon to see our soldiers. The piano is not good enough for me any more. Does that mean you will buy him another one?'

'It does indeed. But more importantly, my love, it means we shall all go to London together. I think it important your brother and Mr Sheldon can try the instrument for themselves.'

'We have never been there. I am so excited. When can we go?'

'I shall have to discuss this with Mr Sheldon before I can make a firm decision. I can see no reason why we could not go immediately the roads are clear. I have no wish to be in Town once the Season starts.'

On the way to the nursery floor she was obliged to explain exactly what she meant by this and her daughter, who had as little interest in her appearance as she did, seemed satisfied with her answer.

To her astonishment she found Mr Sheldon lying prone, theatrically defending his troops from a violent attack on the other side of the carpet from Thomas. This gentleman did not seem the sort of person to enjoy playing soldiers with a child. However, from the ease with which he interacted with both her daughter and her son she must presume he had nieces and nephews somewhere.

'They are having so much fun. Do you think they would mind if I joined in?'

Mr Sheldon answered without looking up. 'I could do with some help, sweetheart. Your brother is soundly trouncing me.'

In a flash Elizabeth was sprawled beside him, eagerly giving him tactical advice on how to position his troops before the next bombardment from her twin.

'I am not needed here. There will be refreshments served in the drawing room in one hour. I would like you to join us, Mr Sheldon, if you are not in a rush to depart.'

When he looked up and his smile did something strange to her insides. 'I should be delighted. Fighting battles is hungry work.'

It would be midday at least before the game was over and the children normally had luncheon in the nursery. Today they could eat with the adults as a special treat. She thought pastries and coffee would not be sufficient for any of them after so much excitement. A message was sent to Cook that cold cuts, bread and cheese, hot pasties, pickles and accompaniments were to be arranged on the sideboard along with the pastries that were already ordered.

As a rule, meals were always consumed in either the breakfast parlour or the dining room but this was her household and she could do as she pleased. Her mama bustled in from her visit to an ailing villager and greeted her with a delighted smile.

'I am told that Mr Sheldon is here, that he rode over. I can hear no piano music – where is he and where are my grandchildren?'

'They are fighting a fierce battle in the nursery and will be down in an hour. Luncheon, just this once, will be served in the drawing room and the children will eat with us.'

'I have not seen Brutus today? He is usually here to greet me if he is in the house.'

'Now that you mention it, I have not seen him since he was let out first thing. I shall send word to the stables for a groom to look for him. I do hope he has not gone to Sir Frederick's kennels again. He threatened to shoot him if he saw him hanging around his hounds.'

Word was sent outside but the dog had not been seen for several hours. This was highly unusual; the dog never stayed away so long from his owners. She could not go to The Rookery, the home of Sir Frederick Watson and his wife, unaccompanied.

She flew upstairs and burst into the nursery. 'Mr Sheldon, I apologise for interrupting, but I urgently need your assistance. Children, you continue with your game. We are eating luncheon in an hour in the drawing room and, as a special treat, you may join us.'

This was enough to keep them happy despite losing their adult companion so abruptly. As soon as they were out of earshot she explained the predicament.

'So, you see, sir, we must go at once. If that man has killed their dog it would be a tragedy of the highest order.'

* * *

Beau had no need to enquire as to why the dog should have ventured somewhere he was so unwelcome. There must be a bitch on heat and this would bring in dogs from miles around.

'How do you propose to go there? Thomas said that nobody rides since his father broke his neck falling from a horse. A carriage could not get through the lanes today.'

'I realise that, Mr Sheldon, and have sent down to the stables for my mare to be saddled as well as your stallion. Does he have a name?'

'Titus, and he is one of the best horses I have ever owned.' As soon as he had spoken he realised he had revealed too much about his real background. 'Tell me more about this Sir Frederick – is he a violent man?'

'He has a similar disposition to my husband. I am sure that he abuses his own wife and also his children. A thoroughly unpleasant individual. I will not call him a gentleman as he is not worthy of that title. He keeps his own pack of hounds and it was hunting with these that Rupert came to grief.'

Beau turned towards the side door, but she shook her head

and walked straight to the front. Sure enough both horses were waiting at the bottom of the steps. He tossed her into the saddle of a pretty bay mare and then mounted himself.

She gestured with her whip. 'There is a direct route through the woods and across the home pastures. It is no more than three miles and we should complete the journey in no time at all. Dee, short for Desdemona, might be shorter than Titus but she is excellent over the country and clears hedges and ditches taller than herself.'

'Devil take it! There will be no jumping anything of that height today. We will find a gate if necessary.'

'Time is of the essence, sir, so you have no option but to follow at whatever speed and in whatever direction I take us.' She touched her heel to the mare's flank and was away, moving from extended canter to gallop in seconds. He had no option but to follow and she was right: for all her lack of size, Dee covered the ground at such a pace his horse was obliged to gallop also.

They covered the distance in less than the time it had taken him to ride from Elveden to Fenchurch Manor. She reined back and he drew alongside. 'Is that the house ahead of us? The owner obviously does not take as much pride in his estate as you do in yours.'

She did not respond to his comment. 'We must walk the horses from here so they will be cool when we arrive. Do you see that gap in the hedge? If we exit the field through that we will be adjacent to the entrance to the drive.'

'Although I have accompanied you, my lady, I am at a loss to know exactly what my role is to be. I cannot see Sir Frederick taking heed of anything I might say to him. If he has had your dog shot...'

'Oh, please do not say that. I am praying it was only a threat and that he would not actually carry it out. It is impossible to keep Brutus confined; he is always able to persuade one of my servants to let him out even though they know they must not.'

'This problem would be solved if he lived in a kennel and was not allowed to wander around the place as if he were a lapdog.'

'Believe me, sir, I have tried that. Initially he did live outside but either climbed over the fence, dug himself out or knocked over the unfortunate boy sent in to feed him and escaped through the door. The bigger he got the harder it was to keep him safe. That is when I agreed to allow him to live in the house because at least then I knew where he was.'

Their approach was noted and he could see two surly servants waiting in the turning circle. 'I think it might be wise to avoid the welcoming committee and go directly to the kennels.'

'I thought I might call Brutus. If he hears me and is free to do so he will come at once to my side.'

'I can do better than that.' Beau dropped the reins, pulled off his gloves with his teeth, and then put two fingers from each hand into his mouth and whistled.

The piercing noise sent the rooks nesting in the trees, which presumably gave the house its name, flying into the air cawing in protest at being disturbed so rudely. Viola was suitably impressed by his prowess and it had the desired effect. How the dog knew the whistle was directed at him he had no idea, but the huge beast appeared from the undergrowth wagging his long feathery tail and looking delighted to see them both.

'Good boy, you must come home at once with us. You must not come here again. Is that clear?'

'One might think he actually understood you. He was certainly listening. I suggest that we make a hasty retreat.' The two men were approaching and he had no wish for a confrontation that would draw attention to himself.

In tandem they turned their horses and cantered back down

the drive with the errant dog loping beside them. They kept up the pace until they were safely in the fields once more and could rein back to a walk.

'You must show me how to whistle in that way, Mr Sheldon, as it seems to have the desired result where this dog is concerned.'

'I shall do no such thing, my lady; it would be highly unsuitable for someone like you to do it.' They exchanged smiles and no more was said on the subject. As the horses had been hard-pressed earlier they decided it would be sensible to remain at a walk, at least for the remainder of the journey.

'There is something I wish to talk to you about, sir, and now is the ideal opportunity as we shall not be disturbed. I intend to buy Thomas a new piano and I am taking the children to London, as soon as the weather clears, in order to do so. Obviously, I know nothing about such instruments and we will need you to accompany us.'

He answered without thinking. 'I should be delighted to do so, my lady. I think a piano made by Graf would be ideal. The instrument I have was made by him and is of recent construction too. When I bought the estate I had no idea the piano that was included in the inventory would be of such high quality.'

'Is there somewhere in London I can purchase one of these? I believe I should like to see what else is available before I make a final decision.'

'Then Thomas can try out what is available before you purchase. I shall make enquiries before we depart.'

'We have a house in Grosvenor Square, which I have not used since my marriage. It is rented for the Season but will be vacant at present. We can stay there.'

At the mention of Grosvenor Square the enormity of what he had just agreed to registered. He had been carried away by the thought of spending time with this charming and delightful young woman and her children. He could not possibly do this as his own town house was in the same place and he would be immediately recognised.

'I could not possibly stay under the same roof as you, my lady; it would give rise to speculation and unpleasant gossip. I shall find my own accommodation and meet you at the appropriate place.'

She was not at all put out by his refusal. 'Of course, how stupid of me to suggest it. We cannot go until the roads are clear, which might not be for another week. I shall have to contact my agent in London and make sure my house will not be occupied by then. If it is...' She stopped mid-sentence and her expression changed. 'In fact, I have changed my mind. I shall ask my agent to find me somewhere I shall not be recognised or run the risk of meeting acquaintances of my husband.'

His hands unclenched at her words. It might just be feasible to remain incognito if he found lodgings in Cheapside or somewhere like that. He was sure that Longman and Heron had premises at 131 Cheapside and they were purveyors of modern pianos. He thought it might be sensible to suggest this was the best place to go and avoid places in a part of Town more likely to be frequented by people who would know him.

'I shall find lodgings in the vicinity of the Tower. I think that the children would enjoy visiting the menagerie.'

'That is an excellent suggestion, Mr Sheldon. It is so far from the better part of Town there would be no danger of my being accosted by any of Rupert's old cronies.' She frowned and then continued. 'When the period of mourning was over I was bombarded by invitations from acquaintances of his hoping to pick up where he left off.'

'You are a young, wealthy and beautiful widow; it would be

more surprising if you were not pestered by hopeful gentlemen. One day you will meet someone that you wish to marry, as I hardly think you will wish to remain alone for the remainder of your life.'

'I shall do no such thing, sir. I have no intention of marrying a second time. Why would I give up my freedom and run the risk of being mistreated?' She raised her hand as he was about to respond. 'I know what you are about to say, but I disagree. I will never trust a gentleman again. The moment I have spoken my vows to him he would change and there would be nothing I could do about it.'

7

Viola regretted her intemperate words. She did not know him well enough to reveal such intimate details. 'The horses are cool. I am going to canter the remainder of the distance. I suggest, sir, that you continue to Elveden now that you are in the saddle.'

This was hardly a hospitable thing to say after he had accompanied her and, with his remarkable whistle, recovered the dog without the necessity of an unpleasant confrontation with her neighbour. However, she was now uncomfortable in his company and had no wish to spend further time with him.

'I was going to suggest that myself, my lady, but was worried the children would be disappointed if I did not join them for luncheon.'

'I am sure they will survive your absence. After all they have only known you a short while. I shall send Thomas to you tomorrow morning – if the carriage cannot travel safely then he can ride with a groom.'

'I have reconsidered my decision not to include your daughter in these visits. Therefore, if Elizabeth wishes to come with her brother she will be welcome.'

After having been so ungrateful she could hardly refuse this request. 'That is most gracious of you, Mr Sheldon. They will arrive at ten o'clock and I shall expect them home in time for luncheon.'

They had now reached her own land. He touched his beaver hat with his whip, nodded politely and cantered off without another word. From the rigidity of his back it was obvious she had offended him. For a second she was tempted to go after him and apologise but the moment passed. She was about to go into the stable yard when she realised Brutus had gone with Mr Sheldon.

It was decidedly annoying that this gentleman had somehow inveigled his way into her family. Her children adored him and now the wretched dog appeared to have changed allegiance as well. She must just hope the animal was merely escorting him home and would return where he belonged immediately afterwards.

It did occur to her that she could very well end up having to repeat the process of fetching him back from her neighbour's kennels. Thomas and Elizabeth would be as cross as she was about this situation.

When she explained why Brutus was not with them Thomas grinned. 'He likes Mr Sheldon, as we do. He's a splendid fellow, Mama. I expect our dog will come back when he's ready.'

'I wish Mr Sheldon had come in. I did not think I liked him, but now I do.' Elizabeth looked genuinely upset.

'Sweetheart, he has said that if you wish to accompany your brother to his lessons he would be happy to have you there.'

Her daughter's look of absolute delight at the news did not please Viola. 'Are you sure you wish to go there, as you will have to sit in silence and behave yourself for two hours. I am sure he will not tolerate any of your bad behaviour.'

'I know he will not, Mama, which is why I have no intention of doing anything to annoy him. I notice there is a harp in his music room. I would like to learn to play that – I wonder if he can show me how to do so.'

'He is a musician, Beth, I am sure he will be able to, even if he cannot play the instrument himself,' Thomas said.

'Shall we eat? I expect you are starving after having had to wait so long. Is your grandmama in the drawing room?'

Her mother called from this chamber. 'I am sharp-set, my dear. I refuse to wait another minute for my meal.'

The children ran ahead laughing, but Viola followed more slowly. She needed time to adjust to this new circumstance. There was no point in denying it to herself. The reason she had sent him away so abruptly was because she was beginning to have unwanted feelings for him.

As long as he remained at Elveden and did not visit here she could push him from her mind. There was an uncomfortable tightness in her bodice and she had difficulty swallowing. Keeping her distance was going to be impossible as she had already invited him to accompany her to London in search of the piano.

Her mother was more interested in her luncheon than discussing the exciting events of the morning. The children asked to be excused in order to go upstairs to continue their battle.

'Thomas, do you not have practising to do for tomorrow's lesson?'

'I have done it whilst you were out chasing Brutus, Mama. I shall do another hour later.'

As soon as the children had gone her mother joined her on the daybed. There was something about her expression that worried her. 'What have you heard on your visits this morning that bothers you?'

'It might be nothing, but Mrs Peabody heard from her son who works as footman for Sir Frederick that he has discovered a distant relative of your husband and is having him fetched so he can take over the estate and become guardian to the children.'

Her substantial luncheon threatened to return. 'How can that be? Rupert was forced to make it very clear in his will that Richard is their guardian and has control of the estate. I cannot believe someone we have never heard of, who has such a tenuous connection, could step into this position.'

'One would think not, but it is better to be prepared. The children told me we are going to London as soon as the roads clear; that would be an ideal opportunity for you to visit your lawyers and make sure Rupert's will stands. I think you should write to Richard at once, send it by express. He will want to be informed that it is possible this person is going to try and wrest control from him.'

'I shall do so. Let us pray that this information is incorrect. I shall ask my lawyers to start making enquiries for themselves.'

The letters were sent and the groom who had taken them to the nearest mailing inn returned with the good news that the lanes were clear. She promptly sent him out again with a message for Mr Sheldon saying that she intended to leave for London the next day, as she had urgent business to attend to.

* * *

Beau had attempted to send the huge hound back to the children, but he had refused to listen. The head groom was watching with some amusement. 'I reckon he wants to stay with you, sir. I can make him nice and snug in an empty stall.'

'Do that if you please. He will do better shut in here, as he can escape too easily at Fenchurch Manor.' He patted the dog's head and pulled his silky ears before striding indoors and divesting himself of his outdoor garments.

After spending a pleasant half an hour preparing a new piece for Thomas to practise the following morning, he was disturbed by the arrival of the footman with a letter on a silver salver. His stomach lurched. The only person who knew his whereabouts was Carstairs, his man of business, and he had strict instructions not to contact him unless there was a desperate family emergency.

He snatched the letter up and his breath hissed through his teeth. It had come from Viola, not Carstairs. He snapped open the wax seal and read the contents. For her to make such a sudden decision must mean something catastrophic had occurred. It was none of his business but nevertheless he was concerned for her.

Another visit was out of the question so he must content himself with a letter. The man who took it would have to wait for a response. Fortunately, there was an ample supply of paper, quills and pots of ink in the study for his use. He sat down and composed what he hoped would be a suitable missive in the circumstances:

Lady Fenchurch,

Thank you for your correspondence. You neglected to inform me where you intend to stay. It will be impossible for us to meet in order for you to purchase a piano for your son if I do not have your direction.

Therefore, I shall remain here until you contact me from London with your whereabouts. Then I shall follow post-haste.

He signed the letter with a flourish and was about to sand it, but then turned the air blue. The signature he had scrawled was not Edward Sheldon but his own. He tore the letter into shreds and tossed it into the fire and began again.

He had no notion if Viola and her family intended to travel in their own carriage or go by post-chaise. If the former they would have to stop to rest the horses and would be unlikely to complete the journey in two days and be obliged to overnight twice somewhere. If the latter they would be there in a day if prepared to journey in the dark.

Travelling this way was exorbitantly expensive but they could both afford it and it certainly would make things easier. Finding lodgings that would also accommodate a carriage and team might well be problematical. He sincerely hoped she had considered this when she made her decision.

Thomas and his sister would not now be coming in the morning as they would be on their way to London. What would happen to Brutus whilst they were all away? He could not be kept shut in and once he was released he would go in search of the children. On finding them gone no doubt he would return to the kennels in order to chase the bitches.

This was a conundrum he had to solve before he too set out for Town.

He could hardly turn up in the metropolis with no clear idea where he was to reside. However, on every other visit he had made he had stayed at the family house in Grosvenor Square. He had told Viola he would find accommodation in Cheapside, but all he knew about that location was that it was on the other side of London and not a particularly salubrious side at that. The only advantage would be no one there would recognise him.

The butler was a young man – perhaps he might know of a

suitable place to stay. When Foster appeared, he put the question to him.

'Yes, sir, I can be of assistance in that matter. There is an excellent hotel in Haydon Square, which is no more than a brisk ten-minute walk from the Tower. Would you like me to send word to them and reserve your accommodation?'

'That would be excellent. I am going to pen a second note to Lady Fenchurch and this must be delivered at the same time as your letter is sent to the hotel.'

He quickly scribbled the address he had been given and the location of the hotel he would be residing in and then handed the folded square to the waiting butler. Now there was no necessity for him to wait until he had heard from Viola. She could contact him at the hotel when eventually she arrived in London.

He instructed Bishop to pack what he would need for a short stay. As he intended to travel by post-chaise he could not take a large trunk anyway. 'There is no necessity to put in my evening clothes. I could manage perfectly well without you, but if you would like to accompany me then I should be glad to have you.'

At Silchester he would never have asked his valet's opinion – was this change in his character permanent or just part of his play-acting?

'I should be delighted to come with you, sir. I have family residing in that area. Perhaps I might have an hour free to visit them whilst we are there?'

'Take as much time as you need. I shall be spending most of my time at Longman and Heron, a piano emporium in Cheapside. I hardly think you will be required there.'

His man beamed. 'I thank you, sir, you are a most generous employer.'

Something occurred to Beau as he was leaving his apartment.

'Foster is familiar with this area – were you acquainted before you came here to work?'

'We are cousins, sir, and both found work here through the same agency.'

'We will be leaving at first light. Arrange for a carriage to be waiting to convey us to the coaching inn. I have already sent a groom to reserve our passage.'

Unless his valet sat on the box with the coachman for the short journey to the coaching inn, he would have to travel inside with him. The Duke of Silchester would not have contemplated such a thing but Edward Sheldon, his new persona, was quite content to travel with Bishop. His mouth twitched. There was no box on a post-chaise so, whether he liked it or not, his valet would be inside with him on the long journey to London.

* * *

Viola received the first note from Mr Sheldon and, after the initial irritation at his presumption, understood that what he said made sense. Mama might have had experience of this part of Town as Papa had shipping interests and was frequently at the docks, which were close by.

'We can hardly set out with no destination in mind, Mama. Do you have any suggestions as to where we might stay for a few nights?'

'I cannot help you, my love, because I rarely travelled with your father. He preferred to do his business without the encumbrance of his wife. Richard is the person to ask. What a pity you already sent his letter by express as you could have asked him.'

'Another thing has occurred to me – where will the carriage, horses and coachmen go? I doubt that any hotels in that area will have accommodation for them.'

'If Mr Sheldon has decided to travel post-chaise then we can do the same. Or, we could catch the common stage if you are unwilling to pay the exorbitant cost of travelling in this way.'

'I shall do no such thing. It is all very inconvenient not being able to use the London house. I cannot see how we can take a nursemaid for the children or our own abigails unless we go in our vehicle.'

'Then, use the house in Grosvenor Square. It is yours by right to use and your son is the Earl of Fenchurch. He should be staying in his own property in the most prestigious part of London, not in some side street in Cheapside.'

'You have convinced me. We will do this visit in style, as is fitting for our station. I shall send someone immediately to have the house prepared for us. The luggage and servants can set off tomorrow first thing and we shall leave later in the morning. I think we will have to overnight somewhere twice, but I am sure that will not be too difficult for them to arrange.'

When a second note arrived from Elveden she also had her plans in place. When they arrived in Town she would send word to him. Hopefully, he would have already visited the places where pianos were to be bought and would know which the best shop was to buy one for Thomas. She rather thought it might cost her in the region of one hundred pounds to acquire what she wanted and that was without the added expense of having it delivered to Fenchurch Manor.

The children were beside themselves with excitement the following day. This would be their first excursion that required an overnight stay. Indeed, it would be their first time away from their ancestral home.

'Mama, if Mr Sheldon has already left why has Brutus not come home?' Thomas asked as he pressed his nose against the carriage window.

'Mr Sheldon will have made arrangements for our pet to remain at Elveden. He is well aware that we too will be absent from home for the next few days,' Elizabeth said.

Viola exchanged an amused glance with her mother. Her daughter often talked like an adult, but she had no notion why this might be.

'As long as he is safe and does not venture to the kennels again that is all that matters, children,' she said and they were satisfied with her answer. The journey was going to be tedious; Viola had never enjoyed travelling. The thought of being cooped up in so small a space for several hours at a time did not appeal to her. Listening to the little ones exclaiming in delight at everything they saw, laughing uproariously when the carriage lurched into a pothole, soon made her forget her reservations and she began to enjoy the journey as much as they were.

8

Beau had never travelled post-chaise. In his normal existence he would have sent his own horses ahead of him and not had the necessity of sitting in a vehicle that had been used by members of the public. No doubt it had been scrubbed clean but he was still aware of the lingering aroma of the previous occupant.

When the postilion pulled into the second inn, in order to change the horses, Beau decided to disembark himself and stretch his legs before the next, and he hoped final, stage of the journey. Bishop descended after him. 'Shall I order you coffee in a private parlour, sir?'

'I had not thought to stop that long, but yes, coffee would be most acceptable. Then inform the postilion I shall be remaining here for half an hour so that the horses are not harnessed too soon.'

This establishment was busy so he was obliged to stand around ignored in the vestibule whilst the landlord dealt with others who were ahead of him. It was a salutary lesson to experience what others did on a daily basis. He had become too used to being treated differently and he vowed that when he returned to his old life he would be more considerate of others less fortunate than himself.

Bishop beckoned him from the doorway and Beau was yet again impressed with his new employee's efficiency. Somehow the young man had bypassed the queue and there was already a jug of coffee, sandwiches and pasties waiting in a private room.

'Make sure that you have something yourself.'

He had given his valet a purse full of coins to pay for incidental expenses on the journey and he was certain that some of them had been slipped into a willing hand as a bribe in order to achieve this miracle.

He had no wish to be seated once he had finished his refreshments so wandered about the place and ended up staring out of the window that overlooked the yard. His attention was drawn to a crowd of people in a corner. His curiosity aroused, he decided to investigate.

He arrived at the same time as Bishop. What he saw astonished him. Greedily drinking from the horse trough was Brutus, the dog that he had left shut up in the stables several hours ago. How the hell did he come to be here?

'Excuse me, that is my dog. He has followed me here.' The crowd parted to let him through and as he approached the hound left the trough and bounded over, almost knocking him from his feet with his enthusiastic greeting.

'Well, old fellow, you are an amazing animal. Let me see your paws.'

'Let me look, Mr Sheldon; he is so muddy you will ruin your garments.'

After careful inspection it was obvious Brutus could not continue to run behind the carriage, as his paws were cracked and bleeding.

'We have no option, Bishop; the wretched animal will have to

The Duke's Bride 75

travel inside with us. I would suggest that you return to Elveden with him but I doubt he would stay there. For some extraordinary reason he has decided to adopt me as his new owner.'

'I'll give him a quick bath, take care of his feet and dry him off before he comes in with us, sir.'

There were various offers from stable boys and ostlers to help with this procedure and Beau returned to the inn to wait. It was far too cold to stand about outside. His mouth curved as he imagined the reaction of his family if they were to hear what he was about to do.

The dog was as reluctant to climb into the carriage as Beau was to have him inside. 'Come along, my boy, the sooner we get on our way the sooner you will be out again.' He snapped his fingers and pointed at the door. The huge animal slunk inside and sprawled in the well of the carriage, leaving neither Bishop nor himself anywhere to put their feet.

They were obliged to rest their boots on the opposite squab, which no doubt would add even more to the cost of the journey. He shuddered to think how much conveying Brutus to London was going to cost him. Although a wealthy man he had always been careful not to waste the family funds.

Whilst the dog sulked on the floor it was hard not to smile at his antics. 'Have you any suggestions as to what we should do with him in Town? I cannot imagine the hotel you have reserved for me will take kindly to having him inside.'

'I'll keep him with me, sir. I reckon he'll be content with that. He's a clever dog. He knows what's what.'

'I am still finding it difficult to credit that not only did he manage to escape the confines of the stables, but he was able to follow us for hours.' Beau leaned down and stroked the dog, who was still ignoring him. 'You are a splendid fellow, Brutus, and even if I am not delighted to have your company I am certain that Thomas and Elizabeth will be pleased to see you.'

The animal recognised these names and his tail thumped twice but he did not raise his head or interact in any other way. After a while Beau was able to doze and did not rouse until the vehicle pulled into The Saracen's Head hours later. They must have stopped to change horses, but he had been unaware of it. This was where they would disembark, pay their dues and find themselves another vehicle to convey them to the hotel.

'We need a collar and leash, Bishop. Is there anything we can use in our luggage until you can purchase the proper items?'

'If you keep him inside with you for a few minutes, Mr Sheldon, I'll soon find some rope we can use.'

His man jumped from the carriage before it was quite stationary and slammed the door shut behind him. The dog deigned to sit up. He was so huge he could see out of the window without difficulty. His tail began to swish from side to side.

'Yes, you will soon be out. You must just remain with me until Bishop returns with your lead.' Why the hell was he talking to a dog as if the animal understood every word he said? Brutus might be intelligent – but he was not human.

The dog whined and then pushed his head into Beau's chest. 'I know, old fellow, you would much prefer to be in the countryside, as would I.'

When the dog was safely restrained he came to a decision. 'It is not more than a mile to the Tower from here. I will walk with Brutus. Hopefully his feet will cope with this. I rely on you to transfer our luggage and give the hotel fair warning of what to expect.'

Once they were moving the dog settled and began to take an interest in his surroundings. His enormous size and apparent docility attracted a lot of attention from other pedestrians and

Beau was obliged to stop half a dozen times for the animal to be petted and admired.

The hotel was everything Bishop had said and he had no complaint about its cleanliness or the size of its rooms. The owner, not unnaturally, refused to allow Brutus inside.

'He can come with me if you are agreeable to me staying away overnight, sir.'

'I can manage perfectly well on my own for a few nights. Enjoy your free time. However, you must report here at least twice a day in case I have errands for you. If you have extra expenses I can...'

'You gave me more than enough, sir, for my short stay. The chef here is excellent; you will not be disappointed if you dine here each night.'

His man departed with the dog, leaving Beau to go in search of the piano emporium in Cheapside.

* * *

The children thought the first overnight stop an exciting adventure. Her mother reminded her that by the time she was their age she had travelled all over the country.

'I could not take them anywhere without Rupert's permission and that he would not give under any circumstances in case I did not return. Since he died I have had no inclination to go anywhere and until now I had not realised how I had deprived them of interesting experiences.'

The children were to sleep with her but her mother had her own chamber next door, which had a communicating door to their room. Their maids had arrived in advance and had unpacked the necessities for the night.

'Mama, I saw a row of shops as we were coming down the

main thoroughfare. Can we go and look at them?' Thomas asked eagerly.

'It is still relatively early and will not be dark for another hour, so I see no reason why not. Why don't you go next door and ask your grandmama if she wishes to come with us?'

Elizabeth knocked politely and when they were bid to enter the children vanished and closed the door behind them so Viola was unable to hear the conversation. A few minutes later they returned.

'Grandmama is going to have a rest so we must go alone,' Elizabeth said.

'Then we had better do so immediately as I have no wish to be out in a strange town when it gets dark.'

They joined like-minded pedestrians on the pavement and her children stopped every few minutes to gaze into the shop windows, even when what was purveyed was no more interesting than ladies' hats and gloves.

There were no shops in the village closest to them and she had never taken them to the market town of Ipswich. This was remiss of her and she would remedy that as soon as the weather improved.

The fifth emporium they came to was a baker and confectioner's. The twins looked imploringly at her and she could not resist. 'Very well, we shall go in. You may choose two small items each and then select something to take back for your grandmother.'

There were two other women, each with a large basket over their arm, and three children about the same age as her two. The girl, smartly dressed in a cherry-red bonnet and matching cape, smiled at Elizabeth and beckoned her over to the display.

'If you are allowed to purchase something, these are the most delicious things in the shop.'

The items she pointed to were sugar mice in a variety of

colours. In a pretty glass bowl next to this tray was a selection of boiled sweets and fudges. On the other side of the shop there were cakes and pastries, but her children were only interested in the sweet treats.

'Grandmama is partial to fudge, children, so I should get her a few ounces of that.'

With their purchases safely wrapped in paper twists they stepped out into the winter night. Suddenly Elizabeth pressed close to her. 'Why is that man staring at us? I don't like him at all.'

Viola glanced across the road and her daughter had not been exaggerating. A tall, thin gentleman wearing a many-caped greatcoat was watching them through narrowed eyes. She had never set eyes on him before but he appeared to recognise them.

'I am not overfond of being stared at, so shall we hold hands and run as fast as we can back to the inn where we shall be warm and safe inside?'

So shocked was she by the unpleasant encounter that she allowed the children to devour their treats before their supper. Once they were safely asleep in the large bed they were to share with her, she went in to join her mother and explain what had happened.

'I fear that man has something to do with the information we had about Sir Frederick looking for a distant relative of Rupert's in order to put him in control of our wealth and livelihood.'

'I hardly think that likely. You have an overactive imagination like your children. We shall be in London tomorrow and be safe in your own house.'

'But will we be? Unlike Fenchurch Manor I have not replaced the staff who were loyal to my husband. If someone is looking for us, is hoping to do us harm, then he will find us easily there.'

'Good heavens, child! Will you listen to yourself? What maggot has got into your brain to make you think you are in danger from anybody? Even if, by some remote chance, there is a distant relative who believes he has a claim on you and your children, he would have to go to court in order to get that ratified. I cannot believe there is any judge in the world who would allow a perfect stranger to step in and take control of the estate in this way.'

'I sincerely hope you are right, Mama. However, I shall not go to Grosvenor Square as planned, but to Heron Square, to the hotel that Mr Sheldon is staying at.'

She sent her maid to give the coachmen their new instructions. The fact that there might be no room for such a large party, a carriage and horses, was something she would not dwell on. For some reason she believed Mr Sheldon would be able to smooth things out for her.

As she fell asleep that night, she realised meeting him at this time was fortuitous. The fact that she had only known him for a few short weeks was irrelevant in the circumstances. He was more than capable of keeping them safe and preventing any unwanted stranger from interfering with their lives.

The journey into the metropolis had begun to pall even for the children by the end of the second day. They trundled over the cobbles behind diligences, carriages and coaches until they turned down towards the river.

'Viola, this is not the sort of area someone of your status would be accustomed to staying in. However, I shall be perfectly at home as I have visited warehouses and sailed in ships that dock nearby.'

Thomas, who was kneeling on the seat, his nose pressed against the window, yelled in her ear. 'Look, Mama, it is Mr Sheldon. He is waiting for us and he has Brutus with him.'

This was extraordinary news indeed. She looked in the direction he was pointing and her son was correct. 'He must have brought the dog with him for some reason. He will explain everything once we are safely settled.'

The carriage rocked to a standstill outside a smart hotel. Mr Sheldon opened the door himself and kicked down the steps. 'Welcome, my lady, madam, and children. Your chambers await. Your servants arrived a few hours ago, which has given me time to make arrangements for your carriage and team.'

He reached in and lifted the children out and they remained obediently beside him whilst he handed her and her mother down. 'I have so much to tell you. Do I have a private sitting room in which we can talk?'

'You do indeed, my lady. Mr and Mrs Grimshaw, the owners of this place, are beside themselves with excitement to have an earl, a countess and a lady staying with them. I believe they have sent some unfortunate guests elsewhere in order to make room for your party.'

He offered his arm to her mother, who gratefully took it, and he led them inside. The vestibule was spacious, impeccably clean and the furniture highly polished; everywhere she looked, she was pleased.

Mrs Grimshaw, a stout woman in navy bombazine, bustled forward and curtsied. 'Welcome to our humble hotel, my lady. You are most welcome. You have the best rooms and I am sure you will be comfortable here. Your servants have good accommodation in a box room adjacent to your own apartment.' She curtsied again, almost overbalancing in the process – it was obviously not a movement she was familiar with. 'If you would care to follow me, my lady, I will conduct you personally to your chambers.'

The suite of rooms they were taken to were excellent. The fires were lit in both bedchambers and the sitting room. The linen was fresh and smelt of lavender. The children had small beds set up for them behind a screen at the end of the commodious chamber she was to sleep in. Her mother was equally delighted with her own accommodation.

'Thank you for your welcome, Mrs Grimshaw. I should like the children to have a nursery tea in the sitting room as soon it can be arranged. Mrs Alston will have her supper on a tray and I shall dine in here.'

'I have left a menu that will inform you of what will be available this evening. If you would care to peruse it and send word down to the kitchen, you can be sure you will get your choice. My chef's famous in these parts and we have a large dining room for non-residents and residents alike. If you change your mind and would prefer to eat downstairs then I shall reserve you a table.'

Sally, the nursemaid, took charge of the children, leaving her free to send for Mr Sheldon and explain her worries.

9

Beau waited in his more modest chamber for the summons to visit Viola. He was as eager as she to hold this conversation. What had happened on the journey to make her change her mind about her destination? He had questioned her servants but they were as much in the dark as he was.

The sitting room door was open and he would leave it so in order to prevent unwanted speculation about their relationship. He hoped she would also have the sense to ask her mother to chaperone them.

He nodded to Mrs Alston who was sitting quietly by the window enjoying the view of the Thames and the many ships that plied their trade upon the river. Viola was pacing the carpet.

'You must think I have run mad to transfer the family to your hotel and not go as planned to Grosvenor Square.' She did not allow him time to answer this but continued. 'I think we had better sit down as I have a lot to tell you and I would value your opinion on the subject.'

When he had heard what Sir Frederick was attempting to do

he was incensed. 'It is none of his business. What possible motive could he have to interfere in your lives?'

'If he has found somebody who is distantly related to my dead husband then whoever it is will be in his pay...'

'I am afraid, my lady, that he would be far more than that. He would be your son's heir and would inherit the title and estates if he were to die.'

He wished he had not been so brutal in his comment as her colour faded and for a moment he thought her about to swoon. Then she rallied and sat upright in her chair.

'I do not think there can be such a person. My son is the last of his line. I was reliably informed that the title would go into abeyance if anything were to happen to him. The estates are not entailed so they would come to me.' Talking about the possible death of her beloved son was almost too much for her. He watched her struggle to maintain her composure and was impressed that she managed to do so. She took a steadying breath and carried on with what she had been saying.

'Although it was stipulated in the will that my brother would take on the role of guardian until Thomas reaches his majority, the lawyers did make a thorough search for a male relative on Rupert's side of the family.'

'They were obviously unsuccessful. Do you employ your own lawyers or do you still use those that have served your husband's family?'

'I was obliged to use Rupert's but I also employed my own – the ones that have looked after the Alston business for twenty years or more. Papa insisted on a copy of the will being lodged with them as well as with the others.'

'A wise decision in the circumstances. If you are certain there is no genuine heir then why did you panic?'

This was hardly a conciliatory question but it was one that

needed answering. There was a simple explanation but it was one he did not wish to consider. He watched her closely as she replied.

'That man we saw in Romford frightened my daughter and, as you might imagine, that does not happen easily. He looked at us in a most particular and unpleasant way – he certainly knew who we were. The staff employed in Town are not loyal to me...'

Something appalling occurred to him and he surged to his feet. 'Your husband would not have been happy with the way the will was set up. Is it possible he had arranged for Sir Frederick to search for someone to replace your brother in the event of his untimely death?'

'Please, sir, will you not sit down again? I find it quite unnerving having such a tall gentleman looming over me as you are.'

He smiled his apology and took his place again. 'You have not answered my question.'

'It is the sort of thing Rupert would do, but the fact that I have only heard about it through my staff, and three years after his death, makes me think it cannot be so. Surely, the obnoxious Sir Frederick would have made his move immediately after the funeral?'

Mrs Alston coughed politely. They both turned and looked at her. 'Forgive me for interrupting, my dear, but I think Mr Sheldon might well be correct. Your husband could not have expected to die so suddenly so nothing would have been in place. Therefore, it is my opinion that it might have taken him three years to find a viable candidate.'

This made sense, but it also sent a chill down his spine. From Viola's expression she understood the significance of this remark.

'He has found a genuine, distant relative and is about to make his move. There can be no other explanation. That man who saw us might be the very person and was on his way to meet Sir Frederick when he saw us unexpectedly in Romford.'

'It is a coincidence that you were both in Romford High Street at the same time. It occurs to me that Sir Frederick might be having you followed...' No sooner had he spoken his thoughts out loud than he regretted it. Now Viola might be too apprehensive to go out.

'Stuff and nonsense, my boy, I think the person they saw was nothing to do with the family. I expect my grandchildren were being noisy and he disapproved of their behaviour.'

Mrs Alston had thrown him a lifeline and he grabbed it willingly. 'That is a far more likely explanation, my lady. Perhaps the fact that you were out without a footman in attendance also added to his displeasure.'

Viola managed a weak smile. 'They also had two packets of sweets each. I think you might both be correct and I am worrying unnecessarily about this stranger. However, I do think I am right to be concerned about Sir Frederick's plans.'

'It is none of my business, my lady, but my advice would be to speak to your own lawyers on this matter and have them look into it. If there is the remotest possibility Sir Frederick has discovered a gentleman who can trace his line directly to your husband, it is as well to be prepared.'

She was not offended by his remark. 'What do you suggest I ask them to do in order for me to be prepared if anything untoward was to happen?'

'I can only speak as to what I would do if I was in your circumstances. It is my opinion only, and I am not in any way connected to your family, so it has little value. I would ask your lawyers to prepare a legal document to present to a judge in the High Court. This document would state how well your brother is fulfilling his role as guardian of the estates and your children, and that any change would be detrimental to both.'

'I shall do so tomorrow. Thomas and Elizabeth are so excited about purchasing a piano and a harp...'

'A harp? I was not aware that your daughter wished to learn to play that instrument. I am not proficient on it myself and would not be a suitable teacher.'

She smiled. 'Actually, Mr Sheldon, I can play the harp. When I got married I was obliged to leave my instrument behind and it has since been sold. Rupert did not hold with music of any description. We only had that inferior piano, so someone could play when he held one of his appalling supper parties.'

Beau nodded. 'I apologise for interrupting. If you wish me to go in search of these instruments with the children, but without you, I should be happy to do so as long as I am accompanied by a nursemaid. I have already visited Longman and Heron and they are, in my opinion, the best company to purchase from. You will be pleased to know they have a fine array of harps as well as pianos.'

'Then I shall leave this in your capable hands, sir. I shall write a note to let them know you are acting on my behalf. Will you be able to buy something from the shop or will it have to be made especially?'

'If that were the case, my lady, your son would have a long wait. No, everything in their shop is for sale. I have tried three of the pianos and I think the Graf that they have has the best tone. Do you wish me to allow Thomas to make the final decision?'

'You might think me an overindulgent parent, sir, but if he is to play it then it must be something he is happy with. I just wish he was not the Earl of Fenchurch. I cannot see how he can pursue his passion and fulfil his responsibilities at the same time.'

'I do not see why he should not keep up with his studies and compose and play as much as he wishes throughout his life. If he has an efficient estate manager and man of affairs he need only keep a light hand on his estate and allow them to do the job he is paying them for.' He paused, and this time thought carefully before he spoke, not wishing to reveal how personal his response was. 'As he will be allowed to develop his talent throughout his life, when he is obliged to pick up the mantle of responsibility I cannot see that he would have to abandon his love of music.'

Her smile was radiant. 'I cannot tell you how happy it makes me to hear you say so. I was in two minds about agreeing to buy Elizabeth a harp. She did not know I am expert on this instrument and was somewhat disappointed that you would not be her teacher too.'

'There is a harp in my music room and she would be welcome to play it if she wishes to accompany her brother. It will be several weeks before their instruments arrive and I would be happy to give her some basic instruction. Or, I could have the harp transported to Fenchurch.'

'No, that will not be necessary, but thank you for your kind offer. If it would not be too inconvenient I should like to come with the children when we return home, not only to hear Thomas play but also to demonstrate to my daughter how a harp should be played.'

The matter settled happily between them, he said his farewell and was on his way to the door when she stopped him. 'I should like to ask you to dine with me, Mr Sheldon. What with one thing and another you never came on the day you were invited. I shall not be dressing for dinner.'

He bowed. 'I should be delighted to accept your invitation. I am equally delighted that you are not dressing as I have neglected to bring my evening clothes with me.'

'We shall eat in here. My mother does not wish to venture downstairs into the public dining room tonight. The children are going to have nursery tea.'

'At what time do we dine? Are you intending to keep to country hours now we are in Town?'

'I thought six o'clock – would that suit you?'

'I shall see you then. I am surprised you have not asked me how Brutus happens to be with me. Are you not curious?'

She clapped her hands to her mouth. 'Fiddlesticks! I had quite forgot. I do indeed wish to know.'

When he explained she was astonished. 'My word, I cannot credit the dog has changed allegiance so fast. And neither can I believe that you actually allowed him to travel inside your carriage – it is not something I should care to do. He is prone to making...'

He laughed. 'There is no need to elaborate, my lady, I am well aware what he is prone to do, but fortunately he did not do so this time. It is my opinion the dog has not abandoned your family but for some extraordinary reason decided to include me in it.'

His comment was spoken in jest but he saw a certain wariness in her eyes as if he was, in fact, hoping to become her husband at some point. If she was to marry then her husband would automatically become custodian of the estate and guardian to her children. He must reassure her at once.

'I am a confirmed bachelor of almost five and thirty; being a music teacher to your children and sharing your dog is the closest I shall come, or ever wish to come, to the married state. I sincerely hope Brutus will agree to travel with you on our return.'

Mrs Alston spoke up with alacrity. 'He shall do no such thing, Viola. He can go in with the servants.'

He walked away smiling to himself at the thought of what the unfortunate maids might think of that suggestion.

* * *

Viola had not realised she was holding her breath until it was released with a gasp as the door closed behind the most attractive gentleman she had ever met. It had not escaped her attention that if she were to marry her problems would be over as far as Sir Frederick and his scheme was concerned. Her vow never to take a husband again was looking less convincing the more she got to know Mr Edward Sheldon.

There was one thing she was not sure about. He was a serious man. He rarely smiled which, of course, made it all the more devastating when he did so. She was going to visit her lawyers tomorrow morning. As well as asking them to draw up the document he had suggested, make enquiries about this possible relation, she would ask them to find out a little more about Mr Sheldon. There was something about him that made her wary.

Her mother had dozed off, which gave her time to consider what it was about him that worried her. She could not quite put her finger on it but then her mother spoke – she had not been asleep after all.

'That man behaves as if he was your equal and not a commoner. He has a very high opinion of himself. You would do well to keep your distance.'

Viola jumped to her feet. 'You have it, Mama. That is exactly how he behaves. He is used to command, expects his opinion to be listened to and followed. I believe he must have been a high-ranking officer in the British Army. It would explain why he is so brown of face and has such an air of authority about him.'

'That makes perfect sense. I wonder why he has not

mentioned it? Do you think he was dishonourably discharged for some reason?'

'Absolutely not. He is the most honourable man I have ever met.'

Her mother made a strange noise somewhere between a cough and a grunt. 'I shall retire to my bedchamber and rest until it is time for dinner. I believe I can hear the children returning, so you will be fully occupied until then.' She pushed herself upright with some difficulty. 'I shall leave you to make your own decision, my love. You have a sensible head on your shoulders.'

Viola, despite saying she was not changing for the informal dinner, decided it would be foolish not to take advantage of the fact that her trunks were now unpacked. She selected a warm, long-sleeved gown in blue velvet and was satisfied that she looked her best, but that it did not appear as if she had made too much effort. She wore no jewellery and had removed her wedding band on the death of her husband.

Mama had also made the effort to put on something fresh. 'Plum silk is a perfect choice, and I much admire the plumes in a similar shade that adorn your turban.'

'The colour of your ensemble is acceptable, my love, but the gown itself is rather plain if you want my opinion.'

'We are dining in our private sitting room with just Mr Sheldon for company. I hardly think it warrants anything more elegant.'

The children were now happily ensconced in their corner of her bedchamber. They had made no objection to retiring early as they were quite exhausted after travelling and then exploring the neighbourhood with their canine companion alongside.

At exactly the appointed hour her guest strolled in through the open door. He had not knocked, which she thought was impolite. 'Good evening, ladies, might I be allowed to compliment you both on your delightful ensembles?'

He was wearing a fresh stock but had on the same garments he had worn before. She now felt overdressed. 'Good evening, Mr Sheldon. Dinner will be served shortly. I have ordered a selection of things as I was not cognisant of your wishes.'

'As long as it's not smothered with a rich cream sauce I shall be content with anything that appears. It is quiet, so might I assume the children are settled?'

'They are indeed. They spent the remainder of the afternoon with their dog. I hope Brutus does not kick up a fuss in the stables, as he is not used to being anywhere but Fenchurch.'

'I checked before I came here, my lady, and he was quite content to curl up in a stall with one of your horses. He is familiar with all four of your team, so I am sure he will be no trouble.'

'I have no idea what to do with him tomorrow. You will be with the children and you can hardly take him, and I am going into the city to visit my lawyers.'

'My man, Bishop, will take care of him. He has family close by and I have given him leave to visit them as long as he takes the dog. He intended to take him tonight but it was not convenient for some reason.'

The conversation was interrupted by two maids who came in staggering under the weight of trays almost as big as they were. He was beside the first in a moment and removed it from her. He put it on the already laid table and then assisted the second girl with the other one.

The girls curtsied but did not wait to help serve, or remove the serving dishes from the trays and put them on the table. She was about to complain when a young man in a frock coat arrived with a jug of claret, one of orgeat and another of freshly made lemonade.

He deftly set the table up and then turned and bowed to her. 'My lady, would you care to be seated? I'm here to serve in any capacity.'

Before she could respond, Mr Sheldon spoke up. 'We can take care of ourselves. Bring coffee in an hour. It can be served with the desserts.'

This was the outside of enough. Why did he think he could act as if he were a host when the meal was being served in her own sitting room? She could hardly countermand his instructions as the servant had already bowed and departed. She was about to remonstrate when her mother tapped her on the arm.

'Thank you, sir, we shall do much better without him hovering over us. I should like a portion of the fish and whatever vegetable is in that dish.'

He served her mother efficiently and then waited for her to state what she wanted. Perversely she ignored him and took a spoonful from the three covers nearest to her. She saw his lips twitch and this made her even more irritated.

He helped himself and resumed his place. The table was large and could have seated a dozen and their places had been laid as far apart as was possible. This meant that in order for her to reach any of the delicious dishes on offer she would be obliged to stand up and lean in a most inelegant way across the table.

The food was excellent and she cleared her plate with enjoyment. There were half a dozen other removes at the far end of the table and she would dearly like to try each of those. But she would rather do without than ask for his assistance.

10

Beau was pleasantly surprised at the quality of the food that had been served to them. He was aware that Viola wanted items from the dishes that were too far for her to reach. He would be quite happy to serve her but was waiting for her to ask for his assistance.

When she put her napkin on the table and the cutlery on top of it he understood she was prepared to forego a satisfying dinner if it meant she had to either stand up and fetch it herself or ask him to do so.

'My lady, I am going to try the other plates. Allow me to do the same for you.' There was no necessity for him to take her dirty plate; there was a pile of clean crockery left on the sideboard. 'Mrs Alston, allow me to serve you from this end of the table.'

When the waiter came back with the coffee he was accompanied by one of the maids with a delectable selection of candied fruit, junkets, jellies and a freshly baked apple pie. By the time they had all eaten their fill, the atmosphere was more relaxed. He rather thought his companions' consumption of the excellent claret had also helped.

'Thank you for inviting me to dine with you, my lady. I do not have a private sitting room, so could I persuade you to join me downstairs tomorrow night so I can return the favour?'

'I should like to do that, Viola. I am sadly starved of company and it will be most enjoyable to sit with others and be able to see what the ladies are wearing.'

Beau was aware that if her mother had not spoken first his offer would have been refused. Now she had no option but to agree.

'We might look sadly out of place, Mama, as we do not have evening clothes with us.'

'This is an informal hotel, my lady, and it is an evening dress that would be out of place.'

He bowed politely, bid them goodnight, and returned to his own chamber well satisfied with how the evening had gone. He was not ready to sleep as the hour was not yet ten o'clock. There was an unread copy of *The Times* on the side table and he settled down to read it. He had not perused more than half when there was a frantic knocking on the door.

He was on his feet in a second and opened it to see the owner of this establishment. 'Sir, it's that dog of yours – he's creating such a racket guests are making complaints.'

'I shall come at once. I did not anticipate him being a nuisance as he is familiar with the horses he was put with.' He snatched up his greatcoat and followed close behind. He could hear the dog barking as soon as he stepped into the yard at the back.

There was no need to enquire as to the whereabouts of Brutus, he just followed the noise.

As he approached he realised the dog wasn't howling but

snarling. He increased his pace and found the animal had cornered a rough-looking individual in the corner of the stall.

'Enough, quiet, sir.' There was instant silence and the gathered grooms and ostlers heaved a collective sigh of relief. The man was a gibbering wreck and made no attempt to move. Beau turned to the spectators. 'Who is that person? Why is he in that stall with the horses of Lady Fenchurch?'

Brutus continued to growl and his hackles were up, but he was no longer making the din that had attracted the attention of the hotel proprietor. Beau looked from one to the other and they shook their heads. 'Don't rightly know, sir,' one of the grooms said. 'We didn't know that varmint was there until your dog set up that racket.'

'Go about your business. I shall take care of this.' The crowd dispersed with some reluctance but they knew better than to argue.

He snapped his fingers and the dog moved a few paces back from the cowering figure. Beau had no intention of getting close as he could see crawlers in the man's hair – his smell was rank too.

'As you can see my dog is now under control. If I snap my fingers and point at you he will take your throat out. Therefore, it behoves you to tell me the truth.'

The man collected his wits and nodded, still unable to utter a word. His breeches were wet – the wretch's bladder had emptied. Small wonder he smelled so appalling.

'What are you doing with Lady Fenchurch's horses? Who sent you?'

'I ain't up to nothing, mister. I was just looking for somewhere to get a bit of shut-eye. Then that dog went for me.'

Beau didn't believe a word of it. The man had a shifty look about him, and despite his fear his eyes were cunning. 'I shall give you one more chance to speak the truth and then what happens is entirely your own fault.'

For a second the wretch remained silent then he nodded. 'I weren't paid enough to have me throat torn out. Some cove spoke to me down the docks and said if I loosened the shoes of one of them horses he would pay me a guinea.'

'Describe him to me.'

'He were about your height, your honour, but half your width. A gentleman like what you are but dressed more like a servant.'

'Go, collect your guinea and tell him you succeeded.' He rested his hand lightly on the dog's head and the man scrambled to his feet and vanished, leaving a noxious aroma behind.

'Good dog, clever boy, I think you deliberately made a fuss to bring me here.' The dog thumped his tail in the straw and then went to sniff the damp patch the villain had left behind. Beau carefully checked the shoes on each horse and they were all securely nailed. He could think of only one reason for this mystery man, and he was certainly the same person that Viola and the children saw in Romford, to want the horses interfered with.

If one cast a shoe in a deserted spot, the carriage and its occupants would be vulnerable to attack, although he was at a loss to think what benefit this could bring to the putative heir to the earldom. His stomach sunk to his boots. There was one reason, but it was so dreadful he could scarcely credit it might be the answer.

A helpful stable boy agreed to find the dog something to eat and make sure he had fresh water to drink. Satisfied Brutus would remain on guard, Beau returned to his bedchamber unsure if he should voice his fears to Viola or keep them to himself.

If Thomas were to die, then anyone in the direct male line, however tenuous the connection, would inherit the title, and possibly the estates if they were entailed, and Viola, her daughter and her mother would be homeless. They would not be penniless as Mr Alston had been rich as Croesus and they could live very well from the interest on his funds without touching the principal. Bishop had gleaned this interesting information and relayed it to him.

He was being as fanciful as a girl – there had to be another more logical explanation. One thing he was quite sure of: it would be over his dead body that anyone would harm any of this family who had become inordinately dear to him over the past few weeks.

His sleep was fitful and he woke unrefreshed to discover Bishop setting up the shaving things. His clothes were already laid out waiting. Green, the valet he had left behind, was no comparison to this young man's efficiency. He would definitely take him back with him and Green could retire to a cottage with a decent pension and would no doubt be happy to do so.

Whilst he was being shaved, Bishop concentrated on his work and there was no opportunity for conversation. As soon as it was done Beau spoke.

'Did you hear what transpired last night in the stables?'

'I did, sir, damn good thing that dog was down there. They think he was a vagrant looking for shelter.'

'I know he was not.' He explained what he had learned without adding his own dreadful interpretation of the events.

'Can't be a coincidence, not two things so close together and both connected to that gentleman Lady Fenchurch and the children saw on the way here.'

'An explanation has occurred to me but I am reluctant to voice it. What interpretation do you put on those events?'

He had never asked Green a question like this in the many years they had been together. But he had come to value his new man's opinion.

'I don't like to say so, sir, but if Lord Thomas met with an accident...'

'Exactly so. I need to know if there is indeed an heir to the title.' He ran his fingers through his hair, quite ruining the careful arrangement of his valet. 'This whole business is like something out of a novel. It is not the sort of thing one expects to be involved with.' He tossed aside the towel and paced the room, trying to marshal his thoughts.

'I think we had better travel back with them. Can you obtain us pistols, powder and shot?' He tossed his man a handful of golden coins. 'There will be sufficient there. Take the dog with you and keep your eyes and ears open.'

* * *

'Mama, can we go now? We have eaten all our breakfast and it is already nine o'clock. Mr Sheldon will think us tardy.'

'No, Elizabeth, you will remain here with me until he comes to collect you. You may ask Sally to put on your outdoor garments as I expect he will be here at any moment.'

Thomas led the charge into the bedchamber. He was beside himself with excitement at the thought of being able to buy his own piano. Viola rather thought that her daughter was not as eager to learn to play the harp as she pretended. Purchasing this instrument was more for herself than for Elizabeth.

Her own mother had yet to appear and this was unusual as her mother was an early riser. She knocked on the communicating door and on receiving no answer a prickle of unease ran through her. 'Mama, it is I. I am coming in.'

She pushed open the door and stopped abruptly. The room was empty, the bed neatly made, no sign of either her mother or her maid. Her heart was thumping painfully and her hands were clammy until she saw the note placed prominently on the mantelshelf.

She tore it open. Good heavens! Mama had decided to breakfast downstairs. It would have been sensible to have spoken about this before she vanished and caused her unnecessary worry. She had no intention of going into the public realm until this evening when she was accompanied by Mr Sheldon. Therefore, she would be obliged to depart without speaking to her parent.

When the children returned from their outing with Mr Sheldon, they were to have their luncheon in the hotel and then go to look at the Tower and the animals in the menagerie. She would be back in good time to accompany them.

Mr Sheldon walked in as the children burst out of the bedchamber, so there was no opportunity to speak to him privately. He smiled and greeted her politely and she responded in kind.

'I thank you for doing this, sir; there are not many unmarried gentlemen who would be prepared to take charge of two lively children.'

'I shall have the good offices of their nursemaid. I can assure you, my lady, I would not venture out entirely on my own with them.'

The children insisted on taking one of his hands each and he did not appear to object to this familiarity. He would make an excellent father and she hoped one day he would have children of his own. The familiar stab of pain twisted her insides at her inability to have more children because of the complications she endured at the birth of the twins. This was another reason she could never marry again, as all gentlemen must wish to fill their nurseries and she could not do that for them.

The hired vehicle was waiting to convey her to her lawyers. Her maid had never been to the city and was impressed by everything she saw. When Viola alighted, a young clerk handed her down from the carriage.

'Lady Fenchurch, it is an honour to meet you in person. Mr Blyth is waiting to see you in his office, if you would kindly come this way.'

The building was of ancient construction, as were all the rest in that area, but it was well maintained and she was pleasantly surprised by the luxurious interior. She was led along a narrow corridor and into a spacious chamber that overlooked a pretty garden at the rear of the building.

An elderly, grey-haired man, dressed in the regulation black, rushed forward and bowed obsequiously. 'Welcome, my lady, I am Mr Blyth the Younger. Would you care for refreshments?'

'That will not be necessary, thank you. Do you have the information I require?' She took a seat by the fire and he returned to his own place behind his desk.

'I am afraid that we have discovered there is in fact a gentleman by the name of Patrick Fenchurch who does indeed have a direct line of descent from Lord Fenchurch. I believe he would be a very distant cousin. However, in law, he does have a good case to apply to become your children's guardian and take control of the estate and its finances instead of your brother.'

This was the worst possible news and for a moment she was too distressed to answer. Then she regained her composure. 'What sort of man is he?'

'He is an Irishman by birth. It appears a cousin of your husband's father married an Irish girl and went to live there many years ago. Mr Patrick Fenchurch has yet to arrive in

England to make a claim. He is a farmer, but not a wealthy one, and certainly not a suitable person to be in charge of your children and estates.'

'Then I must tell you that Sir Frederick Watson is orchestrating this. He will manipulate Mr Fenchurch and this man will be his puppet. Have you drawn up the papers to counteract this claim if it is made? I cannot understand why your original enquiries did not discover him. I am not impressed by this.'

'My lady, I can only apologise for our lack of diligence. As it was clearly stated in the will that Mr Alston was to take over the estates and responsibility for you all, there seemed no necessity to enquire further than we did.'

'How likely do you think it is that this man will do Sir Frederick's bidding? I cannot see any judge in an English court wishing to hand over the care of the Earl of Fenchurch to an Irishman.'

'My lady, Mr Fenchurch might live in Ireland, have an Irish accent, but he is legally English as his father was English. I believe there is nothing for you to worry about at the moment and we will certainly lodge the papers as soon as we hear he is in the country.'

She had to be satisfied with that, but it was not what she had hoped to hear. She would discuss the matter with Mr Sheldon when she saw him as, being an intelligent and well-travelled gentleman, he might have some pertinent suggestions.

As she descended the steps she was hailed by a familiar voice. 'Richard, I had hoped you would be here for the meeting but I am delighted to see you now and I shall tell you everything I have learned.' They embraced, ignoring the shocked expressions of the passers-by as any show of public affection, even for one's brother, was not considered proper.

In the carriage she gave him a brief update on her life since she had last seen him. He was as appalled as she to know there was a genuine candidate to take over his responsibilities.

'There is one alternative, sister; you could marry this Mr Sheldon. He seems a likely sort of fellow, a genuine gentleman. I cannot see him refusing to help you in your hour of need.'

For a moment she thought he was serious and then he laughed. 'You must not tease me like that, Richard. My nerves are already frayed from all this anxiety. I have been thinking furiously for the past half an hour and think I might have a solution. This Patrick Fenchurch is a man of modest means but his roots are in Ireland and I think he might well be reluctant to come here, to bring his family to live in what is, in effect, an alien world.'

'That is probably correct, but the lure of a large sum of money and a means to better himself and his family might prove more compelling.'

'What if you went to speak to him and offered him a substantial sum if he remained where he was? I think it quite possible in those circumstances he would take our offer over one from Sir Frederick.'

'That is certainly something to think about. Do you have the whereabouts of this person?'

She handed him a copy of the letter that the solicitors had received from the investigators listing everything about this gentleman and his location. Her brother glanced at it and then folded the paper and put it in his pocket.

'I will leave tomorrow. The weather is inclement and there are storms at sea. I might not be able to sail to Ireland for a day or two. Then it will take me a further two days to reach him. We must pray I reach him before he has signed any sort of agreement with the other party.'

The carriage rocked to a halt outside the hotel. The doorman was there to let down the steps and hand her down. 'The children should be back at any time. I hope you will remain until they return.'

'Wild horses would not drag me away – I have every intention of inspecting this Mr Sheldon and seeing that he passes muster. I cannot have an inferior gentleman associating with my family.'

He offered his arm and she put hers in it. He was not a tall man by Mr Sheldon's standard, but he was half a head taller than her and they made a handsome pair. Her fair colouring came from her mother; he was the image of their papa and they did not look at all like siblings.

It did not occur to her that erroneous conclusions about their relationship might be drawn by any onlookers.

11

The children kept up a non-stop barrage of questions all the way to the piano emporium. Beau found them charming and relished the opportunity to broaden their knowledge of their capital city.

'Will you come with us to the Tower after luncheon, please, please, Mr Sheldon; do say that you will?'

'I have no objection but we must wait and see what your mama has to say on the subject. Look, that is our destination.'

Thomas snatched his hand away and was about to dash across the road with complete disregard for an enormous diligence that was trundling past. Beau just managed to catch the back of his cape and prevent him from being crushed beneath the horses' hooves.

He swung the boy from his feet and dropped him to the ground. 'What the devil did you think you were doing? Are you so full of your own importance that you do not believe you have to wait for other road users to pass by?' His words were harsh, but they were meant to be. He had aged ten years in that second. If anything had happened to the child he would have been devastated.

Then his sister joined in with her own reprimand. 'You are a stupid boy – Mr Sheldon is right. You could have been killed because you didn't bother to look. Perhaps you need to have leading strings put on again.' This was the kind of comment one would have expected from an adult and his momentary horror turned to amusement.

Thomas hopped from foot to foot completely unmoved by what had been said to him. 'I beg your pardon for almost getting killed, Mr Sheldon, but I am desperate to choose my piano.'

Beau ruffled the boy's hair and then holding both the children firmly he strode across the road when there was a safe space to do so. The nursemaid trotted along behind, having added nothing of value to the expedition so far.

It took less than an hour for both children to have selected the instruments they wished to have delivered to the house at the earliest possible moment. He shook hands with the owner of the establishment and handed over the letter giving him permission to conclude the deal.

'As you can see the children are eager to have these items as soon as possible. If you arrange for a carter to pick them up today I can see no reason why they could not be at Fenchurch within a week. I guarantee that the countess will settle her account immediately, and no doubt there will be a bonus for the speedy arrival of the harp and the piano.'

'Both will have to be tuned when they arrive. Do you wish me to make arrangements for someone to call and do that?'

'That will not be necessary; I shall do it for them.'

The children stopped to gaze into the shops they passed and he instructed their nursemaid to remain at their side at all times. It was a mile to the hotel but it took them over an hour to complete the journey because the children were so interested in everything they saw.

'Look, Mr Sheldon, we can see the Tower from here. I cannot wait to visit.' Thomas and his sister had gained sufficient confidence to walk without holding on to him. He followed the child's pointing finger and saw a hired carriage pull up outside the hotel.

Viola stepped out and walked arm in arm with a handsome gentleman. She was laughing up at him as if he was someone important to her. A surge of rage ran through him. He wanted to draw the man's cork, knock him senseless; then reason returned. With it came a moment of clarity. He was hopelessly in love with her, but how could he reveal his feelings whilst he was hiding his identity?

He stood motionless, for the first time in his life indecisive. Then Elizabeth grabbed his hand.

'Look, Uncle Richard is here to see us. Do we have your permission to run ahead?'

'You do indeed, sweetheart.' Thomas took off immediately, but she hesitated. 'We still want you to accompany us on our expedition. The fact that our uncle is here does not mean that Mama and my brother do not wish to have you there as well.'

He was moved by her entreaty. They were delightful children and would make perfect cousins for Rushton and Giselle's two daughters. The nursemaid had run after the children, leaving him to stroll at his own pace lost in delightful possibilities for his future.

At what point must he reveal his true identity? He did not wish to marry without his family present and in order to accomplish that he would have to take her to Silchester Court. He had only been away for a month and they would not be expecting him to return until July at the earliest.

He increased his pace. He wanted to meet Mr Alston, hear what had been discovered at the lawyers and see what help he could offer. He did not even know how old Viola was. She looked no more than two and twenty but that would be a physical impossibility as her children were approaching their ninth birthday. She was probably nearer his age than he realised, but it would not be polite to enquire.

This was one thing he could not ask Bishop as it would be immediately apparent to this intelligent young man why he had asked the question. He would spend the next few weeks getting to know the family better and hopefully when he did tell her who he was, and make her an offer, she would be more ready to listen. They had both stated categorically they had no intention of marrying, but as he had changed his mind he thought it possible she might too.

To his astonishment when he stepped into the foyer, the children, their mother and their uncle were waiting to greet him.

'Mr Sheldon, I am Richard Alston. I have heard so much about you and I'm delighted to meet you in person.' Alston was about his age, and he liked him immediately. He had an open expression and when he offered his hand Beau was pleased to shake it.

'I too have heard about you, sir, and all of it complimentary I can assure you.'

'Mr Sheldon, I hope the children were well behaved.'

Thomas looked appealingly at him. 'They were exemplary. I have absolutely no complaints on that score and will be delighted to escort them anywhere in future.'

'Children, run along with Sally and have your luncheon. I have reserved a table for us in the dining room and Mama is already there. She has already struck up a firm friendship with another elderly lady who is staying here and I have not been able to pry her away. Shall I see you down here in a quarter of an hour?'

'You will indeed. I think it wise to see how we like the restaurant before we commit ourselves to eating here this evening. I hope you will be able to join us wherever we eat, Mr Alston?'

'I have business to attend to at the docks this afternoon but have reserved a chamber here for tonight.'

It took Beau only seconds to remove his outer garments, wipe the mud and dust from his boots and check his topcoat and cravat were still immaculate. He had never thought to fall in love – had met dozens of hopeful young ladies over the years and none of them had stirred his senses.

The most recent addition to their large family, Sofia, who had married the younger of his twin brothers, Perry, had told him there was somebody out there for him and he would meet her one day. How right she was. Like all his siblings he realised he had known the moment he had met Viola that she would one day become his wife and the mother of his children.

He found infants annoying but enjoyed the company of little ones once they were able to converse sensibly and listen to instructions. Certainly, he had always got on well with Rushton's daughters and he already loved Elizabeth and Thomas as if they were his own.

His mouth curved at that thought. God willing, one day in the not too distant future they would indeed be his children, as he intended to adopt them legally. He was the ideal person to prepare Thomas for his responsibilities when he came of age. He would have to find an excellent tenant for both Elveden and Fenchurch Manor. He found it difficult to stop smiling as he mulled over the prospect of becoming a family man at last.

Viola came from a similar background to Grace, and his sister-in-law, who had married Bennett, the brother closest to him in age and character, would be the ideal friend for her. He did not consider for a second that his suit would be rejected when she discovered his deception. All his life he had snapped his fingers and whatever he wanted had appeared. He was the Duke of Silchester – one of the most eligible bachelors in the country – what possible reason could she have for refusing him?

* * *

During luncheon Viola explained what she had discovered at the lawyers that morning. 'What do you think, Mr Sheldon?'

'Your course of action is exactly what I would have suggested. It is perfectly possible that this Mr Fenchurch is a reasonable man and would not agree to Sir Frederick's nefarious suggestion. I imagine that his father's relocation to Ireland was to get away from the family who appear to have an unpleasant reputation.' He was speaking sincerely and obviously did not consider the impact of his comment.

Her mother was not best pleased by his remark. She banged the table with a spoon, attracting unwanted attention from the other guests in the dining room. 'Are you suggesting, sir, that Mr Alston and I arranged the marriage between my daughter and the earl knowing of his reputation?'

He looked somewhat startled at her attack. Instead of being embarrassed or offended, he smiled. 'As you did not move in the same circles as them, one could not have expected you to know he was not a suitable husband. I am certain you made enquiries and, as Lady Fenchurch said, Lord Fenchurch could be a charming and pleasant companion when he so wished.'

Richard put his hand on mama's arm and immediately she relaxed her rigid stance and smiled at her favourite child. 'If you had been in the country at the time, my love, I'm sure you would have discovered more than we could.' She beamed at Mr Sheldon. 'My son was travelling in India for our shipping business.'

'I have never travelled so far; perhaps one day I will do so. Did you find the country as exotic and interesting as I imagine it to be?'

The conversation continued and moved from one subject to another, and it wasn't until she saw Sally hovering anxiously at the doorway that she realised how long they had been.

'We are tardy. The children will be eager to go out. Do you wish to come with us, Mama?'

'I intend to rest this afternoon, my love, so I can be fully restored in order to enjoy my dinner here tonight. Perhaps Mr Sheldon would agree to accompany you instead?'

'I should be delighted to, my lady. Shall we reconvene in the foyer in ten minutes?' There was a twinkle in his eye as he said this, as if he expected her to demand longer.

'It takes moments to put on my bonnet and cloak, sir, so I will certainly be there within that time.'

* * *

The Tower was deemed to be the most splendid building the children had ever set eyes on, the animals astonishing and the ravens very black. In all it was turning out to be a most successful outing for all concerned.

She had watched with interest the interaction between Mr Sheldon and her little ones. They treated him with affection and respect and she had never known them to behave so impeccably for so long. Her mother had been right to say that what they needed in their lives was the calming influence of a gentleman.

'Mr Sheldon, at what time do you intend to depart tomorrow morning?'

He turned to her, his expression serious. 'That is a subject I have been reluctant to bring up as it will cast a shadow over this delightful adventure.' He looked up to check the children were busy admiring the battlements with their nursemaid before he continued. When he told her what had transpired last night in the stables she was shocked to the core.

'Why have you waited so long to tell me? It is something my brother should be aware of too. This man cannot possibly be Mr Fenchurch, so what can be his motive?'

'I think he must be in the employ of Sir Frederick. It seems an outlandish theory, but I believe he could be trying to remove your son from the line of succession. This Irish Fenchurch would then become the earl... Do I need to go on?'

His expression told her more than any words. He thought the only possible explanation was that her villainous neighbour was planning to murder her son. She wished she had not eaten so much lunch.

'What shall I do? How can I protect him?'

He moved in so he was standing no more than a few inches from her and what he said could not be overheard by the other folk milling about in the courtyard outside the Tower.

'If you will allow me to, I shall take that responsibility upon myself. I give you my word no harm will come to Thomas on my watch.'

'I accept your kind offer, sir; you are most reassuring. Tell me, how do you intend to make it safe for us to return in the carriage? I imagine that man will masquerade as a highwayman and it will appear he has inadvertently shot my son during the hold-up.'

'Bishop can ride ahead – I shall purchase a suitable mount for him – and make sure there is no danger waiting. The obvious place for an attack would be somewhere in Epping Forest, for that is a notorious stamping ground of footpads and other ne'er-do-wells.

'I shall travel in the carriage with you and will be suitably armed. It will be a sad crush with three adults and two children but it cannot be helped.' His smile was warm and despite her fear she responded. She thought she detected something else in his eyes then dismissed this as fanciful.

'I was wondering if Brutus could not run alongside your man? He is a terrifying animal when aroused, from what you tell me. Would he not be a valuable asset?'

'That is an excellent notion, my lady. As we shall be travelling slowly, stopping frequently to rest the team, and breaking our journey twice, he ought to have no difficulty keeping up.'

'I cannot believe that my obnoxious husband is able to cause so much misery three years after his death. If only we could prevent Sir Frederick from interfering in this way. There must be people of influence I could contact who would take the side of a countess over such a person.'

'I do know of people who might be helpful in this instance. If you would like me to, I will write to them as soon as we return to the hotel.'

He did not offer to tell her who these people might be, and she was too polite to enquire. He might be a commoner but so was she by birth – and it was birth that counted in these situations. This just reinforced her belief that he had been a high-ranking officer in the army but had been obliged to leave for some reason. She could not for one instant accept he had left under a cloud.

The children returned, eager to tell them everything they had seen and heard. 'The Yeoman Warders in their splendid red and gold uniforms are my favourite things. You would not believe the tales they can tell about kings and queens having their heads chopped off in the courtyard,' Elizabeth said gleefully.

'I like the crown jewels best, Mr Sheldon. I think they have been here for centuries for people to look at,' Thomas added.

'It is almost dark and I think that we must return immediately to the hotel,' she told them and they did not argue. The two of them skipped along ahead, but not too far, as they had been told to remain close. This gave her a further opportunity to converse with her companion.

'I must thank you for the change you have made to my children in the few weeks you have known them. Elizabeth particularly seems so much happier and she has not had a tantrum since the one she threw the first week you were here.'

'They are, as I have told you more than once, the most delightful children. It will be March tomorrow, the first day of spring. I am eager to see what sort of flowers there are in my park and gardens. I am hoping there will be daffodils and tulips as well as forget-me-nots and primroses.'

She was surprised by his interest and knowledge of plants. One might have thought he had owned a property before to take such an interest in the gardens.

'My favourite flower is the rose. Fortunately, there is a beautiful rose garden at Fenchurch Manor, which was planted by my mother-in-law before she died giving birth to Rupert. I was always surprised that the old earl did not marry again, but he remained a widower until he died.'

'Did you meet him?'

'No, he too died young. Rupert inherited when he was nineteen years of age and by the time he reached his majority he had been running wild for years. He was too young for such responsibility, and I am terrified the same thing will happen to Thomas if I am not careful. That is why I am encouraging him to pursue his love for music and playing the piano.'

'I assume you only found all this out after you were married to him.'

'That is true, sir, but I cannot regret my marriage as without it I would not have my children.'

12

Beau was becoming entangled in his own prevarications and he decided that as soon as they were safely back in Suffolk he would explain the whole to her. He had not told her many direct lies but he was guilty of lying by omission and he was not comfortable with that.

He wrote four letters to close friends of his in the government and asked them to do what they could to prevent this travesty of justice taking place. They would assume he was writing from Silchester Court and would reply there. This necessitated a quick note to Carstairs asking him to forward any letters that arrived from these particular people.

Music no longer consumed him; it would always be an abiding interest, but his passion was now for Viola and her enchanting children. His ancestral home was outdated and needed modernising. The east and west wings, which had been converted to accommodate the twins and their wives, had kitchens that were close enough to the dining room to allow the food to arrive hot.

As soon as he was home he would set in motion the much-

The Duke's Bride

needed improvements but he would do nothing until he had persuaded his beloved Viola to marry him. The more he thought about his reasons for dissembling, the flimsier they seemed. Why should a rational person wish to live someone else's life? He was not a commoner, he had been born to rule, and pretending he was otherwise was the height of folly.

It had taken him far longer than he had anticipated to complete his correspondence and he scarcely had time to change for dinner. He rubbed his bristly chin and thought that if he wished to look his best he must shave for a second time that day.

There was a small dressing room and closet to the left of the large bed and he heard movement in there. Bishop popped his head around the door in a most casual manner that would have irritated him a few weeks ago but now he quite enjoyed the informality. This relaxed attitude was something he would take back with him when he returned.

'I have hot water here, sir, and am about to set out your garments for tonight. I thought the dark blue topcoat and light blue waistcoat might be acceptable to you?'

'Splendid fellow. I need a shave. I barely have enough time to do this and change my raiment. We are to dine downstairs tonight and a table has been reserved for six o'clock and it is already after five now. I need you to purchase yourself a sturdy mount. Can you do this before the morning?'

'No problem at all, sir. I know exactly where to find such an animal.'

* * *

It was the gentleman's duty to escort the ladies of his party to dinner but in this case he must stand aside and allow her brother to do the honours. He emerged from his bedchamber as Mrs Alston emerged from hers.

'There you are, young man; you must take my arm as I am a trifle unsteady on my feet today.'

'It will be my absolute pleasure, ma'am. I am quite prepared to carry you if you would prefer that.'

She chuckled as she put her arm through his. 'I might hold you to that, Mr Sheldon, if I imbibe too much claret tonight. Mr Alston and I were not blessed with our children early in our lives. I am now approaching my sixtieth birthday, which is a venerable age, do not you agree?'

'It is indeed. You wear your years well, ma'am, and I would have put you no more than forty.'

'Now that is doing it too brown, sir, but I thank you for your compliment as I do not get many of those nowadays. You have made a big impression on my grandchildren. I have never seen them so content before.'

'I am not comfortable with infants but I enjoy the company of older children. Lady Fenchurch has given me permission to protect your family and I give you my word as a gentleman that nothing untoward shall happen to any of you whilst I draw breath.' He had spoken too vehemently but it was too late to retract his words. Like her daughter, Mrs Alston was sharp of wit and looked at him with a knowing smile.

'So that is how the land lies. There is something you should know – you will think me a busybody to interfere in this way, but better to speak now before it is too late.'

'I beg you, ma'am, do not reveal any secrets that Lady Fenchurch would not wish me to know.'

'Fiddlesticks to that, young man. My daughter suffered complications when the twins were born and she is unable to have any more children. You must not pursue your interest if you wish for children of your own.'

Mrs Alston had not the right to mention such a thing to him. He stared down at her, his disapproval apparent in every inch of him. 'It is not your place to discuss such things, madam.' The remainder of the journey was completed in stony silence and he removed her hand from his arm as soon as they were on the ground floor and there was no danger of her tripping on the stairs.

He stepped to one side and nodded. She took the hint and turned away, her face pale and her shoulders hunched. A wave of shame engulfed him. What was he thinking to speak to his future mother-in-law in that way? He was behaving out of character and that was inexcusable.

'Mrs Alston, please wait.' He stepped in front of her and reached down and took both her hands, horrified to find they were trembling. 'I should not have spoken to you like that. I apologise most humbly for my appalling rudeness. I understand why you told me such an intimate fact – you were just trying to prevent heartache on both sides. I can assure you, ma'am, the lack of children of my own will not bother me. Can I ask you not to mention this conversation to your daughter? I have not yet reached the point where I think I could speak to her...'

'You are forgiven, Mr Sheldon. At the risk of having my head bitten off a second time I will tell you that Viola is halfway to falling in love with you. I believe that you could speak to her without fear of being rejected when we are safely home.'

The constriction in his chest disappeared and he was able to breathe freely once more. 'Then it shall be our secret, ma'am, until then.' He reclaimed her hand and in perfect harmony he escorted her the remainder of the way.

The dining room was busy but they were bowed to their

table, the menus handed out as if they were the only ones present that evening. The evening sped by and he enjoyed every moment of it but had no recollection of what he had eaten or drunk when it ended.

He assisted Mrs Alston to her feet but she refused to take his arm. 'Richard, you must escort me back as Mr Sheldon brought me down.'

Beau was delighted with this arrangement. He delivered Viola to the entrance to her sitting room – it would not be polite to stop at her bedchamber door, however innocent the move might be. 'Goodnight, I have enjoyed this evening and hope you will dine with me at Elveden when we are returned to Suffolk.'

'We shall be delighted to, sir; you are a most entertaining companion. I have ordered breakfast to be served at seven o'clock in my sitting room and we will be downstairs within half an hour of that time. It will be full light by then and there will be no danger to my horses or the dog from travelling in the dark.'

She gazed up at him and it took all his self-control not to bring her into his embrace and kiss her. That must wait until they were betrothed, but it was going to be damned difficult. Instead he raised her gloved hand to his mouth and pressed a kiss on the knuckles.

Then he bowed and walked away before he did something he might regret.

He finally understood what it was to be truly happy. He had waited all his adult life to experience this feeling of euphoria, to have love envelop him and make everything else seem unimportant.

His man was waiting to help him disrobe. 'Do you have the pistols?'

'I do, sir, and a fine horse. I shall much prefer to be riding than shut up in a carriage.'

Only then did it occur to Beau that he had not enquired if his man could actually ride. He obviously could, so there was no necessity to mention the matter now.

'Wake me at six thirty. Make sure all the baggage is safely stowed at the rear of the vehicle. Check the horses' shoes again before they are harnessed. I am concerned that the dog will suffer, having to run so far on icy roads.'

'I have thought of that; I have had soft leather boots made for him.'

If Bishop had said Brutus was to wear a gown he could not have been more surprised. 'Boots? Now that I cannot wait to see – an excellent notion if the dog allows you to put them on.'

His man grinned. 'He was proud as punch when I tried them. Made no effort to pull them off. They will protect his pads from damage. He has the stamina to complete the journey without difficulty. I've never met such a strong dog before.'

'He is indeed a canine marvel. There is money there for you to settle our account. You have proved an excellent valet, Bishop, and I hope you will stay with me permanently.'

'I should be honoured to do so, sir.'

Beau did not utilise a nightshirt when at home but when travelling he wore one as a precaution. His brother, Bennett, slept in a similar fashion from choice but there had been a fire when he was a guest somewhere and he had been obliged to emerge from his bedchamber enveloped in a bedcover. This was not something he intended to experience himself.

* * *

The more time Viola spent in the company of Mr Sheldon, the more she liked him. She had detected a certain look in his eyes when he had kissed her hand and she rather thought he returned her feelings. As she lay in her bed she viewed the situation carefully, trying to use her head rather than her heart to make a decision.

She had vowed never to marry again after her previous experience, but he was not like Rupert in anyway at all. He was a gentleman to the core; she trusted him implicitly, but was still not sure she could make that final commitment.

The memory of the indignities she had suffered in the bedchamber at the hands of her husband were etched into her very soul. However much she loved... loved? Until that moment she had not realised her feelings had turned from admiration and liking into love.

Did he feel the same way? He would make an excellent father to her children and they were already besotted with him. Even her mother liked him and she was a good judge of character. Loving him might not be enough for her to accept an offer – that is, if he made her one. Her skin crawled and her stomach turned over unpleasantly at the thought of what he would expect her to do once they were married.

Intimacy between a husband and wife who love each other might not be as vile as the ignominies she had endured at the hands of Rupert. Even so, she was not sure she loved Edward enough to put herself through that humiliation again. She could hardly expect him to marry her and not consummate the union, so if he did make her an offer she would refuse. The fact that she could not bear him children was another reason she should not contemplate marrying a second time.

She pushed the idea of becoming Mrs Edward Sheldon to the back of her mind. Time enough to face that question if the gentleman concerned made her an offer. The last thing that occurred to her as she fell asleep was that if she was married, then Sir Frederick's devilish plans would come to nothing.

Her sleep was troubled and she woke with the beginning of a megrim. If this developed then travelling in an overcrowded, closed carriage would be torment for all concerned. Casting up her accounts was a very unpleasant accompaniment to a full-blown megrim.

There was little time to think about her own health as the children demanded her attention. Rather than being horrified at travelling with Mr Sheldon they were delighted.

'Do you think he will tell us a story about his time in the army, Mama?' Thomas asked eagerly.

'We do not know if Mr Sheldon was actually an officer, brother; it is merely conjecture on our part.' Elizabeth had once more reverted to her stilted adult mode of conversation. That was not a good sign and did not bode well for the journey. Why was her daughter so unsettled this morning?

They were down in good time and Richard was waiting to see them off. 'I have paid your account, Viola. One of our own ships is sailing to Ireland this morning and I shall be on it. I will come to you on my return and let you know what transpired.' They fondly embraced. Then he hugged both the children and their mother and stepped back to speak quietly to Mr Sheldon, who had appeared through the archway that led to the stables.

It was not possible to hear what they said but it was serious and they shook hands solemnly when the conversation was done. His valet, Bishop, rode out into the road followed by Brutus. Her mouth dropped open and then she laughed.

'Mama, children, you must see this. Our dog is wearing boots.'

This novelty should be enough to keep the children giggling and laughing as they watched their pet trotting happily alongside Bishop's horse in his smart footwear. He was attracting a deal of attention and he appeared to be enjoying all of it.

The carriage tilted alarmingly as Edward – she could no longer think of him as Mr Sheldon – climbed in. He smiled and took the seat between the children.

'I find that if I am seated centrally the carriage is less likely to tip over when we turn a corner.' He said this with a straight face and the children nodded as if this nonsense was true. He winked at her and she hid her smile behind her hand.

'You are a very big man, Mr Sheldon, twice the size of our mama and grandmama,' Thomas said helpfully.

'Do not be impertinent, Thomas. Apologise immediately to Mr Sheldon.'

Her son turned red and hung his head and muttered his apology. 'I beg your pardon for speaking rudely, sir.'

In answer Edward put his arm around the boy's shoulder. 'There is absolutely no need to apologise to me for speaking the truth. I was jesting; there is no danger of the carriage overturning wherever I might be sitting.'

Elizabeth, who had been staring out of the window, turned her head to look at him. 'I think Brutus should not be wearing human clothes. He is being laughed at and people are pointing their fingers at him and at us.'

'Would you prefer your dog to have cut and bleeding paws by lunchtime, Elizabeth?'

'He should not be expected to walk all the way to Fenchurch. He should be allowed to travel in here with us. Why did he not go with the servants as was planned? I am most displeased at this change.'

'Your opinions are irrelevant, young lady. You will not speak again until you are given leave to do so. Is that clearly understood?' His tone was cold and her daughter's bravado melted like snow in the sunshine.

She was about to remonstrate with him when her mother

touched her hand and shook her head slightly. If she were to marry Edward it would be his right to discipline the children and she knew they would never receive more than a tongue-lashing. He would not raise a hand to her or to them, whatever the provocation.

'How far is Epping Forest from here, Mr Sheldon?'

He understood why she had enquired. His smile was warm and it reassured her. 'We shall be stopping to stretch our legs and allow the horses to rest before we get there. Thomas, is your dog beside the carriage still?'

'No, sir, I can't see him any more. He must be with your man.'

'He is an amazing animal. I am most impressed by his intelligence and obedience.'

She could not keep back her shocked response to this untruth. 'Brutus is a fine animal, but obedient he is not. He does as he pleases and there appears to be nothing I can do about it.'

His deep, baritone laugh filled the carriage. 'Then it is fortuitous is it not, my lady, that what he wishes to do is usually acceptable?'

He had removed his arm from around her son but she noticed her boy was leaning up against him and this moved her deeply. They had never had any connection with their natural father and she could see now that her mother was right: they desperately needed a real father. She came to a decision. If she was asked she would accept for her children's sake and pray that she could endure what came next.

'Elizabeth, if you wish to come with your brother and practise on my harp, you would be very welcome.'

Her daughter's gloved hand slipped into his and harmony was restored. 'Mama has said she will come too and show me how it sounds, so I know what I am to aim for.'

'When will our instruments arrive?'

'Within a week or so of your return, young man, so you will not have long to wait. Until then you must practise on the one you have.'

The conversation drifted from one subject to another whilst her mother dozed in the corner. She was concerned that Mama was sleeping so much when she had always been such an active person until recently.

When the carriage trundled into the courtyard of the splendid coaching inn that had been selected for their break, she was glad to get out. The interior of the carriage had become unpleasantly stuffy and her headache, despite her willing it to go away, was getting worse.

The children stood politely waiting to be told what they should do. He handed down her mother from the carriage. 'Could I impose upon you to take your grandchildren into the private parlour that has been reserved for us, ma'am? I wish to speak to your daughter alone.'

Her heart thumped painfully. Was he intending to propose to her in such a public place? She was not ready for such a declaration. She would go in with the children and prevent him from speaking.

'Viola, what is wrong? Are you unwell? Your complexion is pale and you have become quieter as the journey progressed.'

A wave of relief washed over her. 'I am suffering from a megrim, Edward, and fear I shall be most unwell before we reach the place where we are overnighting.'

He put his arm around her waist and she was glad of the support. 'Then we shall remain here. We can manage without our luggage and servants for one night.'

13

Beau guided his beloved Viola to the chamber that had been hurriedly reserved by Bishop. It was fortunate indeed that the inn they had chosen to make their first stop at had vacant rooms, as it was still early in the day.

The nursemaids and abigails were elsewhere with the luggage, so it would fall to him and Mrs Alston to take care of the children until their mother was well enough to resume her duties. He spoke briefly to her and was told that this indisposition, although unpleasant, would pass within a day or two.

'In which case, ma'am, I shall send my man to fetch back the carriage, the servants and the luggage. It should be here before nightfall.'

'I thank you, young man, and do not look so worried. A megrim is not life-threatening.'

He nodded politely but made no response to this comment. The old lady was deliberately making reference to his interest in her daughter and he was not comfortable with that.

The children had remained under the supervision of Bishop as they intended to spend time with their dog and have a closer look at his footwear. He beckoned his man over and explained what he required.

'Hire another hack, there is no point in ruining your mount. And do the same for the return journey – I shall be more comfortable having you at my side in the present circumstances.

'Children, you may come out and spend time with Brutus later, but now he needs to rest. There is a fine spread set out for us in a private parlour. Whilst your mama is unwell you will be in my charge.'

The children exchanged a look, not of apprehension as one might have expected, but of delight. It would seem that despite the firm set-down he had given Elizabeth, she did not fear him but actually enjoyed his company.

He held out his hands and they took one each. A smart gentleman was exiting the premises and they stood to one side to allow him to come out without hindrance. He nodded and smiled.

'Excellent children you have there, sir, a credit to you.'

Thomas bowed and Elizabeth curtsied and he could not help smiling at the comment.

'Excellent children? I think that is overstating the matter, but I shall say no more on the subject.' His tone belied his words and they giggled.

Their table manners were impeccable. They ate more than he did and appeared happy to stand at the window looking out into the yard whilst he went to check how the patient was progressing. He was concerned that his future mother-in-law had not appeared to eat, as there was one thing he was quite certain of – she did enjoy her food.

Again, he had managed to acquire a small apartment for Viola and her family. His chamber was opposite to her sitting room – close enough to be of assistance if he should be required,

The Duke's Bride

but not too close to raise eyebrows if there happened to be anyone interested in their behaviour.

He knocked on the sitting room door but, on receiving no response, he opened it and stepped in. To his horror he found Mrs Alston apparently comatose on the floor. He could hear nothing from the bedchamber so must suppose Viola was asleep.

He dropped to his knees and chafed her hands, calling her name repeatedly but got no response. Her complexion was pale, but her lips were not blue, which would have indicated she had suffered an apoplexy. Carefully he scooped her up and carried her into her own bedchamber.

Her pulse was regular but she still did not rouse. There was nothing for it, he would have to act as her maid. He had no intention of disturbing Viola if he could avoid it. With gentle fingers he unfastened her cloak and slipped it out from beneath her, then he removed her bonnet and boots.

He took a deep breath before running his hands down her person to check if she was wearing stays, which could be interfering with her ability to breathe. She was not, which was fortunate as he would have had to loosen them and had no wish to cause her further embarrassment when she awoke and realised he had attended to her in such a personal manner.

The room was warm, the fire burning fiercely, so there was no danger of her becoming cold. He unrolled the comforter that had been laid across the end of the bed and placed it over her. He was at a loss to know what to do next. Then a slight sound behind him made him turn.

Viola, in her undergarments, was standing in the doorway. 'You can do no more, Edward. This has happened once before and the physician said that when she overtaxes herself her heart cannot cope and so she faints. Thank you for taking care of her.'

He was at her side in two strides. 'And you? How are you? I

did not wish to disturb you unless I had to. My sister, Giselle, suffers from megrims...'

'I did not know you had any family, Edward. You must tell me more when I am better. I do not believe this will be a very severe attack. I have not cast up my accounts, and I believe if I can sleep for the remainder of the day I shall be restored by morning.'

'What about your mother? Are you sure I should not summon someone professional to attend to her?'

'No, she will sleep for a few hours and then wake refreshed and wonder how she came to be in bed. Who is watching the children in your absence?'

'They are waiting for me in the parlour downstairs. If you are quite sure there is nothing more I can do here, I shall return at once to them. Your servants should be with you in a few hours. I have reserved these chambers for two nights as you and your mother must be fully recovered before we resume our journey.'

'Then I shall return to my rest. We are indebted to you, Edward, and I thank you.'

'I am happy to help you, Viola, and even more pleased that we are now on less formal terms.'

He waited, poised to leap into action if he was required, until she returned safely to her bed. He had no time to dwell on what he had revealed about his real persona; the children had been left unattended for far too long already.

The afternoon did not drag as he had expected. The children were lively companions and they played spillikins until they all tired of this and then he decided to teach them how to play cribbage. The landlord found them the necessary items and soon they were all engrossed in the game.

'Children, you must remain here on your best behaviour whilst I go and check that your grandmother and mother are recovering from their indisposition.'

'Mama often gets these headaches, sir, and Grandmama has fainted clean away at least twice in the last few months. They always recover speedily.'

'Thank you for your reassurance, but as they do not have their maids it is I who must see if they have everything they require.'

Thomas, who was now building a house made of cards, looked up and smiled. 'Will we be having nursery tea or shall we be eating with you tonight, sir?'

'You are half correct, young man. I shall eat nursery tea with you but it will be served a little later than you are accustomed to.'

They were satisfied with his response and he was confident they would not misbehave whilst he was upstairs. It would be dark soon. Hopefully, both Bishop, the maids and the luggage would be here before it got full dark.

* * *

As soon as Edward had left the chamber, Viola returned to check on her mother for herself. Her skin was warm, her pulse steady; she was just deeply asleep. Satisfied there was no danger, she returned to her own bedchamber.

This was not as commodious as the one she had shared with her children in the hotel. They would have to come in the large bed with her tonight, and possibly tomorrow night if they decided to remain here for another twenty-four hours.

The blinding pain that stabbed in her right eye whenever she had a megrim had abated to bearable, but she knew from past experience if she did not rest in a darkened room it would return with a vengeance later on.

Once she was settled under the comforter, she closed her eyes and let her mind drift over all sorts of delightful possibilities. Even the unpleasant duty of being obliged to share her bed and her body with Edward no longer alarmed her as much as it had before. The more she knew him, the more she loved him. If she explained her reservations she was certain he would be prepared to wait until she was ready to become his true wife.

Her lips curved at her presumption. She was already married to him in her own mind and he had yet to declare his feelings or make her an offer. He had mentioned a sister, Giselle, and until that moment for some reason she had thought him alone in the world. She would have to learn more about his background before they tied the knot.

She was able to sleep for a further three hours and then woke almost recovered.

'My lady, do you wish to get up and use the commode? Sally has made the children a comfortable bed on the *chaise longue* in the sitting room and she will sleep with them. They will be perfectly comfortable there. I will sleep in the armchair in here so I can attend to you in the night. Mrs Alston did not wish to get up but has eaten a hearty meal.'

'Thank you, Hughes, that is very efficient of you.' She was tempted to add to this remark that it was also completely out of character for her maid to make any effort over and above what was expected of her. Was it possible she too thought things were going to change at Fenchurch and her position was in jeopardy?

'I take it my luggage is here. I should like to remove my undergarments and put on my nightgown after I have completed my ablutions. I should also like a jug of barley water fetched here. I require nothing to eat tonight.'

It took her longer than usual to prepare for the night. These sick headaches always made her slow and clumsy and affected her vision disastrously. When she was in her nightgown and bedrobe she walked through to see for herself that her children and her mother were safely settled.

Thomas and Elizabeth were sound asleep, the room in darkness apart from the flickering flames of the fire, and their nursemaid was dozing in an armchair close by. She retreated and pushed open the communicating door to the second bedroom.

'Come in, come in, my dear girl. I am so glad that you are also feeling more the thing. I'm sorry if I gave you cause for concern by my silly fit of the vapours. I understand that once again Mr Sheldon came to our rescue.'

'He did indeed, Mama.' She moved closer so she could safely converse without being overheard by the maid who was sewing in the corner. 'I think you have already guessed that I am in love with him.'

'I am delighted to hear you say so, my love, as I know that he returns your feelings. I told him you are unable to give him children and he was unbothered by this information. It would be different if he had a title to protect. I think he will make you an ideal husband. He is exactly the sort of gentleman we should have found for you...'

'No, I will never regret marrying Rupert, as without him I would not have my beloved children.'

'That is quite true, and I shall not mention the subject again. When are you anticipating that he will make you an offer? Do you think that he believes he must apply to Richard before he does so?'

'I am sure he does not. As to when he might propose, I think he will leave it until we are home. He mentioned a sister called Giselle – I must ask him more about his family, but I can hardly do so until we are betrothed. Even though you are sure he reciprocates my feelings it would be presumptuous of me to talk of such things until we actually are engaged.'

'It has occurred to me that if you are married you and the children will be safe from any interloper. I suggest that you marry by special licence.'

Viola leaned forward and kissed her mother affectionately. 'You are running ahead of yourself, Mama; until he has spoken you must not talk of such things, even to me.'

As was usually the case even though she had been asleep for several hours previously, she slept soundly until she was woken early by the noise of a tray being put down on a side table. Her stomach rumbled loudly.

'Hughes, I do hope you have brought me something to eat. I am sharp-set this morning and do not think I could survive until we break our fast at a more civilised time.'

'I have a jug of coffee and some sweet morning rolls. You will be pleased to know, my lady, that your children and Mrs Alston are still asleep. The time is now a little after six o'clock.'

After devouring the delicious, if insubstantial, repast Viola was eager to get up having spent more than enough time in bed. Freshly gowned in a travelling ensemble of moss green chenille, which had a matching bonnet and pelisse, she was eager to seek out the gentleman she hoped would one day be her husband.

The hour was early but she was sure he would already be outside checking the horses were fit and had not been tampered with overnight. She was almost buffeted from her feet by the enthusiastic greeting of the children's dog – or should she say of Edward's dog as he seemed to have changed allegiance recently?

'Enough, silly fellow, you will spoil my gown with your slobber. I can see you have your smart boots on, so there is no need to wave them in my face.'

'He is inordinately proud of those, and has shown them to anyone who is prepared to take a moment to look. I fear he will wish to wear them every time he goes outside in future.'

'Good morning, Edward, I was in need of fresh air as I was cooped up most of yesterday.'

'I cannot tell you how relieved I am to see you looking your usual lovely self. Is your mother also recovered?'

'She was perfectly well last night and able to eat her supper with relish. I was not so fortunate but have had something before I came down, which will keep me going until I have a more substantial breakfast with you and the children.'

'I have arranged for it to be served at eight o'clock and for us to leave at nine. Is that agreeable for you?'

'I shall not be sanguine until we are safely at home. I know you have taken every precaution but I am somewhat unnerved by what has happened over the past few days. I am hoping that whoever arranged for us to be held up has spent a miserable two nights hiding in the forest awaiting our arrival.'

'They will be in for further disappointment as I intend to travel through Epping at a gallop. This is why I needed to be certain the horses are well rested. This time we shall travel in advance of our luggage – that will also cause confusion, as they no doubt will be expecting us to be behind that carriage.'

'That is ingenious, Edward. Presumably our staff do not have to travel at speed through the forest, so will not arrive until sometime after us at our overnight stop.'

'We will not now be stopping in Romford, but in Chelmsford at The Saracen's Head. We shall travel at speed when we have to, but once we are on the more frequented parts of the toll road we shall take things slowly so the horses can complete the distance without distress.'

They were both startled by a sudden shout from the window above them and looked round to see both children leaning out of the window and waving frantically. For a second her stomach lurched but then she saw they were smiling, so there was no emergency inside.

Edward was not amused by this display. He flicked his hand and instantly the children vanished and the window slammed shut behind them. She spoke without heed to the consequences.

'You are not their father, you are their music teacher and it is not your place to discipline my children.'

'Would you have preferred them to continue to make an exhibition of themselves?' His tone was even but she knew him well enough to realise he was displeased – whether with her children or herself she had no idea and had no wish to find out.

Without responding to his comment, she turned on her heel and marched back into the inn. His eyes were boring into her back but she would not falter and she would not apologise. Once inside the safety of the vestibule she was obliged to stop and place a hand on the wall to keep herself upright.

Never in their seven years of marriage had she dared to speak her mind to Rupert. She had once made the catastrophic error of daring to criticise his lurid choice of waistcoats and that had been the first time she had been beaten by him. She had never made the same mistake again.

Then Edward's arm was around her and he gathered her close. 'I overstepped by reprimanding the little ones, my love, but I am hoping in the not too distant future it will be my privilege and honour to share in the raising of your wonderful children.'

They were standing in full view of a dozen or more guests who were watching with considerable interest this unusual display of affection between a couple they thought must, of course, already be husband and wife.

She raised her head and smiled. 'That is a most unusual proposal, sir. I would expect a man of your standing to make me an offer when on one knee.'

To her horror he grinned and did as she had laughingly suggested whilst she desperately tried to pull him back to his feet. 'No, I was jesting – get up, get up please.'

He ignored her protests. 'I love you. Would you do me the inestimable honour of becoming my wife at the earliest possible opportunity?'

'I will, of course, I will, but you must get up immediately and stop making a cake of yourself.'

He surged to his feet and picked her up so her face was on a level with his. She knew at once what he intended and was having none of it. 'If you do not put me down this instant, Edward, I shall scream that you are molesting me and have you thrown into jail.'

In answer he lowered his mouth until it covered hers and she forgot her reservations, her embarrassment at being so publicly kissed, and responded with enthusiasm.

14

Beau was aware he had drawn unwanted attention to himself and his future wife by behaving so recklessly in the vestibule of a well-frequented coaching inn. What was he thinking? If that bastard was indeed having them followed word would soon reach him that he and Viola had come to a very public understanding.

'My darling, I think we have caused enough excitement for one day. You must go at once to speak to your children and your mother and give them the good news. I shall join you for breakfast.'

Her smile was radiant, she had never looked lovelier, and he knew with absolute certainty she was the woman he had waited all his life to meet. He intended to marry her, with or without his family present, and worry about the ramifications once she was legally his.

He returned to the stables where he could gather his thoughts without fear of being disturbed. Sir Frederick would be well aware that as soon as Viola became his wife, his plans would be ruined. It might well cause him to step up his interference in their lives in a more violent way. Doing what he had just done was possibly a grievous error of judgement.

Too late for regrets. Once they were safely back in Suffolk he would send Bishop to London to obtain a special licence. He had no intention of revealing his true identity before the ceremony and risk her changing her mind because of some foolish notion that he must have a direct heir, which she could not give him.

In order for the marriage to be valid he would have to use his full name, Beaumont Edward Charles Peregrine Sheldon. Hopefully she would just think he did not use his first given name as it was too outlandish. There was no necessity for him to have his title mentioned for the ceremony to be legal.

He would not consider the ceremony entitled him to share her bed until they had been married again in front of his family in the chapel at Silchester Court. Until then he must maintain his self-control, although he knew this was going to be damnably difficult. He had never wanted to make love to a woman more than he did to Viola. Finally, at the advanced age of four and thirty, he understood what romantic love was and why his siblings were so happy with their partners.

Bishop cleared his throat noisily behind him and he was jerked from his musings. He turned to see his man beaming from ear to ear. Devil take it, word had spread already of his good fortune.

'May I be permitted to congratulate you, sir?'

'No, you may not. We shall be leaving at nine. Make sure the horses have been well fed and watered as they will have a hard task ahead of them.'

'Do you wish Brutus and I to go ahead as we did yesterday?'

'I think not. Seeing you and the dog will just alert them to the fact that we are about to arrive. For the same reason, the carriage with the luggage and the maids will travel behind us today.'

He explained his plan of action and Bishop nodded. 'I reckon you should...' The man coloured and hastily apologised for presuming to offer advice to his master.

'Go on, man, what were you about to suggest?'

'I was going to say that it might be helpful to have the Bow Street runners involved in this, sir. They have a mounted brigade, they wear red waistcoats and are called the Robin Redbreasts...'

'I do not need a description of their clothing; what I need is for you to tell me why you think they might be prepared to take an interest in our problem.'

'Epping Forest is notorious for highwaymen and it is their job to clear them out. If I were to tell them I had heard there was a gang waiting to pounce on your carriage, they might well ride with us in the hope of apprehending them.'

'I suppose it is not unreasonable to think that the Countess and Earl of Fenchurch would be a target. You have a little over two hours to accomplish this – do you think you can do that and be here ready to depart at nine o'clock?'

The man nodded. 'It's not too great a distance back to the Smoke. If I go post I can do it easily in the time.'

Beau tossed him a handful of coins, more than enough for the purpose. Then something else occurred to him. 'I have changed my mind about you being obligated to return by nine o'clock. We shall delay our departure until you get here. I have no wish for you to break your neck in order to fulfil my orders.'

The dog pressed himself against his thigh and he stroked the silky ears. Obtaining a special licence to marry would mean they could marry wherever they liked at whatever time they liked, but these were rarely given and would have to be applied for in person from the Archbishop of Canterbury himself. A common licence would fit the bill as they could then marry in the local church as long as it was before midday.

This was easier to obtain and could be got from a local bishop. He would ride to Ipswich as soon as he was home and get this organised. He had no wish to have his name read out three times in the local church, as there might well be someone who recognised his unusual first name.

He went in search of Viola. He needed to discuss his plans for their nuptials and not make decisions unilaterally that should be made together. It would be interesting to be obliged to defer to another's opinion, as this was something he had not been required to do. As head of the family he was the one deferred to on domestic matters and, of course, the estate was his concern.

All this would change once he was married. As he would never have children of his own Bennett's sons would inherit the title and the responsibilities. Therefore, the balance of power at Silchester would change. For his nephew to learn what would be expected of him, Bennett would need to be more involved with the running of the vast estates.

He should reveal his identity before the marriage, but he dare not risk the woman he loved to distraction nobly refusing him because she believed he must secretly desire his own progeny. This was underhand and out of character for him, but he had no option in the circumstances. Marrying him would protect the children and herself from interference from her neighbour. This was paramount – he must just pray she would eventually forgive him for his deception.

He was halfway up the stairs when the children saw him and flung themselves into his arms. For a sickening moment he thought they would come to grief but he flung his weight forward and regained his balance.

'Can we call you papa? Will you be living with us at Fenchurch Manor? We are so happy you and our mama are to be married,' Elizabeth said as she clung to his jacket.

'You are lucky we did not all break our necks. I was unprepared for your precipitous arrival.'

Thomas had a handful of his stock in his hand and looked a little pale. 'My word, that was a close-run thing. It is a good thing you are so large, Mr Sheldon, or I am certain we would have tumbled to our deaths.'

Beau put his arms around them and carried them back to the safety of the landing where he put them down. 'I am delighted you are both pleased that your mother and I are now betrothed. I think it a little premature for you to address me as papa, sweetheart, but I appreciate the sentiment.'

Viola emerged from her sitting room. 'Come in, Edward, we have much to discuss. Children, Sally will take you down to visit Brutus.'

An impulse made him lean down and place an affectionate kiss on the forehead of each, and from their expressions he knew he had done the right thing. The nursemaid curtsied and smiled – news of their engagement had travelled fast.

'I hope Mrs Alston is as pleased as the children at our news.'

'She is indeed, my love, and has advised that we marry at the earliest opportunity, as by so doing you will become head of my household and guardian to the children.'

'I had thought the same. On our return I shall discover the nearest bishop and apply for a common licence. We can then be married in your local church but without the necessity of having the banns called and alerting Sir Frederick.'

He could tell from her demeanour that something was bothering her and he thought he knew what it might be. 'Under normal circumstances we would have a longer engagement, have more time to get to know each other. Therefore, I think it would be advisable for the marriage to be in name only until you are ready to move things on.'

The Duke's Bride

Her look of relief gave him pause. He was prepared to do without children of his own in order to marry the woman he loved, but he could not envisage a marriage that did not involve intimacy. Was she so damaged by her abusive husband that she would never be able to share his bed with any pleasure?

He pushed aside his worries. He was being selfish; Viola and her children needed the protection of his name and he would give it to them regardless of the sacrifices he might have to make.

'I was thinking exactly the same thing, my love. We have only known each other a few weeks and being able to spend more time with you before we are... we are truly man and wife will be of benefit to both of us.'

His immediate thought was that he could see no advantage to himself but this was hardly the time to say so. 'I am prepared to wait as long as it takes, my darling, but I pray it will not be too long.'

She flushed under his scrutiny but moved towards him instead of away, which was what he had half expected. The top of her head came to his shoulder but this was no obstacle as far as he was concerned. He bent his knees and swept her up so her feet were dangling in mid-air.

The next five minutes almost broke his iron control, but somehow he managed to step away before things got out of hand. Her response had shown him she was a passionate woman and reassured him that eventually he would be able to make love to her.

He turned his back to hide his embarrassment and spoke whilst gazing out of the window. She was an experienced woman so would be well aware why he was doing so. 'I came to tell you that we will not be leaving at nine o'clock as planned.'

He explained the reason and she spoke from behind him. 'I should be less alarmed at the prospect of crossing Epping Forest if I knew that the Bow Street runners were there to protect us. I shall escort my mother to the private parlour for breakfast in half an hour. Could I ask you to collect the children from outside and bring them in with you?'

'Elizabeth asked if she could call me papa – I told her it was premature. Mr Sheldon or sir is too formal now. I thought they might call me Uncle Edward. Would you have any objection to that?'

'I think it a perfect compromise. Before you go, you mentioned a sister, Giselle. Will she be able to come to our wedding?'

'I am afraid not. She has a small baby and lives the other side of the country. You will meet her eventually.'

He had no wish to prolong this conversation. He had not told any direct lies, but if she enquired further about his family he would either have to reveal his true name or continue to deceive her. He knew without a shadow of a doubt that the more falsehoods he told, the harder it would be to convince her he had done it for her sake and not his.

* * *

The fact that he found her so desirable was flattering but also made her decision to remain out of his bed more difficult. Edward was a red-blooded gentleman and although she was certain he would never break his word, she had no wish to make life difficult for him.

Viola was still glowing from his passionate kisses. There had never been anything like that between her and Rupert even in the beginning. In fact, now she came to think of it, he had never made any attempt to kiss her before they were married and she had misinterpreted this as him being the perfect gentleman.

The Duke's Bride

What had taken place in the marriage bed had not been making love but something closer to rape. This was the first time she had voiced this fact even in her own head. In law a wife was the property of her husband once they were married. He could legally beat her, as long as he used a cane no thicker than his little finger, and he could demand his marital rights whenever he wished.

He had never asked if she was willing to share her body with him but had climbed into her bed and taken what he wanted without involving her at all. The whole experience had been humiliating, painful and she was not sure if she could risk putting herself in the position of having to endure such unpleasantness ever again.

As far as she could recall he had never kissed her on the mouth – or anywhere at all. She had been a receptacle for his seed, nothing more. Once the title was secure he had never come to her again and for that she had thanked God every night. The beatings were preferable to the other.

'Viola, daughter, you are wool-gathering. I have been standing here this age and you have been ignoring me.'

'I was lost in thought – and none of it pleasant. Do you think I have done the right thing accepting Edward's offer? I am now having second thoughts.'

'You will not find a better man anywhere in the kingdom; of that I am quite certain. The good Lord has sent him to you and you must not turn his gift down.'

'I do love him, and the children adore him too. The marriage will be unconsummated initially.' Her mother looked scandalised. 'Not at my suggestion, at his behest. I agreed because it was exactly what I wished to suggest myself. Even after three years I am still terrified of committing myself for the rest of my life to someone who might turn on me...'

'Stuff and nonsense, my girl. Edward Sheldon has given you his word and he is the most honest gentleman I have ever met. He would not lie to you and you must put aside your fears and follow your heart.'

'Wise advice, Mama, which I shall take. I wonder, will he want us to live with him at Elveden or will he join us at Fenchurch?'

'More to the point, have you asked him if he is happy to have me living with you still? I have no wish to be banished to the dower house at either place.'

'You are part of the family. If I thought he would do that I should not marry him under any circumstances. I shall ask him to clarify his position – but not over breakfast as I have no wish for the children to be involved in any of the details. As far as they are concerned they have got a new papa and that is all they need to know.'

'Who would have thought that a month ago you had never heard of Edward Sheldon and yet now you are going to marry him. I believe he was smitten the moment he set eyes on you. I was wrong to tell you he was a confirmed bachelor – he was just waiting to meet the woman he would fall in love with.'

Her mother seemed more sprightly today, which was a relief. These intermittent bouts of fainting were of great concern to her, although Mama made light of it. In future she would do more to keep her dearest parent from overexerting herself.

'I imagine that Richard is already on his way to Ireland. It is going to cost the business a deal of money that it seems we did not need to spend.'

'I think it wise to discover what sort of man this Mr Fenchurch is, as he will be Thomas's heir until my son produces children of his own.'

'I am somewhat reassured by the fact that Fenchurch's father removed himself from the family. I think we had better go down as I heard the children going into the building.'

She offered her arm and her mother took it. They were met in the foyer by her future husband. There was no sign of either Thomas or Elizabeth.

His smile sent waves of heat around her body in a most alarming way. 'Do not look so apprehensive. The little ones asked very politely if they could go in and take their seats. They find eating in a public place fascinating.'

He nodded politely to her mama and offered an arm to each of them. He towered above them both and for the first time his size was a comfort rather than an impediment to liking him.

'Am I to be banished to the dower house, sir, when you are married to my daughter? I was not even allowed to visit when she was married to that other man.'

'I should be bereft without your presence, ma'am; you are an essential part of this family unit.'

'Mama, I expressly asked you not to talk about this over breakfast.'

Her mother laughed. 'As we are yet to enter the dining room, I believe I have not broken my word.'

Viola looked anxiously about the chamber but sure enough the twins were sitting at a table by the window, looking the picture of innocence. She would much prefer to have eaten in the sitting room upstairs but as the children were so eager to be here she had not the heart to deny them.

There were no spare tables and she was conscious of being stared at as they made their way across the room. There must have been around twenty other people breaking their fast. Unlike her own establishment here there was no buffet set out for one to help oneself. One must wait until a waiter came to enquire what one wanted.

'Mama, we have asked what there is this morning and there is not as much choice as there was at the hotel,' Elizabeth said. 'I am going to have ham and eggs with toast and strawberry conserve.'

Edward settled her mother first and then pulled out her chair. Where was the waiter who should be taking care of this task? 'And you, Thomas? What do you want to eat?'

'I shall have just toast and marmalade, thank you, Mama.'

The waiter hurried up and took their orders. An enormous pewter coffee jug appeared first along with the necessary cups and saucers to drink it in. The children preferred it with cream and sugar, but like Edward she liked it black and unsweetened.

This was another thing they had in common. They also had a love of music, were talented musicians themselves, and she rather thought they both preferred to be in the countryside and not the town. 'Edward, when we are married do you wish to open the house in Grosvenor Square and visit every season?'

If she had offered to pull his teeth for him he could not have looked more horrified. 'I have no love of the city. I like to ride in the fresh air and not inhale the polluted atmosphere one finds in Town.'

'Then we are in agreement on that score. I could see at once that you were at home in the saddle, as am I, so we also share a love of outside activities.'

Thomas glanced at him before venturing to speak and he nodded his permission. 'We like to play cricket in the summer. Elizabeth is better at it than I, but we all enjoy the game. Even our grandmama comes out to watch.'

'I am not sure how you achieve a game when there are only three of you.'

'We get the outside men and grooms to join us. It is terrific fun. I do hope you like to play too.'

'I enjoy most outside activities, young man, and have been considered to be a demon bowler by those I play against.'

Edward poured them all a drink and then added the cream and sugar for the children. A large platter of freshly made toast, butter and jam arrived as he completed the task. He ate heartily as did her daughter, but the rest of them were content without a giant plate of ham and eggs.

'I suggest that we repair to your sitting room, Viola, and the children can demonstrate their prowess at the game of cribbage.'

She was almost disappointed when word came up from the yard that Bishop had returned safely and wished to speak to Edward.

15

Beau was unsurprised that Bishop had been unable to interest the magistrate at Bow Street in the possible sighting of a band of highwaymen.

'They were sympathetic, sir, but even knowing who was likely to be held up was not enough to send any of their runners.'

'Then we will have to travel at speed through the danger area as originally planned. You have had an exhausting journey; are you fit enough to ride or do you require an hour or two to recover?'

'I have been sitting in a carriage so will be ready as soon as I have eaten.'

Beau looked up and saw the children watching from the window. He smiled and beckoned, and they understood they were to get ready to descend and begin the next stage of their journey home.

It took them a considerable time to get organised and the carriage was waiting by the time they eventually arrived. He lifted them into it and then assisted the two ladies. The carriage rocked and moved forward. The coachmen had been told to

The Duke's Bride

take it steady and then spring the horses as they entered the forest.

'Would it not be more sensible, Edward, for us to wait until there are other vehicles travelling through this part and then go with them?'

'If there are coaches and carriages approaching at the same time as us then of course we shall travel with them. I have instructed your coachmen to do so if possible. However, one cannot keep horses standing when the temperature is so low. If we are alone, then speed will be our protection.'

The children kept up a running commentary on what they could see from the window whilst Mrs Alston slept in the corner. After travelling for an hour or more the vehicle slowed to a stop. He opened the window and leaned out to speak to the coachman.

'Have you seen anything untoward ahead of us?'

'No, sir, all quiet. We're the only vehicle on this stretch of the road at present. Nothing behind us neither.'

'Then take this mile at a gallop. I thank God the road is well maintained and relatively straight, as I would not wish to endanger the horses or ourselves by this venture.'

He pulled the window up and resumed his seat in between the children. 'This will be an adventure. Elizabeth, Thomas, take tight hold of the straps; I have no wish for you to fly off the seat.'

They did as he instructed and he braced his feet against the seat on the other side of the carriage. His future mother-in-law was tucked in tight beneath the furs and should be relatively stable, however bumpy the ride became. Viola and the twins were similarly covered but he had refused. He disliked being encumbered and was quite warm enough beneath his thick greatcoat.

The driver snapped his whip and the horses moved into a trot, from there to a smooth canter. Once the carriage was bowling along at this speed it would be safe to increase the pace again and get the team to gallop. Horses could not keep this up for more than a mile without becoming blown. This would be more than enough to take them past the trees that grew so densely on either side of the road, which was why it was the favourite haunt of those wishing to hold up a passing carriage.

The children squealed in delight as they were thrown from side to side. He was less enthused about the experience, as he knew only too well that if a wheel dropped into a pothole the carriage could overturn and all of them be killed.

This was madness – he should not be risking their lives with this foolish race. He stood up and hammered on the roof and immediately the coachman responded. The horses dropped back to an extended trot and he unclenched his fists.

'I think we might have been in more danger from overturning than we were from anything else.' He had checked his weapon earlier and it was primed and loaded and ready to fire if needs be.

'This is quite fast enough for me, young man,' came the muffled voice from the corner.

'I agree, ma'am, and we are almost through the forest and will soon be...'

The carriage lurched. He heard the coachman yelling at the horses as the man hauled desperately on the reins. Then his world turned upside down. The children screamed. Viola and her mother did the same. A horrible silence followed for a second.

Beau could not breathe. The air had been pummelled from his chest. There was something heavy adding to his distress. His head cleared and he was able to assess the damage. One door was beneath him the other above.

'Thomas, Elizabeth, are you hurt?'

There was no response and neither was there from his beloved, or her mother. The carriage was on its side. There was no sound of screaming horses, which was a small comfort.

'Viola, talk to me. I dare not move until I know you have no broken limbs as you are resting on top of me.' The children were sprawled across his feet but he could not see the whereabouts of the old lady who was also ominously silent.

'I am perfectly well, Edward, just stunned.'

'We are unhurt, Uncle Edward, but I think that our grandmama is not at all well,' Elizabeth said.

'Can you move all your limbs without pain, sweetheart? What about you, Thomas?'

'I'm a bit bruised, but nothing broken. Is it safe for us to sit up?'

'Remain still for a moment, I need to hear from Bishop or the coachman that we will not turn completely over if we do so.'

Bishop called out to him. 'We will soon have you out of there, sir. There was a tree blocking the road. Thank God you were not travelling any faster.'

'Whoever placed it there might well come. Send Brutus to investigate.'

'The dog's already gone into the trees.' The door, which was now above Beau's head, opened and Bishop looked in. 'We can lift you out, sir, easy enough but I reckon it would be safer to right the carriage with you all still inside.'

'Only Mrs Alston appears to have taken any injury. I am most concerned about her as she has a feeble heart. Pull the carriage onto its wheels and we will brace ourselves.'

He heard the sound of voices that did not belong to his party and guessed another vehicle had stopped to assist. Whoever had caused this accident was not likely to appear if there were others there to witness it.

'Listen, children, they are going to pull us the right way up. We need to position ourselves so we will not be hurt when this happens, but just slide back onto the squabs. Slowly turn so your feet are facing the same way as mine.' He had already swivelled round.

'Why is my mama not speaking? Do you think she has had a fatal apoplexy?'

'I have had no such thing, daughter; I was merely gathering my wits after a very unsettling experience.'

'Thank God, Mama, we all thought you badly hurt. Are you able to move at all?'

'I thought I was having a nightmare so ignored everything about me. I am quite capable of turning so my feet are pointing inwards like everyone else.'

Beau would have preferred to be next to her so he could hold her steady when the carriage began to move. It would begin slowly initially but then, once it was almost upright, it might well be different and he had no wish for anyone to be injured after surviving the first impact.

The children managed to wriggle themselves so they were between him and Viola. Mrs Alston was beside her daughter and closest to the side of the carriage.

'We are ready, Bishop; start to pull the vehicle up.'

There was a deal of shouting, some worrying creaks and groans from the carriage, then it began to right itself. The procedure took less time than he'd expected and they all ended up in a heap for a second time.

He extricated himself from the mêlée of arms and legs. 'Excellent, we are all in one piece.' The carriage door opened, which was in itself a surprise, and willing hands were there to lift out the children and the two ladies.

He jumped down after them. A florid gentleman of middle

years slapped him on the back. 'Well done, well done, sir. A miracle no one was injured and that your carriage has suffered no damage either, apart from a few scratches.'

'I thank you for your assistance.' He looked around and saw that Bishop had already organised the removal of the tree so the road was now clear of obstruction.

The little ones had recovered from the accident and were now bouncing about as if nothing untoward had taken place. Viola was taking care of her mother who also seemed in remarkably high spirits considering what had just happened. This left him free to examine the horses and carriage for himself.

'The axles are undamaged, sir – blooming marvellous, is what it is. If you hadn't got me to slow down we would all have been done for.'

'And the team?'

'Jed, the under-coachman, has checked them all thoroughly and they are ready to go. A few buckles broke on the harness but that's no never mind. It will hold together until we get to the next coaching inn and I can get repairs done.'

'Good man – how soon will you be ready to depart?'

'Give us a quarter of an hour and I reckon the horses will be back in harness.'

'We are blocking the road at the moment so the sooner the better.'

He wandered over to speak to Bishop who was looking into the undergrowth. 'No sign of Brutus? I think he would bark if he had found anyone close by.'

'That's what worries me, sir; we should be able to hear his movements. Do you think the varmints caught him?'

'Absolutely not – the only way they could harm him is if they shot him and we would have heard that. He will probably be back before we leave. If not, then he will follow us.'

The coachman had been correct in his prediction and in the allotted time they were all snugly inside and on their way to the next inn. The dog had yet to return but he had reassured the children he would come eventually and they were satisfied with that.

'First, we were travelling at breakneck speed, young man, at your behest, and now we are progressing at a snail-like pace. If we continue as we are it will take us a week to get home.'

'Mama, until the carriage has been thoroughly checked and the harness mended it would be foolhardy indeed to go any faster.'

'Uncle Edward, why did you suddenly decide we must travel less quickly?' Elizabeth asked.

'A good question. My original decision to take the dangerous part of our route at a gallop was putting us at greater risk, which is why I banged on the roof and had the coachman return to a more sensible pace.'

Mrs Alston stirred in her corner. 'I repeat what I said to you, daughter, this gentleman was heaven-sent. I am certain with him in charge of the family we will all be well protected and happier than ever before. I just wish my dear husband was here to see the change in you.'

* * *

Viola thought this kind of comment was inappropriate when her children were listening but could hardly remonstrate, as this would also be inappropriate. So, she said nothing and the moment passed, but she was certain Edward was not impressed. No doubt the twins agreed with her mother, as they all but worshipped him.

After being upended so violently her bruised body was

feeling every bounce and jounce, and she thought the others must be suffering as she was.

'I hope they have accommodation for us wherever we stop to have the carriage repairs done. I think we all need to rest and recuperate. I certainly do.'

'I hurt all over, Mama,' her daughter moaned. 'I wish there was another way to travel as I don't like being in a carriage any more.'

'Unless you wish to ride or walk, sweetheart, you have no alternative but to endure the discomforts. I certainly think it would be sensible, if there are decent chambers to be had, to remain wherever we halt and give ourselves a chance to recover from the earlier mishap.'

'If we overnight then Brutus will catch up with us, Uncle Edward. I don't like him being missing.'

Edward opened the window and leaned out. Bishop immediately rode alongside and then set off at a canter to organise the matter for them.

The Queen's Head turned out to be a superior hostelry, and they were delighted to provide them with accommodation for the night. The twins had a small room to themselves, and their nursemaid, she and her mother had reasonable chambers, but unfortunately there was no private parlour. Edward was situated at the rear of the premises, rather too far away from them all than he was comfortable with.

They were all in low spirits as one of the horses had become lame and the dog had yet to return. At least they had a private parlour downstairs allotted to them for their stay where they could eat and sit together as a family.

'We will not be able to proceed tomorrow if we have to wait for all the horses to be fit and for Brutus to return. I have therefore decided we shall complete our journey by post-chaise. Your coachmen will remain here until the horse has recovered and they can proceed.'

'It is exorbitantly expensive, young man. I assume you have very deep pockets if you are intending for us to travel this way.'

'I do indeed, ma'am. This journey appears to be fraught with endless difficulties, and the sooner it is over for all of us the better it will be. I have instructed the carriage with the servants and luggage to continue on their journey so they should arrive at roughly the same time as us, late tomorrow.'

'The food here is indifferent. Let us hope the beds are more comfortable than they appear. I am going to retire, daughter, and I require your assistance as I do not have my maid to attend me.' Her mother glared at Edward. 'I think it high-handed of you to send our luggage and servants away without consulting us. We shall be in disarray and sadly travel worn by the time we return, and I am most displeased about that.'

Edward did not seem particularly put out by this reprimand. He shrugged in a very continental way and left her to depart with her parent. By the time this task was done the children had also gone to bed, leaving her alone with him.

Her intention had been to gently remonstrate with him for not discussing his plans before implementing them, but before she could speak she was in his arms and being kissed with a tenderness she had never experienced before.

Her eyes were full when eventually he raised his head. He had no need to say how much he loved her – his expression said it all.

'I could have lost you and your children today and it would have been entirely my fault. I always considered myself an intelligent man, able to make rational choices, but my decision to gallop through the forest almost brought us to our deaths. I hope you can forgive me for my stupidity.'

The Duke's Bride

'There is nothing to forgive, my love. Shall we be seated? It is so much easier to talk to you when I do not have to strain my neck.' There was a comfortable *chaise longue* and they sat together on it. 'As far as I am concerned it was you who saved our lives by slowing our breakneck speed.'

He reached out and cupped her face. His fingers were long, lean and elegant. Everything about him was perfect, and in that moment, she decided she had no reservations about this match. She would be his true wife the night they were married.

When she told him, instead of being overjoyed she saw something she did not recognise in his eyes. Was it regret? Or was it a fleeting glimpse of sadness about something she did not understand?

'I love you, my darling girl, but I shall not share your bed until we are better acquainted. I know why you are hesitant to be intimate and understand exactly. Your experience has made you wary of what, I can assure you, should be a loving and enjoyable experience for both parties.'

'Are you having second thoughts because I cannot give you children?'

'I am not. You have given me two children that already I love as if they were my own flesh and blood. I am content with the size of our family.'

'There are so many things we need to discuss. Do you wish us to move to Elveden or will you come to Fenchurch Manor?'

He turned his face away so she could not see his expression. She was about to ask again when he answered. 'We will remain at Elveden initially.'

She took this to mean he intended that they would move to Fenchurch Manor once the marriage was consummated. This was a reasonable decision but for some reason she got the feeling he was not telling her the whole.

'Edward...'

Their conversation was abruptly terminated as someone hammered on the door. He was on his feet and across the room in two strides. He opened the door and was confronted by an irate young man dressed in the most ridiculous fashion. She believed he would be known as a macaroni, as his shirt points were so high he could not turn his head properly and his waistcoat was a hideous mixture of purple and yellow stripes.

'Well?' That was all that Edward said, but it was sufficient to make the unfortunate gentleman step back.

'I beg your pardon, Mr Sheldon, but I believe you are the owner of a very large and vicious hound. He has spooked my cattle and my phaeton is now quite ruined.'

'I shall come at once. Brutus is the most docile of canines unless provoked. Might I enquire how he came to spook your horses?'

'They are a spirited pair and one of them took a lump out of him as he went past. He turned on them and not unnaturally they tried to bolt.'

'I shall come with you, Edward. I am eager to see that our dog has not come to any harm from this encounter.' She gave the intruder a superior stare. 'I am most displeased to hear that my dog has been savaged by one of your horses.'

'I beg your pardon, my lady, I was misinformed. I thought the dog was Mr Sheldon's.'

'Do not come with me; it is too cold out there for you without your cloak. I am made of sterner stuff and shall come to no harm without my greatcoat.'

His smile made her toes curl in their boots and then he was gone, leaving her with many questions and not enough answers.

16

Beau wanted to punch his fist through the nearest window. He could not go through with this marriage until he had revealed his secret. However, if he did so he ran the risk that she would refuse him, not only because he had deceived her, but also because it would mean she had to relocate to Silchester. He was in a quandary. Once they were married they were committed for the rest of their lives regardless of their feelings.

He pushed this aside. Time to make a decision when he knew how the land lay with regards to Mr Fenchurch and the interference of the noxious Sir Frederick. Bishop greeted him with relief.

'Sir, it wasn't the dog's fault. He came into the yard quiet as you like when one of those vicious chestnuts savaged him as he walked past. All he did was snarl and charge at it. He didn't attempt to bite. If the owner had had them under control there would have been no problem.'

'Having met the owner your story does not surprise me. Does Brutus require sutures?'

'A few teeth marks, but he's not bothered. The horses are fine; it's just the phaeton that's damaged.'

'Well I am damned if I am paying for that. Where is my dog?'

'I was obliged to shut him in a storeroom to stop that gentleman from attacking him with his whip.'

The hound was inordinately pleased to see him, and he did not object when the animal slobbered over his coat in an effort to lick his face.

'Good lad, good boy. I wish you would not wander in the way that you do, but at least you always find us again.'

He checked the injury and was satisfied it needed no further attention. Then he carefully removed each of the leather boots the dog was wearing in order to give his pads some fresh air overnight.

'I shall take the dog in with us tomorrow, Bishop. Leave your mount here and the under-coachman can ride him back when they return.'

'Righto, sir, makes sense to me. What time do we depart?'

* * *

Beau returned to his chamber but slept badly. Viola and her family thought him a gift from the divine, sent especially to take care of them. They would change their minds once they knew how he had deceived them. His only consolation was that his decision had been made with the blessing of his family, not done to deceive anyone or to benefit himself in any way.

He abandoned the attempt to sleep and got dressed in the dark. He was marrying Viola because he loved her and could not live without her or her children, and not for any monetary gain. He would continue with his plans to find a bishop and obtain a common licence, but before they married he would wait for Richard Alston to return from Ireland.

If this gentleman had been successful, had persuaded Mr

Fenchurch to remain where he was in return for a sizeable contribution to his family's well-being, then there would be no urgency to marry in order to protect Viola and her children. If this proved to be the outcome he would reveal who he was and rely on his powers of persuasion to convince her to continue with the engagement.

For the first time in hours his shoulders unknotted and he thought he might be able to sleep. He was damned if he was going to get undressed again – he would do the unthinkable – sleep on top of the bed fully clothed. His mouth curved. At least he did not have his boots on.

After a hasty breakfast the following morning, he settled the children and the ladies into their vehicle and waved them off. He did not envy the postilions who were obliged to ride the lead horse in all weathers. Presumably they changed when the horses did, but he had not thought to enquire. They were paid enough for their service.

* * *

They covered the remaining fifty miles in a dizzyingly short amount of time. As Edward had predicted, they arrived at the last stage as it was getting dark. Viola was well known here and in no time at all a hired vehicle was available to convey them the last few miles.

'I cannot tell you how relieved I am to be on *terra firma*; if I never go in a carriage again I shall be quite content,' Mama said.

'I certainly have no wish to travel at such speed again. I much prefer to take it at a decorous pace and use my own carriage. You have been very well behaved, children. I am very pleased with you both.'

They exchanged a smug smile. 'Uncle Edward told us we must not upset Grandmama by being noisy.'

'Then you can tell him, Thomas, that I am most impressed by the change in both of you since you have met him. He is a good influence on this family.'

Her mother retired immediately saying that she would have a tray sent up to her. The children did not even quibble about the fact their dog would not be returning but go straight to Elveden with Edward.

'We think he is now his dog rather than ours, Mama, but we are quite happy to share.'

'As we will all be living under the same roof very soon, Thomas, you will not do without his company for long. Imagine the difficulty if Brutus had not taken to your future papa!'

'He is a very clever dog and if he had not liked Uncle Edward then neither would we,' Elizabeth chimed in.

She hugged them both and handed them over to Sally who had arrived earlier that day with the other maids and their luggage.

It would be too soon to take the children for a music lesson the following morning – they would all need at least a day to recover from the strictures of the journey. Everyone had an interesting collection of bruises from being tumbled about in the carriage, but she thanked God it had been no worse.

The servants at Fenchurch, unlike those in Grosvenor Square who had been loyal to Rupert, had been dismissed, some without reference, and she had employed new staff. This was another thing she would ask Edward to take care of once they were married. The staff in London must be dismissed and replaced with new before she would go there again.

There was so much she did not know about him. She knew

his age and that he had a sister called Giselle, but apart from that his past was a blank to her. Did it really matter that he did not speak of his life before he came to Suffolk? They had spent a considerable amount of time together, she had watched him interacting with her children and her mother, as well as servants, and he treated them all with the utmost respect and kindness.

He loved animals and they loved him. He was a fine horseman, a handsome man and a formidable character. She had not seen him enraged and had no wish to do so. One thing she did know was that however furious he was he would never harm any of them. She had gone through all these points more than once in her head, so why was she still dwelling on them?

He loved her and she loved him – would that be enough to build a life together? What if he had dark secrets he was hiding from her and these were only revealed after they were married? His air of authority, the way he carried himself, was what had attracted her to him in the first place. There were, of course, dozens of gentlemen who were not members of the aristocracy but were still part of the *ton*. For some reason she believed he had no interest in elevating his status by marrying her.

Did the fact that she was ignorant of his past present an obstacle to them getting married? This was easily solved by asking him the requisite questions next time they were alone together. After dealing with some correspondence, and speaking to the housekeeper, she too decided she would have a tray in her sitting room upstairs and retire early.

The next morning the children expected to be accompanied by her to Elveden and were bitterly disappointed when she informed them they would have to wait until the following day.

'Mama, I am sure that Uncle Edward will be expecting us,' Thomas said.

'We can go anyway – he will be delighted to see us.'

'Elizabeth, I shall compromise. I will send a groom with a message and he can wait for a reply. This should not take more than an hour and we can go if Edward is agreeable to us coming.'

The note was written and dispatched and the children returned to the nursery floor in the expectation of being granted their request. The servant returned with the information that Edward was to be absent from home for several days.

Of course, had he not told her he was going to obtain a marriage licence as soon as he was back? She was about to give the children this bad news when they hurtled down the stairs, already in their outdoor garments and boots. Her heart sank. Would her daughter revert to her bad behaviour if she was thwarted?

'We can see Brutus outside – he has come home. Can we play with him on the lawn?'

'Yes, Thomas, but do not wander off.'

He dashed off and did not even bother to enquire if they were to visit Elveden today, presumably they understood that if the dog was with them, Edward was elsewhere. At least Brutus had not attempted to follow Edward to Ipswich. She could only suppose that the lack of luggage on a carriage indicated to the animal that his owner intended to return soon.

A carriage turned into the drive whilst she was watching the children darting about the park with the dog in hot pursuit. For a moment she was puzzled as she rarely got visitors and it could not be Edward as he was already away. Then it dawned on her she had yet to interview any of the governesses and she had quite forgotten, in all the excitement of the past few days, that they were due to arrive.

There was nothing prepared and she hurried across and

pulled the bell strap. When the footman came in answer to her summons she sent him in search of the housekeeper.

'How can I be of assistance, my lady?'

'I wish for three guest bedrooms to be prepared. They are for the young ladies I am going to interview for the position of governess. They will be staying for several days. They will dine with Mrs Alston and I.'

The housekeeper was efficient and everything would be in place before the carriage pulled into the turning circle. She should really call the children back but having them outside would give her time to talk to each of the candidates before they were introduced to Elizabeth and Thomas.

There was still time for her to rush upstairs and inform her mother. 'How do you know it is the missing governesses, my love? Do they have a banner blowing above the carriage to indicate who they are?'

Viola laughed. 'I suppose it would have made sense to wait, but if you remember they were due to come before the snow and that is now more than a week ago. It can be nobody else as we do not have visitors here.'

'I shall delay until you are certain before coming down. I am fatigued after all the exertions of the past few days and will remain where I am in case you are mistaken in your assumption.' Then her mother sat up in bed. 'Mind you, it will be more interesting if it isn't one of them, so I shall definitely rise and be downstairs within half an hour.'

Viola had not seriously considered this explanation, but now she was a trifle anxious about the impending arrival of the carriage. Who else could it be? Then an awful possibility occurred to her. Was this Mr Fenchurch and his lawyers come to stake their claim?

She beckoned to the footman who was, as always, waiting in the entrance hall. 'If the occupants of the carriage are ladies, then allow them in. If it is gentlemen, then do not open the door under any circumstances.'

What else should she do to keep them safe? The doors – there were many and all of them would be unbolted at this time of the day.

'Make sure everywhere is locked – tell Cook that none of the kitchen maids are to go outside until told otherwise. Also, all the downstairs shutters must be closed. Be quick and get others to assist – the carriage is almost here.'

Now all that remained for her to do was call in her children. If it was actually this man and his lawyers, they could legally take her children from her if they were able to get their hands on them. She ran to the window but they were no longer on the grass. She should be cross for their disobedience but was just relieved they were in no danger. The constriction around her chest began to ease. With Brutus beside them they would be perfectly safe, as he would not let anyone touch them, and these people were not likely to be carrying weapons.

* * *

Beau had been tempted to ride Titus on his search for the nearest bishop but decided it would make more sense to travel in a carriage and not arrive dust-stained. His own Bishop travelled on the box with the coachman as he would have need of his services during the day.

He would be away for several days as his enquiries had discovered the gentleman he would have to apply to resided in Ely, which was a deal further than Ipswich from Elveden. After much thought he had come to the inevitable conclusion that he should tell Viola who he was and why he was masquerading as plain Mr Sheldon before he married her.

He was hoping to delay matters until Richard returned from Ireland and they knew exactly where they stood with regards to the putative heir to the earldom. If they had been too late and Fenchurch had already accepted Sir Frederick's offer, she would have to marry him regardless of the circumstances. What he would have to decide was if the safety of her family was more important than his honour. Marrying her under false pretences might be the only option, but it was not one he relished.

He travelled with the window open as he enjoyed the fresh air even in the cold. It was now March and there was a faint haze of green on the hedgerows. He had noticed in his own grounds that there were patches of golden yellow daffodils around the trees. He had been assured by his head gardener that the weather was set fair for the next week at least and there would be no more snow until next winter.

He sent Bishop to enquire from the church the whereabouts of the cleric used when he occasionally visited Ipswich.

'We're in luck, sir, Bishop Fowley is visiting at Kentwell Hall, which is in Long Melford. He's going to be there for a week or more, so you can speak to him there.'

'I take it this Kentwell is a deal closer than Ely?'

'It is, sir. We can be there before dark and only need to be away one night.'

It took him the best part of the day to locate Fowley. It cost him five pounds – roughly what a chambermaid received for an entire year of dedicated labour. God knows what a special licence would have cost him if he had needed one of those.

'Bishop, the horses are done, we will stop at the next hostelry we approach.' Beau was leaning out of the window in order to yell this command.

The inn was tolerable, but no better than that. As long as he did not acquire crawlers, or was obliged to share his bed with a complete stranger, he would have to be satisfied.

'I shall wish to leave at first light; we will find somewhere better than this place to break our fast.'

17

Beau's carriage pulled up outside Elveden mid-morning. He jumped from the vehicle and strode towards the house. The door was flung open by his butler who, instead of waiting at the head of the steps to greet him, ran down and met him halfway across the turning circle.

Beau increased his pace. There was something very wrong.

'Mr Sheldon, you must go at once to Fenchurch Manor. Lady Fenchurch sent for you yesterday. They are besieged by those who would do them harm.'

'Bishop, with me. We will ride.'

His stallion and Bishop's gelding were led out to him already saddled. His return had been anticipated. He swung into the saddle, rammed his boots into the irons and his magnificent horse sprung from a standstill into a gallop.

He covered the distance flat out, scarcely aware of the massive hedges and ditches they jumped. He sat back in the saddle and pulled Titus to a walk. A few seconds later his man was beside him.

'There is no point in arriving pell-mell and alerting those

who are attempting to get inside. We must be surreptitious about our approach. You are more familiar with this neighbourhood than I – is there another route we can take that will bring us close to the house without being seen?'

'There is, sir, a path that the cattlemen use to bring the herd in at night.'

This track was muddy from the frequent passage of the cows but it served the purpose admirably. It led them to the cowshed and dairy, which was set apart from the main house and the stables. He dismounted.

'The horses are cool; we can put them in that barn. Our coats can be used as protection from the cold.'

Bishop watered both animals at the trough before they led them inside the cowshed. Fortunately, the beasts were outside somewhere. Their sudden appearance startled the cowmen who were busy clearing the muck. It was relatively warm inside, so there was no need for either Bishop or himself to give up their riding coats.

'Take care of our horses. They need hay to keep them busy until we return.' One of the men had approached and touched his cap.

'Yes sir, they'll come to no harm in here.'

'Tell me, do you know what is going on here?'

'I do that, sir; them legal varmints have left four armed men outside the house and have gone to fetch reinforcements so they can break in.'

'When did they go?'

'They did not leave until dark yesterday.'

Beau nodded his thanks and drew his man to one side. 'There must be at least two dozen outside men working here. More than enough to overcome the armed men, but I am reluctant to risk injury to any of them if we can achieve this another way.'

'I have my pistol; you have yours. But I doubt that would be enough.'

'I want you to find me a curate and bring him here immediately. We cannot marry after midday so you only have an hour to complete your mission. I shall find a way to get inside without alerting the guards. It is a damned nuisance Lady Fenchurch has no supporters here as we could dearly use them.'

'I don't see why Sir Frederick is not here with all his men. He only lives a few miles away. They could have broken in easily. Why has this not happened?'

'There can only be one explanation. Fenchurch is not here yet. He is on his way and until they have him they cannot enter forcibly. The armed men are to prevent Lady Fenchurch and her family from leaving. I think it unlikely the lawyers are aware of my plans.'

He turned and walked back to the man he had spoken to before. 'How well do you know the house? Is there a way I can get in without being seen?'

The man grinned. 'The children went in through the trap what the fuel goes in by. That big dog went in too, so I reckons as you will fit in just fine.'

With detailed instructions as to how to find this entrance Beau set off. He kept his collar turned up and had his muffler around his face. This was an army trick one of his brothers had told him about. It was often a flash of skin that revealed the presence of an approaching attacker. He would not make that mistake himself.

Bishop knew he had to persuade the cleric to enter through the coal hole and he had no doubt his man would achieve his ends. If necessary he would forcibly drop the man through. There was no time for niceties – he had to marry Viola immediately or the ceremony could not take place until after midnight and that might well be too late.

The entrance the children and dog had used to get in yesterday was, not unexpectedly, outside the kitchens. He paused and scanned the area. There were no guards patrolling here so he would take his chance and make a run for it.

As he dived head first for the wooden door set into the ground, it occurred to him that one of the children might have had the intelligence to bolt it behind them. If that was the case he had a problem. He was correct. It was fastened tight. He had no option but to climb, using what footholds he could find, and make his entrance through an upstairs window.

He was within arm's reach of his goal when he heard voices approaching. He flattened himself against the wall and prayed they would not look up and that he would not lose his grip before they went away.

His hold was precarious. The toes of his boots were resting on barely discernible promontories and his fingertips were clinging to something equally small. Climbing at speed when there was so little to hold on to was achievable. Remaining still was likely to prove fatal. He was more than five yards from the ground. He held his breath and sent up a fervent prayer to the Almighty to keep him steady for the next few minutes.

His fingers were becoming numb. He could not cling on much longer. The guards walked around the corner. He could move. He completed the last yard like a man possessed; his grip on the windowsill when he reached it was enough to allow him to scramble up so he was sitting with his back to the glass.

A flurry of mortar and stone had descended in his final climb but, thank the good Lord, there had been nobody there to hear it. Like most gentlemen who spent a lot of their time on horseback he carried a stiletto in a specially made sheath inside his left boot.

He reached in and removed it and the narrow blade was perfect to slip between the windows and flick back the catch. The window moved up smoothly and he tumbled in and lay panting on his back on the floor whilst he recovered his equilibrium.

That had been too damn close. But he was in and undetected by those outside. He turned and quietly pushed the window down, then fastened it again just in case someone thought to look upwards.

The room he had entered must be one rarely used as the furniture was draped with holland covers and there was no fire laid ready to light in the grate. As he had never ventured anywhere upstairs apart from the nursery floor he was not sure exactly where he was.

He moved quietly to the door. As he reached to open it, it flew inwards and he was flattened by a huge, hairy body.

'Remove yourself at once, Brutus. Yes, old fellow, I am delighted to see you too. How in God's name did you know I was in here?'

The dog continued to pin him to the floor and lick his face with enthusiasm, Beau snapped his fingers and pointed. The dog responded obediently and allowed him to scramble to his feet.

'Make yourself useful; take me to Thomas and Elizabeth.'

There was no need for his request as when he emerged he heard the patter of childish feet approaching at a run. From around the corner came the children and to his amusement Viola was close behind. He opened his arms and the three of them threw themselves in. He stood for a moment holding them tight, breathing in their scent, relishing the moment.

'Sweetheart, we must talk. Children, can you sit with your grandmama for a few minutes? I promise we shall not be long.'

Reluctantly they stepped out of his embrace. 'It's horrible here, Uncle Edward. We had to come in through the coal hole so those men would not take us away.'

'I know you did, Elizabeth, and you did the right thing. I tried to get in that way myself...'

Thomas was tearful. 'If you had fallen it would have been my fault as I was the one who locked the hatch behind us.'

'No, son, you did exactly what you should have done to protect your family. Actually, there is something important you can both do for me rather than go to Mrs Alston. I need you to go down to the fuel store and listen for the arrival of my man. Then you will have to quickly unbolt the hatch and allow him to come in.'

Immediately the little boy rallied. 'We can do that. We will take Brutus with us as he will know if anyone is approaching long before we do.'

'I am so proud of both of you, and this will all be over soon.' As he spoke Beau prayed he was not telling them a falsehood.

They ran off with the dog loping beside them. 'Is there somewhere more convivial we can converse, darling?' He still had his arm around her waist and she seemed in no hurry to remove it.

'It is too late to be so fussy, my love. Tell me at once what you have planned.'

'I have the licence in my pocket and Bishop has gone to fetch the curate. As long as he is here before midday we can be married and then there will be nothing Fenchurch and his men can do.'

He quickly explained what he thought was happening outside and she nodded. 'Only the lawyers were here yesterday – there was no sign of Mr Fenchurch. I think he must have agreed to support Sir Frederick in his wicked plans or they would not have come yesterday.'

'He must be imminently expected for them to have made their move without him. Perhaps they thought you would acquiesce without a fuss. They must have been most put out by your quick thinking.'

'I was terrified they would grab the children and thus force me to let them in but, as you can see, that did not happen thanks to Brutus. They pushed a legal document under the door, which confirms our worst fears. I had a footman push it back so I cannot show it to you.'

He tilted her face and kissed her gently. 'Are you happy to marry me so swiftly? You still know so little about me. Are you prepared to take me on trust?'

'I know that you love us, and that you will protect us and keep us safe. That is all that matters to me.'

They went to find Mrs Alston and explain what was going to happen. As always, the old woman was quick to understand. 'Do you think you will be able to keep them out until after midnight tonight if the curate fails to arrive in time to carry out the ceremony now?'

'The shutters are closed downstairs so they cannot enter that way. Even with the arrival of Mr Fenchurch himself they cannot get in unless we choose to open the door. They will have to retreat and fetch the militia. I am certain we can accomplish our objectives whether the curate gets here or not.'

* * *

Viola, for the first time since the arrival of the carriage yesterday, began to believe that things were going to be all right after all. She was going to marry the man she loved, the children were going to get a father and finally the evil influence of her first husband would be eradicated from their lives.

'I am not sure if I should change into something more suitable or remain as I am, as it is quite possible we shall not be married today.'

'You look quite enchanting in that russet gown. I shall have to marry in my dishevelled state.' His lopsided smile touched her heart.

'I hope you intend to remove the dust and dirt from your person, young man, before you tie the knot.'

'I shall do so immediately, ma'am. I apologise if my disarray offends you. Climbing up twenty feet of wall after galloping headlong across country for several miles tends to do that to a person, you know.'

Her mother laughed. 'I cannot think why I like you, as you are an arrogant and autocratic sort of gentleman, but for some reason I do. You are a welcome addition to this family even if it does mean my daughter will no longer be a countess.'

For some reason this remark forced him to look away. She was about to reassure him that the title meant nothing to her, as it had belonged to a man she hated, that she would much rather be plain Mrs Sheldon, but he strode out before she could speak.

'I pray we can be married today. If the militia were to arrive before midnight they might well break in and all will be lost. Mr Fenchurch will be able to take the children away from me and there will be nothing we can do about it.'

Her mother snorted inelegantly. 'Fiddlesticks to that! Do you think so little of your future husband that he would allow that to happen? It would be over his dead body.'

'That is what I fear, Mama. I will not let him give up his life for us.'

'You would be prepared to live without him under the thrall of Sir Frederick? That is doing it too brown, daughter, as well you know. The good Lord saw fit to send him here for you and the children and you would do well to remember that.'

'I am going downstairs to check on the children. I cannot be happy with them sitting in the cold damp of the cellars without supervision.'

'More to the point, my dear girl, who will be your second witness to your wedding ceremony?'

'I have no idea. No doubt when it comes to it Edward will have that in hand.'

She glanced nervously at the tall-case clock that ticked the time away in the hall and saw it was fifteen minutes to midday. Then she heard the children and the dog and at least two other people hurrying from the servants' quarters.

'Mama, Bishop is here with Mr Culley. He has come to marry you to Uncle Edward.'

Edward spoke from behind her. 'That is the best news we could have, Thomas. You and your sister run along and tell your grandmother to go at once to the family chapel.'

One might have thought the cleric would be disgruntled at his unusual mode of entry but the young man was smiling. He bowed to her. 'This is most exciting, my lady, and you have my full support. I must perform the ceremony now or it will not be done in time to be legal.'

Edward took her hand and all four of them ran to the chapel. Mr Culley had the licence and he had also brought the parish records in his haversack as he was required to record the ceremony. He would then complete her marriage lines and hand them to her and she would legally be Mrs Sheldon – no longer Lady Fenchurch.

Bishop accompanied them. He was obviously to be the second witness. He had been so closely involved with everything it made sense to use him. The curate said only what was strictly necessary to make the union legal. Her eyes widened when he read out Edward's full name. He must have disliked being called Beaumont so had adopted his middle name, and she did not blame him. She made her responses, as did he, and they were pronounced man and wife as the first strike of the clock heralded the arrival of midday.

Her heart was full. She looked up for her first kiss as Mrs Sheldon. She was shocked to see tears in his eyes and a sliver of doubt about her hasty marriage flickered through her. Neither of them had had any choice if they wished to protect the children so, whatever came next, the alternative would have been so much worse.

Bishop and her mother signed the necessary papers and the matter was concluded. If it hadn't been for the children's happy laughter as they skipped about calling Edward 'Papa' for the first time it would have been a subdued affair.

'There you are, Mrs Sheldon – you will want to keep this safe as it is proof that you are indeed married and responsibility for your children rests with your new husband and nobody else.'

'Edward, would you keep this for me? I would much prefer it if you were the one to show it to the lawyers. I have no wish to speak to them at all and neither do I wish to invite Mr Fenchurch to the house even if he is, at this particular moment, heir to the title.'

He took the document, folded it carefully and slipped it into a pocket inside his topcoat. 'I think it might be sensible for me to escort Mr Culley from the premises.' He smiled at the young cleric who nodded vigorously. 'If you would be kind enough to stand in the turning circle whilst we discuss, in very loud voices, the fact that you have just conducted our marriage service in a consecrated chapel within the required parish, we would be eternally grateful.'

'I should be delighted to do so, Mr Sheldon. Am I to return pillion with Mr Bishop?'

'No, you shall go back in style in our carriage.' He glanced at his man and Bishop immediately vanished to take care of his order. His smile at her was kind but not one to stir her senses. 'Sweetheart, this is not how I imagined our nuptials would be. I think we could all do with our luncheon after the excitement.'

'I shall organise it at once. I think we should suggest that the staff drink a toast to us tonight. We must make an effort and change for dinner. I shall mention it to Cook.'

He frowned. 'We will not be here will we, my love? We shall be at Elveden by then. I think we must postpone any sort of celebration until tomorrow when you are more settled in your new home. Whilst I deal with this Fenchurch, I suggest that you make sure your belongings are packed and ready to transport. No doubt the children will have a trunk full of toys they wish to bring.'

18

Beau waited whilst the footman flung open the front door with a flourish. He half expected the guards to attempt to rush in, but he was able to step outside accompanied by Mr Culley without being accosted.

However, they had only reached the bottom step when all four ruffians approached. He turned to the curate. 'I thank you for your attendance here, Mr Culley. My wife and I are most grateful you were able to come at such short notice and conduct our wedding service.' His voice carried wonderfully, and he was certain that anyone within half a mile now had this interesting nugget of information.

'I was honoured to be asked, Mr Sheldon, and I wish you and Mrs Sheldon all the happiness in the world.'

Beau offered his hand and it was shaken with enthusiasm. The four men would have had to be deaf as wheelbarrows not to have heard what they had said. He looked around at them and to his amusement they slunk off, no doubt to inform both Mr Fenchurch and Sir Frederick they were too late to interfere.

The carriage trundled out through the archway and he acted

as footman. 'I hope my man has paid you handsomely for your services, Mr Culley.'

'More than generous, but I would have conducted your service for nothing. The important families around here might not be sympathetic, but middling folk and the villagers were scandalised at what was being attempted. Mrs Sheldon has a lot of friends although she might not realise it.'

'Thank you for telling me. We will be removing to my property. I have a living vacant and it is yours if you would like it. There is a substantial vicarage, an acre of land and a decent stipend that goes with it. I shall send Bishop with the details in a day or two.'

He had made this offer when the cleric was safely inside the vehicle as he feared he might have been embraced otherwise. 'Thank you, I should be delighted to accept. There is a young lady in the village I should like to marry and now I shall be able to do so. You will not regret your decision, sir.'

Beau stepped away, happy with his accomplishments that morning. If the bishop had been at his residence in Ely he would not have been home in time to prevent an unmitigated disaster.

Was it possible that Mrs Alston was right, that his movements had been directed by divine intervention? He never gave his faith much thought. One believed in God because it was what one did. If he was honest he probably paid lip service rather than true devotion when he attended church on a Sunday.

This was of some comfort to him, as he felt wretched about marrying Viola without having told her who he really was. He must let his family know and tell them there would be a second service in the family chapel, as there had been for Perry and Sofia, when he eventually returned. The Duke of Silchester always married at Silchester Court and he had broken this tradition today. He would rectify matters as soon as possible.

He would send Bishop to Elveden to have the house prepared. God's teeth! He had no idea how many of her staff she would wish to bring with her – or even if the rooms on the nursery floor were habitable.

There was no time to waste if they were to effect the move before it got dark. Bishop was waiting to speak to him in the entrance hall.

'Sir, I have located two diligences and the necessary farm horses to pull them and have sent word to Elveden to set things in motion. Is anything else you wish me to do?'

'I shall eat with my new family and then return with you to make sure everything is as it should be when Mrs Sheldon, my children and my mother-in-law arrive later today.'

When he broached the subject of staff, Viola reacted oddly. She did not seem particularly pleased with his question. 'Presumably the nursemaids will accompany the children, your personal maid and that of Mrs Alston, but is there anyone else you particularly wish to come with you?'

'It is all very well, Edward, demanding that we transfer immediately to your house, but we are hardly prepared. What will happen to the remainder of my staff? Will they now be out of work? What about my horses and my carriages? Will they also be redundant as we are combining two households?'

'I think this is something we must discuss once we are safely at Elveden. I have a nasty suspicion we have not heard the last from Fenchurch and I will be in a better position to protect you when you are living on my property. Maybe it would make sense for Fenchurch and his family to become tenants here?'

'Why should he be rewarded for turning against us? If he is working for Sir Frederick, then I do not wish him to set foot upon my son's property.'

'Then he shall not, sweetheart. The staff can occupy themselves cleaning the house from top to bottom and making it ready for whoever might be living there in future. They will not be laid off. You have yet to answer my question about who you wish to bring with you. My house is fully staffed but I am prepared to accommodate any servants that you will feel more comfortable having around you.'

'That will not be necessary, my love. Only the nursemaids and our personal dressers will be coming with us. Which reminds me, I have yet to receive a visit from any of the candidates I wish to interview for the position of governess, and the snow has been gone for some time.'

'That is certainly strange. You must look into it as I imagine a post with you would be something any governess would like to have. Did you wish Thomas to go away to school when he is ten years of age?'

'Certainly not. I would like to employ tutors for him – I think those public schools do nothing but harm to a child's character.'

'I was educated by tutors and then went up to Oxford. That will be ideal for our son.' He deliberately used this term. 'We have much to organise and discuss about the future of our children and ourselves but that can wait until we are settled together and there is no further annoyance from Mr Fenchurch or your neighbour.'

Beau had almost said that none of his brothers had gone away to school but remembered in time that she did not as yet know how many siblings he had. There was nothing he could do until Richard returned from Ireland and confirmed that Fenchurch had sided with the opposition.

The children were so excited by the new arrangements that there was no time for him to dwell on things that he could not remedy at present. The servants had been given permission to bring the trunks down the main staircase, so their luncheon had been accompanied by the thumps and bangs that this entailed.

'When do you expect us to be at Elveden, young man?'

'Come before dark, ma'am; it is safer to travel in the light. I am leaving now to ensure that everything is made ready for you. Children, you had better check your playroom and nursery to see that nothing you require has been left behind.'

They scampered off and he stood up and nodded politely to his mother-in-law and then kissed his wife on top of her head. As he did so he inhaled her unique aroma, a mixture of cloves and rose water, he thought, and it inflamed his senses. Her hair was soft beneath his lips; he was eagerly anticipating being able to run his hands through the length of it.

She looked up and her smile was loving but somehow lacked the radiance it had before. Was she already regretting this hasty union? They had the rest of their lives to get to know each other and he was quite certain, even if it took months rather than weeks to achieve this, he would eventually win her love again and be able to share her bed.

* * *

All too soon Viola and her family were travelling from Fenchurch Manor for the last time. Well, probably not the last time as no doubt she would visit when Thomas was resident there. She sincerely hoped she had not made a catastrophic error by marrying a man whom she was now convinced had not been entirely open with her about his past.

The removal of various precious pieces of furniture and the larger items that she wanted with her in her new home could take place over the next few days as long as the weather remained clement. Also, her summer clothes remained in tissue paper in the box room and they would have to come too.

'I have not had my bride clothes made, Mama. I think I should like to go to Town, and this time stay at Grosvenor Square, and replenish my wardrobe and that of the children. I expect you would like some new gowns too?'

'That would be most agreeable. However, I think it might be wise to change the staff and have the house cleaned from top to bottom before we visit. Grosvenor Square will be busy in a few weeks when people return from their country estates for the Season which starts, as you know, sometime in April.'

'I am not sure I am prepared to mingle with the *ton*.'

'Despite the fact that you are no longer a titled lady, you are the wife of a wealthy and powerful man and your children are aristocrats. So why do you not wish to go when there are others around?'

'I only had the one Season, but I was aware that I was looked down on as inferior to those born with blue blood.'

'That might well have been the case ten years ago, but it is not so now. In any case, daughter, there is no obligation to make morning calls or attend parties in the evenings if you do not wish to do so.'

'I wonder if Edward would agree to transfer my entire staff from Fenchurch to Grosvenor Square? Then those who are there can be dismissed without reference and I shall be confident I am surrounded by those I trust.'

'I cannot see why he would object. I think it a fine idea.'

They had both forgotten the children were listening avidly to everything that was said. She should not have mentioned her insecurities in front of them.

Elizabeth, who was sitting next to her, took her hand. 'Papa will not let anyone distress you ever again. He is a formidable gentleman and with him at your side no one will dare be impolite.'

'Thank you, my love, for saying that. We are almost there. Are you looking forward to living here?'

'We are, Mama, but something else has occurred to me. We no longer need another piano or harp as both instruments are already in place in our new home,' Thomas said from the other side of the carriage.

'Good heavens! You are quite right to point that out, but there is nothing we can do about it now as they will be on their way. I shall have to discuss with your papa how best to deal with the surfeit of musical instruments that we shall have.'

The children filled the silence with their chatter as they eagerly pointed out various landmarks that were now part of their own domain – places they would spend the next few years happily exploring.

'When the governesses finally arrive, Mama, they will be most surprised to discover there is no longer a Lady Fenchurch and that they must now apply to Mrs Sheldon for employment.'

'Very true, Elizabeth, but as they are now more than two weeks past the allotted time for their interviews I suspect they are not coming. I shall have to begin again to look for someone suitable for you both.'

'I expect Papa will have the matter in hand. It is he who will arrange things for us in future, is it not?'

Viola was about to make a sharp retort but reconsidered. 'He will not wish to be concerned with domestic matters, my love, but no doubt I shall discuss it with him.'

Thomas asked permission to lower the window so he could look out as they turned into the drive.

'I suppose that you may do so, but only because it is a special day.'

Elizabeth lowered the window on the other side of the carriage without asking and the two of them leaned out like village urchins.

'Mama, the house looks bigger than I remember. There are a dozen servants waiting to greet us and Papa is there too.'

'I would expect him to be, Thomas, and for the staff to do the same. Remember to be on your best behaviour; you do not wish to disappoint today.'

Edward was beside the carriage himself and opened the door and kicked down the steps. 'Allow me to assist you to the ground, ma'am, and then my housekeeper will show you to your apartment. It is on the ground floor and your drawing room opens onto the terrace.'

'No stairs? How thoughtful of you, my boy. I much appreciate your kindness.'

Her mother did not wait for the rest of them but hurried off, obviously consumed with curiosity to see her new accommodation.

'Out you come, little ones, your nursemaid is waiting to conduct you to your new chambers. No doubt you will wish to arrange your toys and playthings yourselves.'

He reached in and swung Elizabeth out and then did the same for Thomas. They were both quite capable of exiting a carriage without being lifted like infants. They did not object, but she must explain to her new husband that they were too old to be referred to as little ones and carried about the place as he was doing.

When he turned to her she was already out. 'There are several items of furniture that I should like to have here and I hope you will agree they can be fetched over the next few days.'

'This house is sparsely furnished; there is ample room for anything you wish to have with you. I cannot tell you how delighted I am that you will all be living here with me for the moment.'

'I am surprised the dog is not dancing around the children. I hope he has not gone to the kennels again.'

'I am ashamed to admit it, but I have allowed him into the house against my better judgement. I think he deserves to be treated like one of the family after what he has done for us. I hope I do not live to regret it.'

Hearing him say this was exactly what she needed to settle her nerves. Impulsively she stood on tiptoe and placed a kiss on his cheek. This was only possible as he was looking down at her. The joy in his eyes at her gesture made her head spin. Whatever her doubts about this rushed arrangement, one thing she was certain of was that he loved her as much as she loved him. What more could a woman want in a marriage?

He had his arm around her shoulders and when they arrived under the portico, to her surprise, he swept her up into his arms. 'It is customary in some places in the world for the groom to carry the bride across the threshold the first time she arrives at the marital home.'

'Then it is fortunate you are a large gentleman and I am so small.' She was smiling at him and the rest of the world faded so only the two of them were in it. 'Imagine the difficulty if I was two yards tall and you no bigger than my papa was.'

He lowered his head so he could whisper in her ear. The touch of his hot breath sent heat racing to her nether regions. 'I love you so much, my darling, and you have made me the happiest man in Christendom.'

'I love you too, and I pray that will be enough to see us through any difficulties that might arise.'

His smile slipped for a second and something flickered in his eyes that she did not recognise. Then he placed her gently on her feet and she turned to greet the assembled servants.

She had only visited this place once and had not realised it was so grand, not as large as Fenchurch Manor, but certainly a substantial and impressive property. Everywhere sparkled and shone; she was astonished his staff had been able to prepare the house so speedily.

The tour included the nursery floor, which was in need of redecoration but perfectly serviceable for the present. The children were busy rearranging their books and other items on freshly polished shelves.

'Mama, Papa we love it up here,' Thomas said happily. 'It isn't as big as before but much warmer and friendlier somehow. Can we sleep on this floor, as Sally and Meg have rooms next to us?'

'Of course you can. The schoolroom is more than adequate for when your lessons resume in earnest. I shall begin teaching you tomorrow as you have already had more than two weeks free from your studies.'

'Papa, can my piano lessons begin again tomorrow morning?'

'They can, Thomas. Perhaps your mama would play for us later, as I cannot wait to hear the harp put to its proper use.'

'Could you play a duet? We can be your audience.' Elizabeth looked hopefully from one to the other.

'I am willing, if we can find music that we are both familiar with. We shall leave you to your tidying as I have yet to show your mama her new apartment.'

When they were private he stopped and encircled her waist and turned her to face him. He waited a heartbeat for her permission. She reached out and put her hands around his neck. He needed no further encouragement. His kiss was passionate and she returned it in full measure. If he had carried her to the bedroom she could not have denied him at that moment.

However, he replaced her to the boards before things got out of hand. 'Well, Mrs Sheldon, I believe that is our first legal kiss. Was it to your satisfaction?'

'You cannot ask me something of that sort, my love; it is most improper of you to do so.'

His smile was infectious and his eyes held a wicked glint. 'I am your husband, your lord and master, and I can ask whatever I wish of you.'

This could have been the moment when her fears returned but instead she laughed. 'Then I shall tell you, sir, that it was most enjoyable and I should be happy to repeat the experience whenever you wish.'

'Then I think it's better if I do not show you my bedchamber. Your room has a communicating door to mine. This is locked on your side. You have your own boudoir and I have an adjacent sitting room. I shall leave you to explore those on your own.'

He kissed her once more, his lips hard on hers, and then strode off and she could hear him laughing to himself. There were still things she had not asked him, that they had not arranged; she would not allow him to desert her like this. She ran to the head of the nursery stairs and put her fingers in her mouth as he had shown her and whistled. To her astonishment it worked and the noise echoed.

She heard him swear and stumble. Then he was pounding up the stairs. He did not look particularly impressed with her prowess.

'Good God, if you wish to speak to me, there is no need to do that to attract my attention.'

He sounded cross but his eyes belied this. 'Edward, you cannot rush off without telling me where you are going and when I shall see you again. I have yet to hear where we are to go for a wedding trip, when I am to get my bride clothes made, if the matter with Mr Fenchurch has been settled...'

He held his hands up in mock surrender. 'Then we had better go to the drawing room so we can discuss these matters.' They were about to leave when the children arrived, closely followed by the dog who thought the noise had been to summon him.

'That was capital, Mama. We did not know you could do that. Will you show us how to?'

'Your papa taught me; I am sure he would do the same for you. No, Brutus, you are not needed downstairs; you may remain in the nursery with Thomas and Elizabeth.'

'I shall show you, Thomas, but it is not a suitable thing for a young lady to do. I intend to have firm words with your mama on the subject when we are alone.'

He was smiling as he spoke so they were not alarmed at his threat. 'Our tea is arriving. Will you both come up and say goodnight to us later?'

'We shall, of course, be delighted to do so; it will be a novel experience for me and one I am sincerely looking forward to.'

Her heart was full as she walked at his side, his arm draped around her shoulders, knowing she was finally truly happy, as were her children and her mama.

19

Beau knew he should tell her he was a duke and she was now his duchess, that he should do it before he made love to her. The only thing preventing him from doing the honourable thing was the thought that once she knew she would withdraw her love and leave him bereft. It wasn't just the deception but the fact that in the next few months he must take them back with him to Silchester. She was under the erroneous impression they would be living at Elveden initially and then when Thomas was older would return to Fenchurch Manor.

With any other woman, in any other circumstances, he would not hesitate. After all, it was the husband's prerogative to take care of his wife and family in whatever way he thought was best. If Viola had not been married to an abusive bastard, things would be different. He had promised her he would respect her wishes, would not impose his will, so by telling her he ran the risk that she would refuse to come. He would be left in the invidious position of abandoning his duties and his siblings, or abandoning his new wife and her family. Neither option was acceptable to him.

'What time are we to dine tonight, Edward? Obviously not early, as it is already past five o'clock. Are we still to make this a celebration dinner and put on our finery?'

'I thought we would leave it until tomorrow night. Your mother needs to recuperate after the stress of moving and she might well prefer to dine in her apartment.'

'I have no wish to eat on a tray. I want to sit in our dining room with you, evening dress or not.'

'If you wish me to change then I am happy to do so. I am yours to command, my darling.'

Her delightful laughter filled the hall. 'And I, my love, am the Queen of Sheba. Shall we remain as we are? I must admit that I have not changed for dinner since Rupert died and think it a ridiculous habit when there are only family present.'

'Then that is the first thing as a married couple that we are in complete agreement on. Let us hope there are hundreds more occasions in the future.'

'If you will excuse me for a while, I am going to see Mama, just to be sure she is comfortable. Do you have a gong that is banged when we are to go to the dining room?'

'I do not. Shall we say in half an hour? I have some correspondence to attend to whilst you are with your mother.'

He watched her walk gracefully away, loving every inch of her. She was petite, but perfect. His mouth curved when he compared her to her new sisters – all the women in the Sheldon family were tall and slender, whereas she was small and rounded. She was also the only one with abundant golden curls.

There were still small items of furniture, trunks and boxes waiting to come in, but he had told the men to put the carts in the carriage house until tomorrow. As he approached the music room door he went in instead of retreating to his study.

He opened the piano, ran his fingers along the keys and

began to play. Music soothed his ragged nerves, made him more optimistic about the future. If two people loved each other as much as they did then they could overcome the greatest obstacles. He came to the end of the piece he was playing and was aware she had joined him.

'That was quite beautiful. I had no idea you could play so well. Small wonder our son wishes to learn from you. Your butler has been pacing anxiously, trying to attract your attention to tell you that dinner is served.'

He joined her at the door. 'After we have dined I should like to hear you play. The harp needs tuning, but that will not take me long.'

'I can do that for myself, my love. I did not recognise what you were playing. Is it something of your own composition?'

'It is something I am working on – not the finished article as yet. Over dinner we shall decide what we are going to perform for the children and we can rehearse that as well.'

Dinner was no doubt delicious but he ate little of it. He noticed she barely touched hers either. He was too absorbed in his beautiful wife and what she had to say. They talked of politics, the king, the prince regent and the problems that the enclosures were causing for rural communities.

He managed to keep the conversation away from anything personal as he had no intention of telling her another lie. If she asked a question direct he would tell her the truth.

'I am far too full and have taken more wine than is good for me, my love, and think that my harp playing must wait until the morning.' She stood up to leave the table and he did the same. He was hardly going to remain drinking port on his own.

'I have asked for coffee to be served in the drawing room in half an hour.'

She pouted, put her finger on her lips in a parody of a young lady who has been thwarted. 'Am I not to have the tea tray, sir? I am most put out by your assumption.'

He snatched her off her feet. 'You are a baggage, and I love you to distraction.'

She nestled into his shoulder and he drew her closer, loving her softness against his chest. Then what she said next changed everything.

'I know I said I wished to wait but I find I am eager to become your true wife. I shall expect you to come to me later.'

If he did not go to her that would be the biggest hurt of all, but he could not until she knew the truth. Was he to be allowed only a few short hours of happiness before it was all in ruins about his feet?

'There are things you need to know before that happens. I have been putting off talking to you and that was reprehensible of me.'

He escorted her to the drawing room. She was looking at him anxiously, and well she might. He was possibly about to ruin her life as well as his, but he had no option. He waited until she was seated and then took his place opposite.

'I have a long story to tell you and I beg you do not interrupt until you have heard the whole.'

* * *

Viola listened with growing incredulity to what he had to say. She had married plain Mr Sheldon and now she found she was actually married to the Duke of Silchester. It beggared belief that he could have deceived her so roundly.

'Why did you not tell me this when you discovered you had feelings for me? I am not sure our marriage is even legal as you have not used your true name.'

'I did use my name; it is not necessary to mention a title in a marriage ceremony. I did not come here for any other reason than to take a few months' respite from my heavy responsibilities. My family fully supported me in this endeavour and it was only intended to last for a few months.'

'You married me under false pretences. I have been calling you Edward these past weeks and your name is Beau. I would not have married you if I had known who you were. I have no wish to be a duchess. I believe it might be possible to have this marriage dissolved or annulled...'

'No, sweetheart, it is not. The only grounds for this would be if you were underage, I had used a false name or was committing bigamy. None of those apply. If I had not married you, you would have been in a far worse situation.'

'This is all very well for you to say so, but I should have been given the option. You might not have lied directly but you certainly lied by omission. I thought you were an honourable man and you have proved to be the reverse.'

'I think it would be better if we continue this conversation tomorrow morning, before we both say something we will regret.'

She was on her feet immediately. 'At least this explains why you have such a high opinion of yourself. I should have guessed you were a toplofty aristocrat from the way you behaved.'

With her head held high she stalked out and managed to maintain her composure until she was safely in her bedchamber. How could she have been so stupid as to fall in love with a man she knew nothing about? Her heart was breaking, not just for her, but for her children and for Edward – no she must call him Beau in future.

He was a duke and he had given up the possibility of having a direct heir to his title and estates for her. She would contact her lawyers and see if there was some possibility the marriage could be set aside. He had a duty to his name and he had reneged on this for her. She loved him too much to allow him to ruin his life.

She could not settle and wanted to speak to her mother in order to get her sage advice but had no wish to burden her with an insoluble problem. She curled up in a chair in front of the fire and let the tears flow. She must have drifted off to sleep because when she awoke the room was in darkness and the fire almost out. It was strange Hughes had not come in to help her disrobe or put fuel on the fire.

Her legs were stiff and she shivered as she stood up. There were no sounds from next door so she must assume her husband had retired. With logs and coal placed in the embers the fire soon picked up. She checked the overmantel clock and saw the time to be a little after midnight.

Where was the tray that should have come up with her supper? Normally she would not have bothered but as she had eaten little at dinner she was now hungry. This was all very strange. Her stomach rumbled loudly and she was glad she was still dressed and could go downstairs without becoming even colder. She frowned. She was not entirely sure where the kitchens were. Even if she did find them they would be unfamiliar to her, unlike those in her own house.

Certain things had become clear to her and one of them was that Beau was the very opposite of Rupert. He could have kept this information to himself until he had shared her bed but had chosen to speak and risk losing her. If she was able to give him children she would go to him now and they could be the happiest couple in the kingdom.

Whatever he said to the contrary she knew he would not have allowed himself to fall in love with her if he had known how things stood. It was his duty to his title and his family to marry a woman who could provide him with heirs. She could see only one way forward and that was for her to conceal her true feelings and send them away.

He was the Duke of Silchester, one of a handful of gentlemen with such a grand title, and she was certain he could get the marriage set aside if he cared to. It would break her heart and her children would be devastated, but she had no option. She must do the right thing.

As she came to this decision she heard movement next door and called out, 'Your grace, I wish to speak to you.'

'Do I have your permission to come in to your sitting room?'

'The door is unlocked.'

She retreated so she was standing behind a chair and could cling onto it for support if need be. He stepped in and she saw he too was fully clothed. His hair was in disarray and his expression was sad. He must have guessed what she was going to say because she had referred to him so formally.

'I wish you to return to Silchester immediately. I shall remain here with my children and keep up the pretence that we are man and wife until the matter with Fenchurch is legally settled. You married me under false pretences and that is reason enough for the marriage to be set aside, whatever you might think to the contrary. I have no wish to be a duchess. If I cannot be Mrs Sheldon, then I shall be Lady Fenchurch once more.'

'I told you last night that there are no valid reasons to have our marriage annulled. I cannot leave you and the children unprotected until I am certain you are safe from Fenchurch and Sir Frederick.' He bowed. 'However, I shall respect your wishes and leave as soon as I can. There is one thing you must know, Viola: if I cannot be married to you and father to your children then I shall remain a bachelor until I die.'

It took all her resolve not to call him back, not to run after him and say that she loved him, that she did not care who he was as long as they were together. He might say he would not marry again if he was free, but she knew he would. He was the most honourable gentleman she had ever met and when his heart was mended he would put his duty first and find himself a suitable wife and fill his nursery.

* * *

Beau was fully aware why she was sending him away. She was convinced he was lying, did not believe that having no children of his own did not bother him, that all he wanted was to be her husband and father to her children.

He could only pray that her love for him was strong enough to eventually overcome her scruples. He would remain at Elveden for the next few weeks and spend this precious time with what might prove to be his temporary family. He could only hope that her mother would take his part and convince her daughter to change her mind.

His misery was disturbed by her knocking on the communicating door. He was not foolish enough to think she had changed her mind so soon. He strode across and opened the door.

'I'm sorry to disturb you, your grace, but I want to know what has happened to my maid, Hughes; I have not seen her since I came up. Did you tell her not to attend to me tonight?'

She had his full attention now. 'I did not. Have you rung?'

'I have no notion where she is sleeping or who is at the other end of the bell strap so thought this would be a pointless exercise.'

'I assume she is upstairs with the female servants somewhere. I can hardly go in search of her. Is there something I can do for you in her absence?'

'I hesitate to ask, your grace…'

'Dammit to hell! If you refer to me as *your grace* again I shall not be answerable for the consequences. I am either Edward or Beau, I care not which you use, but you will not talk to me as if I am a stranger.' He had not meant to sound so fierce and was about to apologise when she smiled. It was a feeble attempt, but the first one he had had since she gave him her ultimatum.

'Very well, I shall call you Beau, as it is your name. It hardly seems sensible to use Edward when that person no longer exists as far as I am concerned. If you are to remain here for a week or two at least we must appear to be in perfect harmony for the children's sake. I have no intention of telling them you are leaving us until I have to.'

'I am not leaving you, you are sending me away. That is what we shall tell Elizabeth and Thomas. I wish them to know I would not desert them if I was not being forced to.'

His comment brought back the woman he loved and recognised. She glared at him and he braced himself for an all-out attack. His ploy had worked and he had broken through her reserve. He would never involve the twins in their dispute or set them against their mother.

'You will do no such thing. You must tell them who you really are and that you have to go back and tell your family you have married. They will accept that. They do not have to know you will not be returning.'

'I will not lie to them, Viola. If they ask me directly they will hear the truth, however unpalatable it might be.'

'You are despicable. If you tell them why you are going they will hate me. Is that what you want?'

'You know what I want. But as you appear to be unable to comprehend I shall repeat them very slowly and clearly.' He could almost see her teeth grinding and if he was not so despondent he would be enjoying this confrontation. He hoped that by forcing her to see how her decision would make four people miserable, she would reconsider. 'I love you; I wish to be your husband and father to your children. I have sufficient heirs and need no more from my own loins. I shall not marry again under any circumstances.'

There was a pause in hostilities and the silence was filled by the loud rumble of her stomach followed closely by a similar gurgling from his own. He could not hold back his snort of laughter. Then she too was laughing.

'I think we could fight better if we were replete. Come, I shall take you to the kitchens and find us something to eat.'

20

The wall sconces in the main part of the house were left burning when the servants retired, so this meant they did not need to take candles. Beau made sure he did not touch her, made no attempt to put his arm around her or take a hand as he had done previously. He must keep his distance, remain friendly, but keep his love in check. She must come to him if they were to mend this unnecessary rift.

He shouldered open the kitchen door and was pleased to find this large chamber pleasantly warm. He had never visited here himself so was as much at a loss as to where they would find what they needed as she was.

'The range is alight, Beau, so I will revive it so we can make coffee.' She raised an eyebrow and he shook his head. 'You have no more idea about the ramifications of your kitchens than I do. I suggest that you be seated and allow me to find us what we need.'

'I can make coffee. I can also prepare a reasonable omelette, but that is as far as my culinary skills go.'

Her smile was genuine this time. 'That is more than most

gentlemen of your status, so I am impressed. You can deal with the beverage whilst I go in search of the food.'

Half an hour later they were sitting on opposite sides of the long table that ran down the centre of the kitchen eating a tasty supper.

'Did you get a tray in your room, Beau?'

'I did, but I sent it back untouched, which is why I am here now enjoying the excellent repast you have prepared for me.'

'Then it is even more peculiar that nothing was sent to me. I had been intending to talk to you about staff, but after your revelation it seemed unimportant. Nevertheless, I might as well mention it now as it would seem you have no intention of departing in the immediate future.'

'Then I am all agog. What about my staff do you wish to change?'

'Not yours, but those at Grosvenor Square. They were appointed by Rupert; they could be dismissed and replaced, I thought, by the staff at Fenchurch. Those are all loyal to me and will have nothing to do now I am living here.'

'I think that an excellent idea. After I have spoken to Fenchurch I will set that in motion. Once you have everything you require from there, do you wish the house to be put under covers? There will need to be a handful of inside staff who remain to light fires and so on. As the horses have been transferred here, along with the grooms, the stables can be closed down too. The outside men must be retained as it would not do for the grounds to become unkempt.'

'I agree, but what about the dairy and kitchen garden?'

'Perhaps you would like the produce from the gardens and orchards to be distributed to your tenants. The milk, butter and cheese could also go to the village.'

'I am happy with that. The interior of the building is in need of refurbishment and redecoration so this would be a good time to do it. I should like it to be modernised as well. After all, if there are to be tenants taking care of it until Thomas is of age, there will be no other opportunity for building works to be carried out without inconveniencing the occupants.'

This was a strange conversation to be having in the middle of the night with someone who had quite vehemently told him she wished to sever the connection at the earliest possible opportunity. Was it possible things were not as dire between them as he had feared?

* * *

When Viola eventually retired she was feeling more sanguine about the outcome of her relationship with Beau. He had every right to be furious with her, to treat her with contempt, but he was behaving as if nothing untoward had happened between them. No, that was not quite correct. He was relaxed and friendly, but no longer loving and affectionate.

In a few hours she would have to break the news to her mother and children that she had married a duke and not a commoner. She would have to pretend to be pleased about the situation and she was quite certain that they would be overjoyed she was now someone of such importance.

Dissembling was as much against her nature as it was his, and it was going to be torment keeping the truth from them. She fully understood why he had not told her his secret and forgave him for his minor deception. She doubted that the twins or her parent would be so lenient with her when they discovered her perfidy.

What she could do was enjoy the brief time they had together and pray that when he returned to his family they would agree with her that he had made a catastrophic error by marrying an infertile woman. Whatever was required of her in order to get him released from this union she would do, but she dreaded to think how Thomas and Elizabeth would react if Beau was no longer to be their papa.

Despite her misery and heartache, she slept heavily and did not stir until someone knocked loudly on her bedchamber door.

'Viola, the children are becoming anxious about your absence at the breakfast table. It is now after eight o'clock.' It was her husband come to find her.

'Hughes has not appeared again this morning, so I did not wake. I shall be down shortly. Please do not make your announcement until I am there.'

'Then you had better be quick, as I intend to tell them immediately after breakfast.'

She was out of bed and into the dressing room before he had finished speaking. There was no point in arguing; she must get downstairs as speedily as possible. She snatched up the nearest undergarments she could find and stepped into them. Next, she grabbed a blue velvet gown that required no help to fasten, as the buttons were at the front.

Her stockings were mismatched, her indoor slippers the same ones she had worn with a different gown, and her hair had been bundled up inside a lace cap. Not ideal, but it would have to do as she was determined to be downstairs before the revelation was made.

Everyone was in the breakfast parlour, so she was not too late. 'I am so sorry I have kept you waiting, but Hughes has vanished. I have sent one of your chambermaids in search of her, as I fear she must have been taken ill to not have fulfilled her duties.'

She had been careful not to address Beau by his real name

but had no wish to call him by the false one. 'I find I am not hungry. Did Papa not tell you we had a midnight feast?'

The children were eager to know what this meant and talking about their visit to the kitchens was enough to lighten the atmosphere and hopefully not draw attention to the fact that she was only taking coffee. He too did not have his usual piled plate but was toying with a slice of toast.

Something made her decide to pre-empt his announcement. 'I have a most extraordinary thing to tell you. Mr Sheldon does not exist; my husband is actually the Duke of Silchester. I am now a duchess.'

The only one who appeared unsurprised by her dramatic revelation was her mother. 'Your papa would have been delighted you have gone up in the world. I always suspected there was more to you, my boy, than you were telling us.'

Thomas was staring at Beau as if he were a stranger and Elizabeth looked equally upset. She had thought the children would be delighted and her mother dismayed. His eyes were cold; he was like a stranger to her.

'Well, are you not going to explain to everyone how this deception came to take place?' She addressed him too sharply.

His lips tightened and she feared she had made an irredeemable error of judgement by blurting out something he had intended to tell himself at a more suitable time.

He told them exactly what he had told her. When he had finished it was Thomas who spoke first.

'Papa, if you are a duke, should you not have had a grand wedding in a big church and not married in a little chapel with none of your family present?'

'Circumstances caught up with us, Thomas, but...' He hesitated and glanced at her. She knew what was coming but could do nothing to prevent it. 'But that will be rectified in due course.

Your mama and I fell in love so quickly, and then the imminent arrival of Mr Fenchurch and his lawyers meant we had to get married immediately.'

'Your papa has yet to inform his family he is now married. He will be returning there soon to do so.'

'Please don't go soon, Papa; we have only just got you with us. Promise you will stay for a few weeks more before you leave,' Elizabeth said tearfully. 'How long will you be away? Can we come with you? When will we be moving to Silchester?'

Viola closed her eyes and waited for him to say he would not be coming back. This would break her heart as well, but no one had ever died from a broken heart and they would all recover eventually.

Her mother prevented him from speaking by standing up so abruptly all attention was centred on her. 'I am feeling most unwell. I wish to go to my room.'

Beau was on his feet and beside her immediately, his face etched with concern. 'Allow me to assist you, ma'am, and I can only apologise that my deception has caused so much upset for all of you.'

'No, thank you, my daughter can take me, your grace.'

She had no option but to hold her mother's arm and lead her from the room. As soon as they were a few yards away it became clear her mother was perfectly well.

'We need to talk, daughter; we can do so in my sitting room where we will not be disturbed. There have been too many strange occurrences in this family of late. The man you saw in Romford, the attempt to lame our horses, the tree across the road and all this related to the arrival of Mr Fenchurch.'

Viola attempted to stem the flow of words, but her mother raised a finger, something she had used to do when Viola was a child and misbehaving.

'Now your abigail is missing and your husband is about to abandon us. Do not shake your head, my girl. He was about to say that he would not be coming back, so I was forced to interrupt. My head is spinning. I thought he loved you – why else would he marry you when he knows you cannot give him children?'

She bundled her parent into her sitting room and closed the door firmly behind them. 'You are very indiscreet, Mama. You should not have been speaking of such things where servants can hear. You know very well it is I who is sending him away, not he who is leaving voluntarily.'

'Then you have bats in your attic. Why would you choose to ruin all our lives in this way?'

Even after explaining in great detail her reasons, and how she expected Beau would eventually be glad she had taken this stand, her mother remained unconvinced.

* * *

Viola should not have told the family – that was his prerogative. She had put him in an invidious position and now he was going to have to lie to the children. Whatever he might have said to her, he had no intention of upsetting them unnecessarily. He was still hoping he could persuade her to change her mind. Then he recalled what Thomas had told him the first time they met – that once she had made up her mind she would not change it.

The two of them were watching him anxiously. 'Do not look so worried, both of you, your grandmama will be well after she has had a rest. I believe the shock of knowing she is now mama to someone so important as myself was too much for her.' His intention was to make them smile. He failed miserably.

'I liked it better when you were just Mr Sheldon, Papa,' Thomas said.

'Life was certainly simpler. However, I intended to tell you myself and hope you understand why I misled you. If you finish your breakfast quickly, we can go to the music room and I shall show you both how to tune a harp.'

They were not so easily distracted. Elizabeth would not be fobbed off with half-truths and prevarications. 'Papa, you must promise us you will not be gone for long. We shall be miserable without you here. What if this Mr Fenchurch tries to take us away again?'

'I am not going anywhere until that matter is settled. Do you think I would leave you or your mama in any kind of danger?'

'You have not answered my question...'

'Do not be impertinent, young lady. You will show me respect at all times. Is that quite clear?' His tone was firm and he regretted having to speak to her like that but the alternative would be so much worse.

'I do not want to know anything about your harp, your grace. I am going to the schoolroom to study my books.'

She ran away and he wanted to call her back, not to reprimand her, but to reassure her that her fears were groundless. It would be hard to forgive his wife for the misery she was causing so unnecessarily.

Soon he and Thomas were engrossed in their music and he was able to temporarily push his worries aside. They had been playing for some time when Elizabeth crept up beside him and he made room for her on the piano stool. He put his arm around her shoulders and she leaned into him trustingly. He would be devastated to give up these children. This could not happen – he would not lose them as well as her.

'You have done well this morning, son; the more I hear you

play the more convinced I am you are an exceptional musician. Elizabeth, sweetheart, are you quite sure you do not wish me to tune the harp so you can have your first lesson?'

'No, thank you. I just want to sit with you. I don't understand what is happening. I thought you and Mama loved each other, so why are things going wrong so soon?'

He should not have been surprised that a child so young was so observant. 'Shall we sit in front of the fire and I will try and explain things to you?'

What he was going to do would push Viola further away, might well turn her love to hatred, but the children were legally his now and he had no intention of giving them up.

'I have responsibilities that I escaped for a few weeks but must now return to. My life is at Silchester Court and you will come with me when I go. You have aunts and uncles and seven cousins, and there might well be more on the way by now.'

He spent the next hour telling them about their new family and what their life would be like in future. He did not mention that their mother did not intend to come with them and they did not ask. Of course, their grandmother would also remain behind and they were very fond of her. If he left for Silchester as soon as he had confirmation that Fenchurch had returned to Ireland, Sofia and Perry would still be living at his ancestral home, as well as Mary and Aubrey. The children would be most welcome and he could not wait to introduce them to his siblings.

'You must return to your nursemaid, children, as I have business to attend to.' He kissed each of them in turn and was pleased to see they no longer looked pale and sad. Taking them away from their devoted parent might well be considered the act of a tyrant, little better than what Mr Fenchurch had planned to do. He had no doubt in his mind that his beloved wife could not remain apart from her children for long but would follow soon enough.

It might take months, possibly years, to repair the damage he was going to do, but it would be worth it if eventually she was at his side. She loved him as much as he loved her and living in close proximity, sharing in the parenting of their children, seeing how happy her new family were in their own relationships, might well be enough to convince her he had done the right thing.

Before he went to visit Watson he must discover what had happened to Hughes. He was on his way upstairs when he met his wife coming down.

'Have you found your maid?'

'She has gone. I believe her to have been in league with Sir Frederick. She was his spy here and it was your arrival in our lives that prompted his actions.'

'I am about to ride over and speak to that gentleman. I am not convinced we know the whole of it.' He did not offer to take her with him and she did not ask to come. Belatedly he recalled his mother-in-law was supposedly unwell and he should have enquired after her health. 'Is Mrs Alston recovered?'

'She is perfectly fine. It was a ruse to stop you speaking, as well you know. I shall not hold you up any further; this matter must be settled before you leave. The sooner it is done the sooner you can go.' Her tone was cool. For a moment he almost doubted that she actually loved him, but such strong emotions were not switched off so easily.

'Then I shall see you at dinner, Viola. Perhaps you would be kind enough to tune the harp so your daughter can begin her instruction on that instrument. By the by, I have cancelled the order coming from London. I have, naturally, paid for the inconvenience.'

He was hoping to provoke a response from her. The reserve she was displaying was unsettling. 'I was going to suggest you did so. There is no need for there to be two harps in this house.' She smiled, but it did not reach her eyes, and sailed past him on her way back to see her mother, no doubt.

Bishop was waiting to hand him his outdoor garments. 'The horses are waiting, your grace, and I am assuming that you wish me to accompany you.'

'I do indeed. I am hoping you will remain my valet and able assistant when I resume my normal life.'

He bowed deeply. 'I should be honoured, your grace, to serve you in whatever capacity you wish.'

Beau was finding it strange hearing himself addressed correctly after several weeks of being plain Mr Sheldon. God knows what the staff thought of this charade – but it was none of their damn business to speculate about the lives of their betters.

He was becoming curmudgeonly. Being thwarted in his desires was not good for him. He had already broken his promise to his wife that he would not impose his will on her, and this was only the second day of their marriage. What sort of gentleman had he become?

21

Viola watched Beau ride away on his stallion and wished with all her heart that things could be different between them. She would write to her lawyers, and send it by express, in the faint hope that they could come up with a way of dissolving the marriage so she could set him free.

There was also the matter of finding herself a new personal dresser. She had never had to look after herself and had no wish to do so now. She would speak to the housekeeper, as it was possible there might be a girl here suitable to replace the missing Hughes.

Her mama had been right to say things had been very confused these past few weeks. She retired to her sitting room to write the letter but instead sat thoughtfully at the escritoire. Her life had been perfectly acceptable, her children happy, until Beau had arrived in their lives. He had turned everything upside down and she was now convinced Sir Frederick would not have gone in search of this Mr Fenchurch if he had not thought she might marry and ruin his plans.

Therefore, he was not the bringer of happiness but the

destroyer of her peaceful life. If she had never met him the children would not love him and neither would she. They would all be better off without him and the sooner he left the better.

With the letter ready to be taken, she went downstairs in search of a footman to run this errand for her. She was waylaid by the young butler.

'Your grace, there's a hired vehicle approaching. Are you receiving today?'

What now? She went to the window and stood where she could not be seen by the approaching vehicle. It was impossible to see into the interior of the carriage, therefore she would have to wait until it pulled up and was parallel to the house. She was on edge, not sure if she should be panicking and having all the doors locked, or if this was just a random neighbour coming to congratulate her on her marriage. She frowned. It could not possibly be that, as they would use their own carriage.

Two young ladies descended and both looked decidedly dishevelled. Their bonnets were askew, their promenade gowns sadly creased and she understood at once they were two of the missing governesses.

She beckoned to the vigilant footman. 'Ask the housekeeper to prepare two guest bedrooms on the upper floor. These are candidates for the position of governess to my children. Send someone up to the nursery floor and let Lord Thomas and Lady Elizabeth know as well. Also inform Mrs Alston of their arrival.'

She hastily retreated to the drawing room where she would receive the visitors when they were announced. Where on earth had they been for so long? Her curiosity would be satisfied when they came in. She was certain her mother would join her as soon as she could, so she too could hear what had transpired over these past days to delay them so drastically.

She had left the door ajar in order to hear what was said in the entrance hall. Both young ladies were well spoken and asked the butler if they could be shown to their accommodation so they could repair the damage to their appearance before speaking to her.

She was out of the door before she had time to reconsider. 'Welcome, I am Mrs Sheldon now not Lady Fenchurch and I am pleased to see you. Your rooms are not yet ready, so would you care to come into the drawing room with me and get warm? Refreshments will be here at any moment and I can assure you I am not off-put by your travel-worn appearance.'

The young women were of similar height but there the resemblance ended. Miss Blackstone was senior to Miss Fellows and had darker colouring and hair, whereas her companion was much fairer.

'My lady... I beg your pardon, Mrs Sheldon; if there is something to eat and drink, and a warm fire we can thaw out in front of, that would be most acceptable. I can assure you that neither of us are accustomed to being seen in public as we are.'

They handed their cloaks to the footman and, after a moment's hesitation, also removed their bonnets. This would be considered impolite in the best houses as a lady always went to her chamber to do something so personal. However, Viola did not give a fig for such rules.

She asked no questions whilst the two of them devoured the sandwiches and cakes that had arrived and drank several cups of coffee. Her mother arrived just as they were completing their repast.

The two young ladies were introduced and both curtsied politely and sat side by side on the daybed, ankles crossed neatly and hands in their laps just as one would expect from someone in their position in life.

'If you have fully recovered from your journey, perhaps one of you would be kind enough to explain why it has taken so long for you to reach me.'

'First, we were marooned by snow, ma'am, then the coach we were travelling in suffered from a broken axle and we were obliged to disembark and walk several miles to the nearest inn. Then Miss Fellows became extremely unwell so I remained with her and took care of her until she was fully recovered. It was somewhat of a surprise to us as you might imagine, to discover you were now married to a Mr Sheldon and living elsewhere.'

'Thank you for explaining, Miss Blackstone. My housekeeper has come to show you to your chambers. I suggest that you take the remainder of the day to recover and I will have your supper sent to you on a tray. Tomorrow you will each spend time with the children. I shall speak to whoever is not with them and then reverse the process.'

So far, she was impressed with both ladies and it was going to be difficult making a choice between the two. Then something occurred to her. Perhaps the unsuccessful candidate would be prepared to take a position as her companion. She had already set in motion the replacement of her personal maid – the housekeeper was making the selection for her from those already employed at the house. At least she could be certain whoever was chosen would be loyal to her.

The children appeared shortly after the two candidates had retired to their chambers. Her son was in the lead, which was unusual.

'Mama, when can we meet our new governess?'

'They have had a long and unpleasant journey. Miss Fellows was taken ill, which is why their arrival was delayed. Miss Blackstone took care of her. I have told them to spend the remainder of the day recovering and you will spend tomorrow morning with Miss Blackstone and the afternoon with Miss Fellows.'

'What are they like, Mama?' Elizabeth asked.

She gave them a brief description and they seemed satisfied with that. They were more concerned with the fact that their new papa was absent from the house. She explained that he had gone to attend to some business and would be back later that day. It was going to break their hearts when they understood she intended to send him away.

They asked permission to spend time in the music room. 'That is an excellent notion, children. I can start your instruction on the harp, Elizabeth, whilst your brother practises on the piano.'

Her mother appeared. 'Run along, children. Your grandmama wishes to speak privately to your mother and will join you in a moment.'

Obediently they trotted off and Viola turned to see what it was that had agitated her mother.

'Viola, I am shocked by your failure to inform those young ladies of your elevated status. What were you thinking of to allow them to call you Mrs Sheldon?'

'Good heavens! How dreadful – I did not do it deliberately, I can assure you, Mama. I quite forgot. They will think I am fit for Bedlam!'

'I shall go up and speak to them and explain that you have...'

'I'm not surprised you hesitated, Mama. The fact that my husband masqueraded as plain Mr Sheldon and only revealed his true identity after we were married will seem extraordinary to them. I should think they will both wish to leave immediately and not work in such a household.'

Her mother snorted inelegantly. 'Fiddlesticks to that, my girl. I can assure you that both of them will be even more eager to be appointed. Working in the household of a duke will seem highly advantageous.'

'This is such a muddle. It would have been better if I had never met him.'

She dashed from the room, allowing her mother no chance to respond. She joined the children and their enthusiasm and delight in her performance on the harp pushed her misery aside.

The morning flew past and she was surprised when the nursery maid appeared to collect the twins.

'You must go upstairs for your midday meal. Make the most of your freedom, as I shall be appointing one of the two candidates and your lessons will resume the day after tomorrow.'

Elizabeth pouted. 'I thought that we were to be allowed to select someone who we liked.'

'Then you were wrong in your assumption. I agreed that I would not appoint anyone you did not like, not that you could choose. I am certain you will like both of them, as I was most impressed.'

'Then can we be allowed to express a preference for a candidate?' Her daughter sounded like an adult. Since Beau had come into their lives, she had reverted to being a normal child. Viola hoped this stilted way of talking was only temporary. Heaven knows how the child would behave when her beloved papa left them.

'I shall ask your opinion after they have both spent time with you, but the final decision must be mine...'

Thomas looked somewhat surprised by her comment. 'Is Papa not to meet them and help you to make your choice?'

'No, he has left the matter to me. After all I have been your mama all your lives and he has only just become your papa.'

They scampered off and she wandered disconsolately into the breakfast parlour where she had been informed her luncheon was served. As she picked at her food she wondered how Miss Fellows and Miss Blackstone had reacted to the news that they were to be interviewed by a duchess and not Mrs Sheldon.

* * *

Beau was almost unseated when his horse shied at the sudden appearance of Brutus. 'Dammit, dog, what the devil do you think you're doing?'

The animal loped along beside him, head cocked to one side, his tongue lolling; he looked as if he was laughing at him and this made Beau smile.

'I suppose it could do me no harm to have you at my side. Stay close and do not dare to venture to the kennels. Is that quite clear, sir?'

Talking to the dog as if he understood every word was ridiculous, but one did it anyway. This time he did not charge across the fields with disregard for his mount's, and his own, safety. He used the lanes and thus it took him almost an hour to complete the journey.

He had his loaded pistol in his jacket pocket but hoped this would not be needed. His horse was cool and so was he. He had no intention of arriving at the home of the man who had orchestrated the attacks looking anything but immaculate. The two ruffians guarding the property approached him, trying to look menacing.

He remained in the saddle and straightened his shoulders. It was possible they did not know who he was, but he would leave them in no doubt of his authority this time.

'I am Silchester. Fetch your master out here to speak to me. Do it now.' His voice snapped like a whip and they exchanged worried glances.

'We knows who you are, and you ain't anyone what's called Silchester,' one of them ventured nervously.

'I was living incognito for reasons that do not concern you. I am the Duke of Silchester. I do not intend to repeat myself a third time. Fetch Sir Frederick at once.'

This time they reacted. No one argued with a duke. The one who had spoken touched his forelock then ran up the steps to hammer on the door. Beau stared haughtily in front of him as if the other man was invisible. Brutus was at his heel, his growls the only sound apart from birdsong.

In less than five minutes his quarry emerged looking decidedly uncomfortable. Beau swung from the saddle and took a step forward.

'Your grace, if you would care to come inside...'

'I have come to tell you that if you venture anywhere near my properties or my family in future I shall destroy you. Do I make myself clear?'

The man's face flushed an unbecoming shade of beetroot. He nodded. 'Yes, your grace, I understand exactly. I most humbly apologise if anything I have done has offended you. I...'

Beau raised his hand. 'I do not wish to hear your lies. You will tell me what you hoped to gain by this? Did you expect to get your grubby hands on my son's fortune?'

The wretched man wrung his hands. 'I made a dreadful error of judgement and deeply regret my actions. The previous earl was my dearest friend and my intention was to carry out his wishes...'

'I have heard quite enough. Only because no one was hurt by your actions am I prepared to let the matter rest and not have you thrown into jail. You will do well to remember who you have offended. I might still wreak my revenge on you and your family.

I only have to raise a finger and your life will be ruined and your family destitute.'

The man bowed his head, shifted from foot to foot, but made no answer. Beau had intended to enquire about Mr Fenchurch but had wasted more than enough time here. He wanted to return to Elveden to start the slow process of convincing his reluctant duchess that being married to him was not the disaster she thought it to be.

He deliberately turned his back and remounted. He rammed his feet into the stirrup irons, squeezed Titus gently, then cantered away satisfied there would be no further trouble from this particular gentleman. Now that everybody in the neighbourhood would be aware of his identity he must send word at once to his family to let them know not only was he married but also that he would be returning with his wife and family imminently.

He had yet to work out how he was to convince Viola to accompany him, but he had no doubt eventually he would prevail. No one refused the Duke of Silchester.

When he strode into the house he was greeted by the children who flung themselves at him. He leaned down and lifted them into the air as if they were much younger. They did not object to his treatment and clung on as he swung them about.

'Papa, you will never guess who is here,' Elizabeth said as she clung onto his collar.

'In which case you must tell me at once.'

'We have two governesses here. They were tired after their journey so you will not meet them until tomorrow. Mama said you did not wish to be involved in the selection. Don't you want to inspect who will be teaching your children before they are appointed?'

'I am sure that your mama has the matter in hand. I need to

write some letters. I shall see you later.' He put them down but not before he had dropped a kiss on each of their heads.

'You will never guess what happened, Papa,' Thomas said as he danced around him. 'She quite forgot she is now the Duchess of Silchester and Miss Fellows and Miss Blackstone were quite astounded when they were told.'

He forced a laugh. 'It's hardly surprising, son, that she should be confused. Good heavens, in one week she has been Lady Fenchurch, Mrs Sheldon and now the Duchess of Silchester. Run along, I have work to do.'

'Mama is in the drawing room with Grandmama. We shall tell her you are home again,' Elizabeth said and she skipped off, unaware that this information might not be as welcome as she thought.

He retreated to his study and not until he had closed the door did he allow himself to react to this latest indication that his beloved had not accepted her new role.

First, he would write the necessary letters and then when he had adjusted to this latest setback he would consider how he could move forward. Carstairs, his man of business, would need to come to Elveden in order to organise tenants for both properties. He completed this missive first, sanded the paper, folded it carefully and pressed his ducal signet ring into the molten wax. He had brought with him this one indication of his status – it had been kept securely in his waistcoat pocket until he had been able to wear it once more.

He then wrote a short letter to Bennett informing him that he had married Viola and was now a parent to her children. He informed his brother he hoped to be returning with his family in the next few weeks and asked him to inform his household to prepare for the arrival of his duchess. The nursery floor would also have to be refurbished and made ready for Thomas and Elizabeth. There was no necessity for him to write to his other siblings as Bennett would give them the good news.

The third letter he wrote was to Lord Rushton, now his brother-in-law since he had married Giselle. His close friend had two daughters of similar age to the twins and he wished the four of them to become better acquainted. The children of his other siblings were still in leading strings and too young to be companions.

He rang the bell and handed the letters to the footman who came in answer to his summons. 'These must go by express.'

The man took them with a bow and backed out as if leaving royalty. This was one of the aspects about being a duke that he disliked. He wished he could have remained plain Mr Sheldon and not be treated with such deference.

His business concluded, he strolled to the windows and stared out at the park. There was already a sprinkling of green on the hedges indicating spring was on its way. Would he still be here to see the garden in its summer splendour?

With a sigh he turned and headed for the door. He needed to tell Viola what had transpired during his visit to Sir Frederick. He was halfway across the room when there was a tentative knock on the door. 'Come in,' he called.

'Beau, why did you not come at once and tell me what happened?'

'I was about to do so. Shall we remain here so we can converse in private?'

She hesitated but then with some reluctance took her place on the padded settle. There was ample room for him to join her but he deliberately sat some yards from her.

When she heard that there would be no further trouble from Sir Frederick or Mr Fenchurch, her expression lightened and she smiled. 'That is a great relief. Which brings me on to something else, and I am certain you will not be pleased with what I'm going to say to you.'

He raised an eyebrow and waved his hand to indicate she should continue hoping that his dismay had been hidden from her. He had already guessed what she was going to say.

'I wish you to return to Silchester but I intend to remain here with my mother and my children. I do not wish to be married to you but will be forever grateful that you stepped in and prevented Mr Fenchurch from intruding in our lives.'

He swallowed the lump in his throat. 'Whatever your feelings on the matter, Viola, you are my wife and there is nothing either of us can do about it. There are no grounds for having it annulled or declared invalid.'

'You are one of a handful of dukes in the country. You are second only to royalty in importance. I'm quite certain that you can arrange things if you so wish. You can tell them that I am barren, that I kept this from you until we were married. I am sure they will sympathise and find you a loophole in the law so you can set the marriage aside.'

'It is possible I could do this if I wished to. However, I have no intention of setting the marriage aside. I married you because I love you and whether you like it or not you are now my responsibility and your children are under my control.' His voice was commendably firm and betrayed none of his heartbreak at her words.

She stood up and shook her head. 'Then so be it. I shall not come with you to Silchester and I will never be your true wife. Pray excuse me...'

He slowly rose and moved closer. He had no intention of physically removing her from Elveden but there was one thing he could do that would bring her to him eventually. He had hoped not to be obliged to take this drastic step but she left him no alternative.

'If you wish to remain at Elveden that is your prerogative. You cannot return to Fenchurch as there will be tenants living in the house very soon. I shall be leaving for Silchester next week and the children will come with me.'

Her eyes rounded and for a moment she was too shocked to respond. He braced himself for her outburst and it was not long in coming.

'You cannot take Thomas and Elizabeth away from me and their grandmama. They belong here with us. I will not allow it.'

'I am sorry to cause you so much unhappiness, but as I explained to you the children are now mine. I could insist that you accompany them but I gave you my word I would not coerce you into doing anything you did not wish to do. The twins were not included in this promise. Do you wish to inform them or shall I?'

22

Viola wanted to throw herself at Beau, pummel him with her fists, throw the largest object she could find at his arrogant head. She did none of these things as she knew it would only exacerbate the situation. From somewhere she found the strength to maintain her dignity.

'I will tell them myself. As they are not to reside with me I suggest that you appoint the governess. The two young ladies arrived today and I intended to interview them tomorrow. Unless you have other plans for my children.'

'You are being childish; it does not become you. I am your husband. Any other gentleman would insist that his wife accompany him, would not allow her to dictate the terms of their marriage. If you wish to be with your children then you must come to Silchester. I will make it abundantly clear to Elizabeth and Thomas that it is your choice that you remain behind.'

This last statement broke the fragile hold she had on her temper. She was standing by the fire and without a second thought she snatched up the fire irons and hurled them at his head. He reacted instantly and raised his arm so the items were deflected from his face.

Not waiting for him to retaliate, she gathered her skirts and fled from the room, expecting at any moment to be caught and dragged back to get her punishment. She was halfway down the passageway when she realised he had not pursued her. She abhorred violence of any kind and yet had attempted to cause him serious harm.

A wave of nausea caused her to clap her hands across her mouth. She was going to cast up her accounts and doubted she could find a receptacle in time. Then his strong arm was around her waist and she was whisked into a small room in which a commode was placed behind a lacquered screen.

'Here, use this.'

A bowl was pushed into her arms not a moment too soon. After an unpleasant and humiliating five minutes she had recovered. He handed her his handkerchief to wipe her mouth and in exchange he took the noxious bowl away from her.

'I am so sorry, Beau, I should not have thrown things at you. Did I injure your arm?' Nervously she raised her head to see him leaning nonchalantly against the panelling, apparently unbothered by her appalling behaviour.

'My arm is bruised, but nothing to worry about. More to the point, my love, are you now well enough to go upstairs and speak to our children?'

She blinked back her tears. 'You tell them. I need time to compose myself. I have no wish for them to know that having them leave will break my heart.'

'The solution is in your hands. You can remain here alone on your high horse or come with me and begin a new life as my duchess.'

'I cannot do that. Until I am quite certain there is no legal loophole that will release me from this arrangement I shall remain here.'

'Then I am satisfied that eventually you will understand the marriage is a binding contract between us. Sweetheart, I know why you are doing this. How many times do I have to tell you I have no wish to have children from my own loins? Although we married in haste I would not have done so if I did not love you and knew that you returned my feelings.'

She was about to deny this, but he raised his hand and she held her peace.

'By remaining here you will make not only yourself miserable, but also your children and myself. I hope you will reconsider your decision. I shall not change my mind about taking Thomas and Elizabeth with me.'

'When do you intend to go?'

'I have sent for my travelling carriage. There will be horses positioned at the necessary hostelries. The governess, my valet and the luggage can travel in the carriage I arrived in. It will take us two days to reach my home. The team will need to rest and then I shall send my carriage back for you. It will remain here until you see sense and come and join your family.'

His answer was deliberately vague. Her irritation was enough to overcome her distress. 'Answer the question if you please, sir. How long do I have before you abscond with my children?'

A flash of annoyance crossed his face but he hid it well. 'I have informed my staff at Silchester to expect me in two weeks. I'm sure you can work out from that exactly when I intend to depart.' He nodded formally and strode away without another word.

His treatment of her when she had been unwell could not be faulted. Was she wrong to remain aloof from him in the hope that he would be able to eventually marry a woman who could give him children? He had told her repeatedly that he loved her and she certainly reciprocated his feelings – therefore, by her recalcitrance she was denying them all a life of love and contentment.

She needed to speak to someone in his family, as they could tell her he truly was content that the title would not pass in the direct line. There was only one thing she could do and it would scandalise her mother, infuriate her husband and bewilder her children.

She hurried upstairs and found the girl who had been appointed as her dresser busy folding clothes. She curtsied. 'I am Annie, your grace.'

'Good, I need you to pack me a valise that can accompany me on the stagecoach. Then you must do the same for yourself, but on no account must you reveal to anyone what you are doing. Is that quite clear?'

'My loyalties are to you alone, your grace. The under-groom here is my betrothed. I will send word to him to get the gig harnessed. The next coach leaves Ipswich at five o'clock. We should be able to catch that easily.'

'I can see we are going to get along famously, Annie. I want your betrothed to accompany us. Having a male servant alongside should make things easier when we alight.'

She had no intention of leaving a note for Beau, as he would immediately set off after her on his stallion. With luck he would think her in bed after her bilious attack and not check until the morning.

'Annie, when you go down to speak to your young man, call into the kitchen and ask Cook to prepare me a tisane and make much of the fact that I am very unwell. Tell them you intend to remain with me all night and have no wish for any supper trays to be sent up.'

The girl grinned. 'We should be in London before anyone is any the wiser. You can trust me, your grace. I will not let you down.'

Viola put a bolster in the bed and then pulled the covers over it so it appeared she was there. Then she pulled the curtains almost closed. She went to the door and stood there to see how it would look if he came to check. Yes – from that distance the shape definitely looked like a human form.

By the time she had changed into a travelling ensemble, the plainest she could find in her wardrobe, Annie was back carrying her own small bag. She had also written Beau a note explaining she had gone to speak to her lawyers in London and would be back within two days. For good measure she added that she was meeting her brother so he would be with her. Telling falsehoods to her husband was not something she was happy with, but she had no choice. What she was doing was for his benefit – not hers or the children's. This missive was put on the pillow where he would find it when eventually he came in to investigate her non-appearance.

'It won't take me but a moment to pack what you need for a short stay, your grace, and then we can leave. I shall take you down the servants' staircase and out through a little-used side door. I am certain no one will see us.'

The under-groom handed her into the carriage, snapped his whip, and the horse set off at a brisk trot. They did not go down the drive but through the tradesmen's track and in no time at all they were bowling along the road to Ipswich.

Sam purchased inside tickets for them both whilst Annie stood beside her guarding the luggage. He returned and handed them into the coach and then saw their luggage safely stowed at the rear of the vehicle and clambered in to join them. In the time it had taken her to clamber inside, the four horses had been changed and the driver was ready to leave. The gig and horse would remain at the inn for their return.

There were only two other occupants, which meant they had ample room for the moment. One of them was a soldier in scarlet regimentals and the other a clerical gentleman. The bonnet she had chosen had such a deep brim that if she kept her head facing forward it was impossible for anyone sitting on either side of her to see her face.

They remained with the vehicle throughout the long, tedious journey although they could have reserved accommodation at Colchester or Romford. By the time they trundled into The Saracen's Head in London, in the small hours, she was bruised all over, exhausted, and deeply regretting her impulsive decision to go to Silchester Court and speak to Beau's siblings.

Poor Miss Blackstone and Miss Fellows would have to be interviewed by her husband in the morning. She did not intend to stay at Silchester, merely speak to any of his family that were available, and then return immediately. With luck she would be back the day after tomorrow – scarcely time for a hue and cry to be set up.

* * *

Beau decided he would tell the children they would be coming with him but refrained from mentioning that their mama intended to remain behind, as he still hoped she would change her mind.

'What about Miss Fellows and Miss Blackstone? Will one of them accompany us, Papa?' Elizabeth asked anxiously.

'They will indeed, but I have no idea which one it will be. Shall we play cribbage until your mother comes down to join us?'

Viola failed to appear before the nursemaid came to collect

the children for nursery tea. He kissed them warmly and promised to come up and say goodnight later on. His mother-in-law had also vanished, but he could hardly knock on her apartment, so he would go and see where his wife was. Her sudden attack of sickness could herald a megrim or could just have been a reaction to her extraordinary behaviour.

He flexed his injured arm and smiled ruefully. He was fortunate it had not been broken by the impact of the metal fire irons. He was waylaid by the butler in the hall. 'Excuse me, your grace, word has come from the kitchen that a tisane has been requested as her grace is indisposed.'

'Thank you, that explains why her grace has not joined us this afternoon.'

He knocked and looked into her bedchamber when he was retiring and saw Viola was sleeping. Hopefully she would be fully recovered tomorrow and in a better frame of mind. The letters he had sent by express would have arrived by now and Carstairs would no doubt set off first thing in the morning and would be with him the day after.

It was early when he got up and he went straight to her rooms. He knocked and was surprised that her maid did not answer. After being ignored for several minutes he went in without invitation. The curtains were still drawn, the fire dead in the grate. There was a sinking feeling in his stomach and he covered the remaining distance to her bedchamber in seconds.

As he feared the bed was empty, a bolster in place representing his wife. He snatched up the note and read it. Dammit to hell! What maggot had got into her brain to think she could find a solution to their problem by dashing off to London to see her lawyers? He thanked the Lord that her brother would be there to escort her about the place. He had been unaware that Alston had returned from Ireland – so much had happened in the interim he had quite forgotten about this.

Mrs Alston was in the breakfast parlour and he nodded politely. 'Good morning, ma'am, I assume that you are aware Viola has rushed off to London in the hope that she can have the marriage set aside.'

The old lady stared at him as if he was speaking in tongues. 'Good heavens! The girl has run mad. I had no idea, your grace, that my daughter planned to do anything so stupid.'

'The visit will prove what I have been trying to tell her. There is no way our marriage can be annulled and the sooner she realises that, the happier we will all be.' He filled his plate and joined her at the table. 'I shall be leaving for Silchester in ten days' time. Your grandchildren will be accompanying me. I assume you will remain here with my wife until she sees sense.'

'I'm tempted to come with you, your grace, and leave her isolated here. I shall not do that, but I can assure you I will do everything in my power to persuade her to forget her nonsense and be happy that she has married not only for expedience, but also for love.'

He buried his nose in his newspaper so he was not obliged to keep up a conversation. He bid her a polite farewell and headed for the stables. A gallop around the park would settle his nerves and Titus needed the exercise.

After an exhilarating and enjoyable excursion he was cantering around the extremity of the park when he saw someone turn into the drive on what was obviously a hired hack. When he was close enough to see the identity of the rider he cursed volubly under his breath.

'Alston, hold up, I need to speak to you.' His brother-in-law was supposed to be in London with Viola, so what the devil was he doing here? They both drew rein so they could converse more comfortably.

'Good morning, sir, I am returned from Ireland with the most extraordinary news.'

'I thought you meeting Viola in London. We are married now, and I must inform you I am not Mr Sheldon but the Duke of Silchester.'

'The devil you are! You have trumped my news with your own, your grace. I found the residence of the family and discovered Fenchurch had already departed for London.'

Beau dismounted in the turning circle and tossed his reins to a waiting groom and his companion did the same. He strode into the house and headed straight for his study. Alston's reunion with his mama could wait until this business had been fully discussed.

As soon as the doors closed he turned. 'Tell me what you know.'

'Initially I was horrified I had arrived too late but then made further enquiries which led me to the conclusion that this Fenchurch is not in any way related to Viola. Several of the local families told me categorically he had no connection to any aristocratic English family.'

'How did Sir Frederick come to make such an error? Surely the man concerned must be aware of his own ancestry?'

'Indeed he is. I then returned and spoke to his wife who was unhappy at her husband's deception. The man had taken the opportunity to make himself rich regardless of the consequences. On further investigation I did in fact find the genuine relatives, but this man did not produce any male heirs, only females. It is a coincidence that there happens to be a second family with the same name living no more than fifty miles away.'

'No doubt this imposter has now scuttled back to Ireland. I

had better tell you how it comes that we are married and why I was living incognito.'

When he had finished his story he added that his wife refused to accept the fact that not only was the marriage permanent but also that he did not care one jot that she could not give him children.

'She will come around – never fear. She loves you to distraction and will make an excellent chatelaine and duchess. I travelled post and am fatigued. Forgive me, sir, but I should like to get some shut-eye before I see my mother.'

'I am concerned that Viola is gallivanting about Town unchaperoned. What might have been acceptable for Mrs Sheldon is certainly not for the Duchess of Silchester.' He sighed. 'I suppose I am obliged to go in search of her…'

There was a sharp knock on the door and it flew open before he could make a response. His mother-in-law surged in and, ignoring him, bustled across and hugged her son.

'You should have come to me first, my boy. I am agog to hear your news.'

Beau left them to their conversation and went in search of his valet. He was in two minds about trekking to London as it was quite possible he would arrive when she was already returning. His man informed him that one of the grooms had gone with her as well as her maid. He told him that there was in fact no heir so the danger to the family was gone.

'If you will permit me to comment, your grace, I believe her grace will be perfectly safe. I cannot see the necessity for us to rush after her in the circumstances.'

'That is the conclusion I came to. I am glad to have it confirmed by yourself. However, I need to know how she travelled. She did not take a carriage so I suppose she either went post-chaise or took the common stage.'

Again, his man surprised him. 'I cannot see that it makes any difference to the outcome, your grace. Either way she will be safe and return in a day or two.'

He slapped him on the back. 'You are an excellent fellow. I cannot imagine how I managed without you. I shall wait here until she comes back.'

He went to the nursery floor to inform the children that their uncle had arrived and found them busy at their lessons with not one, but two, ladies in charge. He had quite forgotten about the governesses.

They both curtsied politely and the children looked for permission to stand up before they rushed over to him. 'Forgive me for interrupting, but I have come to inform the children that their uncle has arrived. He will not be available for an hour or two as he needs to rest after his exertions.'

'Why has Mama gone away without telling us, Papa?'

23

Viola and her two companions disembarked from the stagecoach at the inn that was nearest to Silchester Court. 'We must rest and repair the damage to our appearances before we continue to our destination. Sam, please find us a vehicle to convey us there. Then go to the kitchen and you will find a meal awaiting you.'

She and Annie headed for the vestibule and were immediately shown to a chamber where they could wash and change their garments. By the time this was completed a maid had arrived with refreshments.

'There, your grace, I doubt anyone would know you had just spent the past twenty-four hours bouncing around in a coach.'

'I might not look as though I have but I certainly feel it in every bone in my body. To think we have to repeat the process on the way back. I give you my word that both you and Sam shall be well rewarded for your diligence and excellent care.'

The girl hesitated. 'Your grace, will we be coming with you or shall we be left behind when you move here?'

If even her personal maid believed that eventually she must

set aside her concerns and take up her new role, then this was indeed a wasted journey.

'If and when I come you will both come with me. I shall ask the duke to provide you with a cottage so you might be married but I am loath to do so, as inevitably you will leave my service to have children of your own.'

'I will never have babes, although I would like to have done. I would rather be married to my Sam than married to another and have a cottage full of infants.'

Intrigued Viola enquired further. 'Why do you say that? How can you possibly know such a thing?'

'My Sam and I have been intimate many times over the past three years and I reckon I would have caught on by now if I was going to.' Annie realised how indiscreet she had been and the colour drained from her face.

'No, do not look so stricken for telling me, Annie. I am not bothered by your admission and will forget that you told me.'

The food consumed, she was ready to complete her journey. Sam was waiting outside with a smart gig and he handed them both in. The drive was no more than a few miles and they turned into the long, immaculate drive far too early.

Too late to turn back. She was the Duchess of Silchester and this probably would be her home one day and she could arrive and depart whenever she so pleased.

Sam pulled up in front of the magnificent building. For a moment she was unable to descend, too awestruck to do more than stare like a child at a fairground. Their arrival had been noted and the front door swung open. She expected to see a footman or perhaps the butler come out to investigate, but instead a young lady appeared under the portico.

'Your grace, you must get down. Someone is coming to greet you.'

Viola had scarcely set foot to the ground when she was embraced. 'You must be Viola – you fit Beau's description exactly. I am your sister Sofia. I am married to Perry, the younger of the twins. I shall not ask why you are here – come in, come in, you must be exhausted after your long journey.'

'I thank you for your warm welcome, my lady. You must think it odd of me to come uninvited and without Beau.'

'Fiddlesticks to that! This is your home now. We Sheldon ladies are independent and our gentlemen prefer it so.'

She was guided up the steps and whisked through a cavernous entrance hall, down a broad passageway and into a small, beautifully decorated drawing room.

'This is my private parlour, Viola. I hope you do not intend that we call you by your title, as we stand on no ceremony here. I am addressed as Sofia.'

Coffee and pastries were fetched but she ignored both. In stumbling words, she explained the reason for her arrival. Instead of being shocked or scandalised Sofia nodded sympathetically.

'I understand exactly how you feel about this. It makes me love you more. I can assure you that Beau has no interest in filling his nursery and indeed, sincerely dislikes small children. I am increasing, so is Mary – much to her surprise – she is the wife of the older twin, Aubrey. Bennett already has two infants, both of them boys, so there is already a surfeit of heirs, and you have nothing to worry about on that score.'

Viola wondered if all the Sheldon ladies were as vocal as Sofia. Then her new sister-in-law leaned forward and squeezed her hand. 'You must think me a rattletrap. I do not normally say so much but I wished to reassure you immediately that you have nothing to worry about.'

'This is all astonishing to me...' There was no time to

complete her sentence as the door burst open and they were joined by a matching pair of Sheldon gentlemen. She was warmly greeted and both Perry and Aubrey confirmed what Sofia had told her.

'We only heard late last night that Beau had finally fallen in love and married you,' Aubrey said. 'Like all the Sheldons he knew within a day or two that he had met the woman he wanted to spend the remainder of his life with. Welcome to the family.'

'I second that. Our older brother always said he had no wish for children of his own, but he admitted he envied us our happiness with our partners. Now he has found someone for himself and we can be content for him.' Perry was perched on the edge of Sofia's chair and it was patently obvious how much the couple were in love.

A slightly older lady rushed in. 'Forgive me for my tardiness. I am Mary and cannot tell you how delighted I am to meet you, Viola.'

'And I you. I lied to Beau and told him I was going to see my lawyers and that I was meeting my brother in London. He is going to be most displeased when he discovers the truth.'

The four exchanged looks and all of them laughed. For a moment she thought their amusement was directed at her, then Sofia explained.

'He will just be overjoyed that you are now prepared to be his true wife, that you are now convinced he has no desire for children of his own.' She leaped from the chair, dislodging her husband who barely retained his balance. 'The teams have already left so they will be in place for the carriage. That will not depart until the morning. You must go in it. It will take two days to travel to him – the horses must rest overnight – and then two days to return.'

Mary was now on her feet looking as excited as Sofia. 'So, we have a week or more to arrange for the blessing of your wedding to be held in our chapel. If a letter is sent by express to Rushton and Giselle, they can be here within the week as well.'

She was overwhelmed by their kindness and already felt part of this large family. 'I know that Beau was disappointed he could not be married here, so having a second service will be the perfect start to our new life together.'

Perry laughed. 'We took a wager that our big brother would not remain away from Silchester for the full six months, but it did not cross our minds the reason for his premature return would be to bring a wife and family home.'

* * *

Beau prowled around the house, unable to settle. He was in two minds about going after his errant wife. Despite the fact that he knew she was in no danger, he was uncomfortable with her gallivanting about the country with no male escort apart from a servant.

The children were equally disturbed by their mother's absence and this gave him pause for thought. Taking them with him was the only way to persuade his beloved to come to Silchester but if it meant Thomas and Elizabeth were unhappy then he would not bring them. He must pray all three of them would miss him and eventually they would join him at Silchester.

Richard joined him in the billiard room later that day. 'I have been speaking to my mother and gather Viola has decided you would be better off without her and is refusing to accompany you to Silchester.'

'I'm hoping that she might listen to you as she has not to either myself or Mrs Alston. I have told her repeatedly that I have enough heirs but she will not listen. She has got it into her head that I will be better off without her, so I can find myself a fertile wife.'

'She was always stubborn and once she makes up her mind it's almost impossible to get her to change her opinion. Hopefully the lawyers will confirm what you have told her and she will return, happy to become your duchess.' He picked up a cue. 'Shall we play or is there something you need to do?'

'I should be making arrangements for the transfer of my belongings and my horses, but I have not the heart to do it. I intended to stay here until the summer – I can hardly credit I have only been here a little over a month and yet I am now married with two children. I have sent word to my family and no doubt they are equally astounded at the turn of events.'

'They will be even more astonished if you arrive without your bride so, I suggest that you leave it for a few weeks until Viola has become accustomed to the idea.'

They played several frames and the score was equal when it was time to change for dinner. As a duke he was now obligated to change – it was what his staff expected. Informality was not possible when one was in his elevated position in the world. Being a commoner had suited him.

The governesses had completed the day with their charges and would be dining with them. He would use this opportunity to talk to them and thus be able to decide which one would be most suitable. The twins liked them both and would be content with whomever he chose.

At the end of the meal, his mother-in-law stood up and led the two young ladies through to the drawing room.

'Well, Alston, I am at a loss to select from Miss Fellows and Miss Blackstone. Both are equally well qualified and either would fit into my household. Who do you prefer?'

'I am remaining out of this, my friend, and if I were you I

would wait until my sister returns and allow her to make the final decision. Both young ladies made no objection when you asked them if they would remain for another day or two.'

'Then that is what I shall do. Viola has now been gone for two days so I'm expecting her to return sometime tomorrow. I hope you will remain here until she does put in an appearance.'

'Unfortunately, I cannot. I have obligations elsewhere and have urgent business to attend to. I am betrothed to my childhood sweetheart and we intend to be married in June. I hope you will be able to attend.'

'Do you have somewhere to live once you are married?'

'I expect we will live with my in-laws until I have time to find myself an estate. My father invested all his income into the business, which is why we have two fleets of ships trading successfully all around the world. He rented a smart house in Town for the Season that my sister attended and also rented a decent property in St Albans. When they came to live with Viola after that bastard died he obviously let this go.'

'Then you must accept this property as your wedding gift from us. Unless it is too far from the capital to be suitable for your needs.'

'I'm overwhelmed by your generosity, sir, and gratefully accept your offer. Are you quite sure you wish to give this to us? You have only recently purchased this estate for your own use.'

'This estate has been in the family for generations. I merely took up residence when the tenant died. If it would make you more comfortable, I can put in a stipulation that it must be passed down through your family and that it cannot be sold.'

'I would be happier with that arrangement. Will the house come furnished?'

Beau laughed. 'It will indeed – although I must remove the harp from the music room, as I do not possess one at Silchester. I should like to meet your future wife. Would you be prepared to bring her here before I depart?'

'I still have the hired hack so will take that back to the posting inn first thing tomorrow morning and then travel post-chaise to St Albans and collect my betrothed.'

Beau ignored the port as did his companion. 'Forgive me, Alston, I must say goodnight to the children before I come through and join the ladies.'

They were both wide awake and waiting for his appearance, and he was glad he had remembered his promise. 'Your uncle is to leave first thing, so if you wish to say goodbye you must rise at six o'clock. You may eat breakfast downstairs tomorrow if you would like to. It will be served at half past the hour – an hour earlier than usual.'

'Papa, that would be splendid. Will Mama be home soon? We don't like it without her,' Thomas said.

'I hope that she will be back with us very soon. I am not happy without her here either. Now, you must both go to sleep if you intend to get up early tomorrow.' He hugged each in turn and they returned his embrace with enthusiasm.

Both young ladies were charming. It would be an impossible task to choose between them and he was glad he had decided to leave this to Viola. On his arrival his mother-in-law stood up.

'I am going to retire now, your grace. It has been a most pleasant evening. Goodnight, sir.'

'Would you like me to escort you to your apartment, ma'am?' He had noticed she was becoming frailer by the day and he was most concerned about her health.

'That would be kind of you, your grace...'

'Please, ma'am, desist from addressing me so formally. If you cannot bring yourself to use my given name then please call me Sheldon.'

'I shall do so if *you* stop calling me ma'am. I dislike that appellation intensely.'

He took her arm and together they journeyed down the long passageway to her rooms. Her maid was waiting to attend to her. In all conscience he could not abandon any of this family and return to Silchester. He would remain here where he could take care of them all until Viola changed her mind.

He paused at the drawing room to speak to the three remaining guests. 'I have letters to write, so will bid you all goodnight. Alston, your niece and nephew will be coming down to breakfast as they wish to say farewell. I neglected to tell them you were returning in a day or two with your future wife.'

The young ladies had been about to stand at his entrance but he waved them back. 'Miss Blackstone, Miss Fellows, there is no need for you to come down so early. Goodnight.'

He hurriedly penned a letter to Bennett telling him of the change of plans. The letter could go by express in the morning – Alston could hand it in for him. He missed Viola; she was part of his life now, as were her children and her mother. He did not feel complete without her in the house with him.

The following morning Alston rode away whilst the twins waved frantically. The hound was standing in the turning circle, his long, plumy tail waving, his head tilted as if asking a question. The children looked at him hopefully.

'Very well, you may go with him but stay within earshot of the house. I shall whistle if I want you to return.'

They thanked him and scampered off. Only as they vanished around the corner of the house did he realise they had no outdoor garments on. At least they were wearing boots and not indoor slippers.

'Your grace,' a quiet voice said from behind him. 'I have their coats here. Do I have your permission to go after them and make sure they put them on?'

'Miss Fellows, I did not expect to see you so early. Yes, thank you, I should not have let them go as they are. I have a lot to learn about being a parent.'

'Elizabeth and Thomas consider you their papa, your grace, and could not be happier. They are old enough to have remembered they needed an outdoor garment for themselves. I shall remind them of that when I catch up with them.'

He grinned. 'Remain where you are. I shall recall them.' He put his fingers in his mouth and whistled. The young lady laughed, which made him like her more. The dog bounded back first, hotly pursued by the little ones.

'I shall leave you to deal with this, Miss Fellows.'

He spent the remainder of the day on estate matters. When Carstairs arrived, he could transfer the ownership of Elveden to his new brother as well as set about finding a suitable tenant for Fenchurch.

Mid-afternoon he was perusing a journal, the twins upstairs at their lessons and Mrs Alston in her rooms resting, when he looked up and saw the Silchester travelling carriage bowling down the drive.

He surged to his feet. Someone in the family had decided to visit him after receiving his news. He strode into the hall and snapped his fingers at the footman. 'Send word to the stables that a carriage is coming and the horses will need attending to.' He had no need to ask for a guest room to be prepared, as all the rooms were kept permanently in a state of readiness by his efficient housekeeper.

When the vehicle rocked to a halt he was waiting under the portico to greet whoever it was. A footman was there to open the door and let down the steps. To his astonishment Viola stepped out.

He took the steps in one and raced across to sweep her into his arms. 'My darling, I am so pleased to have you home. What the hell are you doing in this carriage?'

She linked her arms around his neck and tilted her face to him. 'Isn't it obvious? I have been to speak to your family and they have convinced me I am wrong to think you unhappy with our marriage. I love you and want to be your true wife.'

His roar of triumph caused the team to plunge and only the quick thinking of the coachmen prevented a disaster.

'I had decided I would remain here until you changed your mind, however long it took. Now we can all transfer to Silchester and begin our lives together.'

24

Viola had no time to regale Beau with her adventure as her children hurtled down the stairs and threw themselves at her. 'Where have you been? We're so pleased to have you home. Are we going to Silchester Court soon?' Elizabeth said as she clung to her hand.

'That is up to your papa, but I imagine it will be very soon. I hope you have both been behaving yourselves in my absence.'

Thomas was leaning against her as if afraid she would disappear again. 'We have, Mama. Miss Fellows and Miss Blackstone have been teaching us. Can they both be our governesses?'

'Too many questions, my loves – I must go and see your grandmama and you must return to the schoolroom. I shall come up to you when I am ready.'

They scampered off and she could hear them laughing and chattering. She turned to Beau who was staring at her in a most particular way. Her heart increased its pace and her bodice became unaccountably tight. Surely he did not wish to take her to bed right now?

'I must speak to Mama. Then I must go up to the schoolroom

and put my proposition to the two young ladies. Following that, I am so fatigued after my travelling that I intend to retire to my bedchamber for an afternoon rest.'

His eyes darkened and his smile was wicked. He said nothing, merely bowed and strolled away, but she was certain he was as eager as she to spend private time together.

Her mother told her that Richard had visited and was coming back with his betrothed. Viola was astounded and delighted to discover Elveden was to become her brother's abode on his marriage.

'I cannot tell you how much I enjoyed my brief visit, Mama. The Sheldon brothers are almost as handsome as my husband and their wives equally attractive. There is to be a second ceremony in the family chapel as soon as we return.'

'It is about time you came to your senses, my girl, so we can all relocate to our new home. I sincerely hope there is an apartment on the ground floor, as I no longer wish to negotiate stairs.'

'I shall ask him when I see him next. I must now go up and speak to the ladies who have been teaching the children. I shall be taking a tray in my apartment so will not see you until the morning.'

Her mother smiled knowingly. 'I expect his grace will also take his dinner on a tray tonight. Off you go, my love, and set things in motion.'

In the schoolroom both children were busy at whatever task had been set for them. She beckoned the two ladies to the far end of the room so they could converse in private.

'His grace, Mrs Alston and the children are impressed by your capabilities. Obviously, I cannot employ both of you in the role of governess so I have a suggestion. Would one of you be prepared to become my companion and secretary? I thought perhaps that, Miss Blackstone, you might prefer this employment, but I shall leave the decision to you.'

There was no hesitation. 'Your grace, I should be honoured and delighted to become your companion and secretary. Miss Fellows is considerably younger than me and will make an excellent tutor to your delightful children.'

'Then it only remains to ask you if you are both prepared to live at Silchester? We shall be moving there as soon as it can be arranged.'

'I cannot tell you how happy I am that we can both remain with your family, your grace. I have one trunk to collect from the lodgings I took whilst I was searching for a new position,' Miss Blackstone said.

'I too have a trunk that I would like to bring with me, but mine remains with my previous employers. They said they would be happy to forward it when I furnish them with my new address.'

'Write the necessary letters and his grace will frank them for you. It will probably be several days before we are ready to depart, so with luck your belongings will arrive in good time at Silchester.'

When she told the children they were overjoyed as they were already fond of both ladies. There was no necessity to discuss the exact duties Miss Blackstone would have – such details could wait until the morrow.

What couldn't wait was her rendezvous with Beau. Her knees were weak, her pulse skittering; she scarcely knew how she managed to convey herself from the nursery floor to her own apartment. Annie had been told to make herself scarce and not to appear unless she rang for her.

She was unsurprised to find him pacing her bedchamber. He had already removed his topcoat, neckcloth and boots. 'At last, my darling, I have been waiting here this age,' Beau almost growled at her.

'I have come as quickly as I could. Heaven knows what the staff will think of our reprehensible behaviour...'

'I don't give a damn what anyone says. I am the Duke of Silchester and you are my duchess and we can do exactly what we please.'

* * *

They soon discovered that what pleased one of them delighted the other. The fact that neither the duke nor the duchess appeared for breakfast surprised no one in the household.

* * *

MORE FROM FENELLA J. MILLER

The first book in another brilliant Regency romance series from Fenella J .Miller, *Return to Pemberley*, is available to order now here:

www.mybook.to/ReturnPemberleyBackAd

ABOUT THE AUTHOR

Fenella J. Miller is the bestselling writer of over eighteen historical sagas. She also has a passion for Regency romantic adventures and has published over fifty to great acclaim. Her father was a Yorkshireman and her mother the daughter of a Rajah. She lives in a small village in Essex with her British Shorthair cat.

Sign up to Fenella J. Miller's mailing list for news, competitions and updates on future books.

Visit Fenella's website: www.fenellajmiller.co.uk

Follow Fenella on social media here:

facebook.com/fenella.miller
x.com/fenellawriter

ALSO BY FENELLA J MILLER

Goodwill House Series

The War Girls of Goodwill House

New Recruits at Goodwill House

Duty Calls at Goodwill House

The Land Girls of Goodwill House

A Wartime Reunion at Goodwill House

Wedding Bells at Goodwill House

A Christmas Baby at Goodwill House

The Army Girls Series

Army Girls Reporting For Duty

Army Girls: Heartbreak and Hope

Army Girls: Behind the Guns

Army Girls: Operation Winter Wedding

The Pilot's Girl Series

The Pilot's Girl

A Wedding for the Pilot's Girl

A Dilemma for the Pilot's Girl

A Second Chance for the Pilot's Girl

The Nightingale Family Series

A Pocketful of Pennies

A Capful of Courage

A Basket Full of Babies

A Home Full of Hope

At Pemberley Series

Return to Pemberley

Trouble at Pemberley

Scandal at Pemberley

Danger at Pemberley

Harbour House Series

Wartime Arrivals at Harbour House

Stormy Waters at Harbour House

The Duke's Alliance Series

A Suitable Bride

A Dangerous Husband

An Unconventional Bride

An Accommodating Husband

A Rebellious Bride

The Duke's Bride

Standalone Novels

The Land Girl's Secret

The Pilot's Story

You're cordially invited to

The Scandal Sheet

The home of swoon-worthy historical romance from the Regency to the Victorian era!

Warning: may contain spice 🌶

Sign up to the newsletter
https://bit.ly/thescandalsheet

Boldwood

Boldwood Books is an award-winning fiction publishing company seeking out the best stories from around the world.

Find out more at www.boldwoodbooks.com

Join our reader community for brilliant books, competitions and offers!

Follow us
@BoldwoodBooks
@TheBoldBookClub

Sign up to our weekly deals newsletter

https://bit.ly/BoldwoodBNewsletter

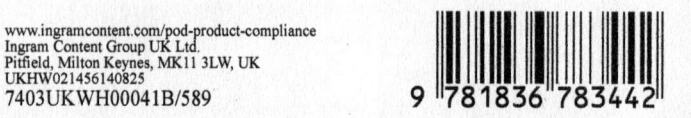